“You need only … of my obligation… I shall fulfill then…

“Your obligations? I should be surprised, my lord, to hear that you knew what an obligation was,” his bride said tartly.

The headache receded a pace, and to his own surprise, Severn laughed. “If you have been listening to my sisters, Lady Severn, I am surprised that you are talking to me now.”

“But not surprised I married you,” Primula said flatly.

A Viscountcy is worth such small sacrifice, don't you think? *The words ran through Severn's mind, but he found he could not say them. Though she had no reason to marry him except his title, he clung to the slender hope that Primula Greetwell had found some other reason to wed. . . .*

Also by Rosemary Edghill
Published by Fawcett Books:

THE ILL-BRED BRIDE
TWO OF A KIND
TURKISH DELIGHT

FLEETING FANCY

Rosemary Edghill

FAWCETT CREST • NEW YORK

A Fawcett Crest Book
Published by Ballantine Books

Library of Congress Catalog Card Number: 91-39255

ISBN 0-449-22186-5

This edition published by arrangement with St. Martin's Press, Inc.

Manufactured in the United States of America

First Ballantine Books Edition: April 1993

For Jennara, of course and at last.

Fleet Marriages

"In London, Fleet marriages . . . were notorious. They were performed without license, first in the chapel of the Fleet Prison and then in nearby taverns and houses, several of which bore signs depicting a male and female hand clasped together above the legend 'Marriages performed within.' The marriages were mostly conducted by clergymen who were imprisoned in the Fleet for debt and were allowed the 'Liberties of the Fleet,' that is to say, were permitted to move about freely within a certain area immediately surrounding the prison." (*The English, a Social History*, Christopher Hibbert, p. 382)

"Fleet Prison, not far from Newgate, was one of three prisons chiefly for debtors administered by the Royal Courts of Justice at Westminster; the other two, the King's Bench and the Marshalsea, were located to the south of the river." (*Thieves' Kitchen*, Donald A. Low, p. 56)

"Lord Hardwicke's [Marriage] Act of 1753 directed that any person solemnizing matrimony in any other than a church or public chapel without banns or license should on conviction be adjudged guilty of felony and be transported for fourteen years, and all such marriages should be void.

"These clandestine marriages (especially of minors) were performed in rooms and taverns near the Fleet, a notorious debtor's prison on Farringdon Street. Defrocked . . . ministers, imprisoned for debt in the Fleet, earned the ready by performing surreptitious marriages. Until Lord Hardwicke's Act went into effect as law in 1754, such marriages were perfectly legal.

"Members of the royal family, Quakers, and Jews were exempt under the Act, but Catholics were not. The only legal marriage a Roman Catholic could contract under English law had to be performed by an Anglican. . . . Scotland was declared exempt from the new law." (*The Regency Companion*, Laudermilk and Hamlin, p. 80)

Prologue

MARCH 1807

"I AM AFRAID, Severn, that this time you've gone too far."

The light seeping through the library curtains was the dismal illumination of late afternoon, but Malhythe's servants had been forced to drag Lord Severn from his bed for this interview. Severn regarded his father with mingled amusement and shock.

"I am afraid, my lord father, that I haven't the slightest idea what you're talking about." With an indifference just shy of insolence, Severn seated himself. Crossing his legs, he concentrated his attention on the gleam of one silk-stockinged calf.

"Pity—as the matter has gone far beyond the realm of boyish prank. And you, my lord, are no longer a boy. I lunched last week with Lord Childwall—his son, you will recall, is one of your cronies."

Bewildered by the abrupt change of subject, Severn ran a careless hand through his disordered curls to conceal his unease. "Ah, yes, Lucius the Anatomist—a man with an eye for neck but no bottom."

"If you choose to mock me, Severn, you show yourself to be far stupider than I had given you credit for. And I did, once, cherish some hopes of your intellect."

The arid acid in Malhythe's voice brought Severn to attention—whatever he was babbling on about, the old man thought it was serious, and the Earl of Malhythe was not a man noted for either scruples or nerves. Severn straightened slowly in his chair and set both feet on the floor. For a brief moment he wished his cuffs less ornate and his toilette less hurried.

"I meant no disrespect, sir. Pray continue."

Lord Malhythe leaned forward in his chair. The periwig that he affected despite changes in fashion gave him an antique severity, like a magistrate out of an old painting. His lace cuffs were brilliant in the gloom, and the large garnet on his forefinger flashed fire as he clasped his hands.

"As I told you, I lunched with Childwall. His son had come to him with a tale of an exploit so disturbing that he felt compelled to confess his part in it. Childwall found it difficult to credit that such a thing could actually take place in this century—but, hearing of your involvement, I did not."

Severn experienced a distinct sensation of unease. Mr. Lucius Foley—Lucius the Anatomist—had been Severn's agent in an enterprise of breathtaking scope—and now seemed to have published the affair to the world.

"I . . . see. And might one know what this third-hand report consisted of?" Severn still thought it unlikely that the Earl wished to tax him with his peccadillos—Malhythe had been a notable rake in his day.

"So the young fox has a few leagues left in him? Very well. Mr. Foley represented himself to his father as your agent in the seduction and spoilation of a young virgin of good family whom you cozened with false promises of matrimony, going so far as to have a sham marriage ceremony read over the two of you—"

"Oh, no, Father—the marriage ceremony was quite real—it was only the priest who was a sham!" interjected Severn irrepressibly. Now that the matter was out he found it difficult to take seriously. His mind was already turning on the matter of a suitable repayment to Mr. Lucius Foley for his treason.

"Indeed," said Malhythe frigidly. "And is that your sole offering with regard to this matter?"

Severn thrust himself to his feet and moved toward the sideboard. He splashed a careless peg of brandy into a glass, downed it, and took another. Much soothed, he turned back to his father. "Oh, very well. I shall take myself off to Rudbek for as long as you please. The chit won't grass—you may satisfy yourself on that head—I called myself Cunningham and she hasn't a clue to the identity of her loving husband. It is a famous joke, sir, I do assure you." His volatile spirits lightening by the instant—when his father had called him to this interview he had thought it was a matter of his debts—Severn turned and arranged himself to indolent advantage by the fireplace.

Malhythe was by nature a cold man, with little in the way of warmth or fellowship to offer any of his children. Born into a mannered age, he valued the semblance of virtue even more than the assumption of it. He was far less concerned with the lost honor of the outraged virgin—whose name it had been little trouble to him to discover—than with the cavalier indifference to appearance and consequence that had caused his heir to go raking among members of his own class. One way or another, this behavior would cease. Malhythe opened a drawer and placed a slim calfskin wallet of papers on the desktop.

" 'A famous joke.' Well, sir, perhaps you will find another as amusing. You are indeed, as you have foretold, to leave London—but not for Rudbek Manor." Malhythe placed a large purse beside the wallet of papers. "Your man has been instructed to pack what you will require, and the coach is waiting to take you to Dover. I will be sincerely sorry if I should hear that your ship has been sunk. If you are boarded you may, of course, apply to my man of business for any reasonable ransom."

"To Dover," Severn echoed blankly.

"Your espoused standard of behavior has been in my mind for some time—boyish pranks from a man of five-and-twenty are as unsuitable to your station as they seem impossible for you to forgo. I have secured for you a position with the East India Company, which you may exploit to what advantage you will. I shall expect to hear that you have made your fortune. Or died," the Earl added as an afterthought.

Severn stared at his father. "Banished to India? Over a trifle like this? It's infamous—how can you consider such a thing?"

"I will thank you not to take that tone with me, my lord; I assure you, I could have made your penance far more onerous. As for infamy, I hardly think it is less infamous to trick a young girl not yet even out upon the town with promises that amount to little more than lies—or are you prepared to make good upon your word?"

"My word? What the devil do you mean?" Annoyed in good earnest now—for even his enemies could not accuse Lord Severn of timidity—Severn rounded heedlessly upon his father.

"You promised the girl—Miss Primula Greetwell, to be precise—the protection of your name."

Severn stared at his father for a long moment of incomprehension. When he did understand he began to laugh, until he was forced to cling to the mantelpiece for support.

"Marriage! To Miss No One, daughter of Sir Nothing?" he said in derision. "Are you that desperate for me to wed? If that is your game you will catch cold at it—before I marry that whey-faced little ninny, I'll—I'll enlist, and there's precious little you can do to stop me—or to make me go to India, for that matter!"

Father and son regarded each other long enough for Severn to regret his momentary levity. Lord Malhythe's indifference to moralities and legalities alike was a legend that Severn's set constantly hoped to outshine, and Severn wasn't quite as comfortable in his defiance of the formidable old man as he hoped to sound.

"You leave regardless," the Earl said passionlessly. "You have some say in the destination, that is all. Gretna—or Dover. Choose any other destination, my posturing young hotspur, and you will find yourself without a brass farthing with which to buy the allegiance of your pot-valiant cronies. Every door I can close to you I shall close, and when you are taken up for debt—as seems quite inevitable—you will have infinite leisure in which to reflect upon what an unlucky precinct the Fleet is to frequent."

Severn stared, his green cat's eyes wide with shock. The old man knew everything—the scrape, the name of the girl, even the shift by which he deceived her. He tried to summon up her face and could not—only the memory of a trick of youth and freshness that had marked her as his lawful prey. To marry her now would be to become the laughingstock of all he knew.

Any fate would be preferable. He was certain—or nearly so—that his father would intervene before he was hanged or transported for debt. He was equally certain that the old devil would ensure that every unpleasantness inherent in the situation short of those final ones would be his to experience in full measure.

"Very well then," Lord Severn said ungraciously. "I've always had a mind to travel. Dover it is, then. Now, if there's nothing more . . . ?"

"Nothing at all," his father agreed. "You've done quite enough already."

Chapter 1

DECEMBER 1815

"OH, NO COLLEY, really! Marriage?" The speaker, known to all of her friends and most of her enemies as Aspasia, reclined in a welter of lace-trimmed pillows and stared at her companion incredulously.

"Marriage, my dear, is said to be the making of a man," Lord Malhythe said. "Perhaps it will be the making of my son as well."

Aspasia favored him with a sidewise stare and tapped her carmined lips with one exquisite finger. Her short dark curls bobbed with the gesture, and her sapphire eyes gleamed. "That depends, my lord, on what you want to make of him. Of course, by the time you know what you have it will be far too late to do anything about it." She sat up decisively and leaned forward. "And who can you possibly find to marry him?"

"That, my pet, will remain my secret for the moment. I'll tell you this much—she is of good family, will definitely accept my proposal—and is known to be to Severn's taste."

"So, they say, were half the ladies in London—and all the muslin company, though that was before my time." She paused in the conversation to select a *confit* from a plate by her bedside, admiring as she did so the sparkle of the sapphire bracelet she wore. She bit into the sweetmeat, and the gems flashed brightly in the weak winter sunlight. Malhythe gave her gifts and liked to see her wearing them. "Oh, you needn't rip up at me—it's only common gossip."

"No gossip you repeat could ever be common, my dear Aspasia." Lord Malhythe patted the couch beside him invitingly, and after a moment she joined him, fluttering gracefully to rest in a welter of silk and swansdown. He liked to see her *en négligée*, too, and so she appeared. Everything in her charming jewel-box house in St. John's Woods was to Lord Malhythe's taste. After all, he paid for it.

"How kind you are today, my lord—or is it laziness? But tell me—who is the bride, and how will you get Severn home from India to wed her?"

Lord Malhythe's son Severn had been banished to India for almost as long as Malhythe had had Aspasia in keeping, and she could number the times the Earl had spoken of him on the gilded toenails of one pretty foot. It did not seem a relationship of such warmth and filial devotion as to allow the Viscount's wedding, sight unseen, a bride of his father's choosing.

"Now that is the simplest part of the entire matter," the Earl said, pulling her comfortably closer. "My gentle son and heir has been petitioning me these past few years by every passing ship—though I warrant Bonaparte hasn't made that too easy—to be returned to the so-loving bosom of his family, not to mention the felicities of the English climate. Now that peace has broken out I suppose his letters will come more often—and I am tired of reading them."

"So you allow him to return, and marry him off, and hope he will settle down," Aspasia said doubtfully. Malhythe was minded to be expansive, it seemed, but Aspasia's experience of human nature did not make it seem likely that his plan would succeed.

"Child, I am giving him the best of all reasons to do so. If his marriage is not to my taste I will cut him off without a *sou*—and marry."

Not one gilded fingernail twitched, though their possessor felt a cold pang of dread. Aspasia had learned economics in a hard school. She knew exactly how the Earldom was situated, and what the Earl's marriage would mean to both Severn and herself.

The Earldom of Malhythe was a ramshackle creation of Charles II, and none of the peerage's holders had ever seen reason to improve on the merry monarch's works. Not a stick nor stone of Malhythe was entailed, all—houses, horses, lands—passed at the whim of the current Earl. In fact, it had passed to its present holder from an irritable great-uncle long before the title had. Only the Glorious '92 and the continental bloodbath that followed had winnowed the lines of descent to the point that Colworth Rudwell was Earl of Malhythe as well as master of Rudbek Manor. He could will it all—house, lands, income—away as easily as it had come.

"Well, am I to wish you very happy? I shan't, you know," she said candidly. "I think I shall be insulted, instead." Malhythe loved to tease her until she ripped up at him—let him find disappointment this time.

"You may be insulted if you like," the Earl said blandly. "I imagine Severn will be appalled—his expected inheritance wasted on what I trust will be a large and happy family—"

"My felicitations, my lord," Aspasia interjected.

"—and, if a son is born, the possibility that I will find some way of transferring the Earldom thither, instead of to his own unbowed head."

" 'How art thou fallen from heaven, O Lucifer, son of the morning.' I ought to have been more suspicious when you brought me sapphires, but this—! To be turned out of my own house into the worst snows in ten years . . ."

"I would find the image more affecting did I not know that the Deed of Gift I gave you for the place reposes with your bankers. Sheathe your claws, pet—I have no intention of reentering the happy state of matrimony. Unless, of course, Severn does something to displease me."

"I hope, in that case, that you have already chosen your own bride, as well as your son's!"

Malhythe laughed, as she had meant him to, and conversation turned to the victory celebrations and the effect on England of free trade with France again after almost twenty years.

But long after he had left Aspasia turned the disturbing intelligence over in her thoughts. Severn was to marry as the price for being allowed to return home, and Malhythe was to pick the bride. Well and good: but if Severn's behavior did not suit the Earl, Malhythe would marry to disoblige him.

And that was not well and good. Above all things Malhythe valued discretion; the name of Aspasia's protector was a mystery to the *ton*; he did not speak of his mistress nor did she disclose the name of her lover. A man of such discretion would be wise enough to know that the happy marriage he spoke of so blythely could hardly be a reality while Aspasia reigned over a more familiar and comfortable household.

Nor would she beg to stay, only to see his wife replace his mistress in his affections, as had happened to some of her friends. No, if Malhythe chose to marry, Aspasia would leave him immediately—and at the moment she could see nothing to prevent it.

Severn's behavior? The sullen wild boy she vaguely remembered was not likely to moderate his behavior to suit his father—Viscount Severn was a reckless rake, and ninety years in India could not have changed him, let alone nine.

After due consideration, Aspasia flung herself down among her pillows and wept.

"A visitor, Miss."

"For me? Good heavens, Badgley." Primula glanced up from her embroidery to see the butler—the very image of a family retainer gone grey in service—bending over her to offer the stiff cream pasteboard on the polished silver salver.

"He did ask for Miss Greetwell, Miss."

"And I am certainly the only Miss Greetwell there is—unless he wants Papa's sister, and she has not stirred from Harrowgate spa since before the Peace of Amiens. I wonder who it could be?" As she spoke she turned the card over and studied it, glad of the interruption. Even in full daylight the December sun was not quite strong enough to do fancywork by, and her tidy soul rebelled at the thought of having candles lit in the middle of the day.

Neither the very grand embossed crest muddled with its many quarterings nor the title meant anything to her for a moment. Then she remembered.

The Earl of Malhythe was Viscount Severn's father.

"Oh, dear," Primula said faintly, half-rising. Conscious of Badgley's curious gaze upon her, she subsided again, one hand pressed to her bosom just below the brooch that closed her lace fichu at the throat. Warring with the strong instinct to refuse to see him was the conviction that he had come to bring her news of Severn, impossible as that was.

"What shall I say to his lordship, Miss?" the butler said, and by his tone had said it more than once.

Primula gathered herself together. She must see Lord Malhythe. To refuse would be inutterably missish.

"Please conduct his lordship to the Egyptian Room, and offer him a glass of wine. Tell him I will join him directly."

"Yes, Miss."

It could only be her imagination that Badgley looked surprised. Surprised . . . and disapproving.

Hard upon Badgley's heels she whisked up the stairs to her room and glanced anxiously in her mirror. Well enough, she supposed; brown eyes and brown hair—when she was younger she might have been pretty but now had settled on serenity as a good second-best. The dress would have to do—she could not bear to keep the Earl waiting as long as it would take to change it—but she brushed cologne through her short brown curls and changed her sensible wool shawl for an opulent silk one brought all the way from India.

India! Everyone knew that was where Lord Malhythe had banished his heir—even people like Sir Rowland knew that, though Papa had no idea why.

Nor would he have. Lines of determination leapt to bracket Primula's mouth as she looked into the mirror. If, at five-and-twenty, Miss Primula Miranda Greetwell, beloved and only daughter of Sir Rowland and Lady Jane Greetwell, was not precisely entitled to the spinster title she had taken to herself with such unshakable determination, it was a secret that was hers to keep.

She had been sixteen, a giddy girl still in the schoolroom. Mr. Cunningham had been tall, auburn-haired, and dazzling. Her parasol had blown away from her as she left Hatchard's one day, and from the rescue of it he had scraped an acquaintance with her. John Cunningham had no trouble convincing the sixteen-year-old Primula of his fatal attraction to her—nor of the reality of the draconian guardian who would never allow them to marry openly.

She had been far too young to question why the secret marriage he proposed could not be celebrated with her parents' connivance, or to find this mythical guardian's behavior odd. Sometimes at night when she closed her eyes it seemed she could still see the signboard with the two clasped hands swing back and forth above her head. "Marriages Performed Within" it said on it, and she huddled close by John's side, terrified to be out alone and in the district that held the notorious Fleet Prison besides.

But greater than her fear had been her love—a love that had lasted all of two weeks, until her new-wedded lord explained the exact nature of his deceit and left her standing on her own doorstep at nine o'clock in the morning.

Fortunately, her parents weren't there. The day before her elopement her father had traveled to Kent upon business. Her mother had elected to accompany him. They were not yet back.

It left her a grace period in which to be thankful that "Mr. Cunningham" had not dispatched to them the letter she had written, and to prepare the story she would tell, when the servants came to them with the tale of her disappearance.

Only it wasn't a story, just a flat refusal ever to discuss where she had been those two weeks. She had always been stubborn, and when "Mr. Cunningham" was through with her she had learned to be sensible as well.

Her parents were kind; in their place many would have beaten the errant daughter until she confessed, or turned her out into the streets to pursue the career she had apparently embraced. But Papa and Mama made no such threats, and eventually stopped asking for answers Primula would not give. Primula was glad of that; it would have made her unhappy, even though it would not have made her tell.

Of course there had been a little gossip—and Mama had made defiantly sure that Primula was on very public display at every afternoon tea she gave for the next nine months, until even the gossips saw that there was nothing to see. But not even Mama had suggested a Season when Primula was eighteen, and so the years went by, leaving behind only a faint bitter regret for "Could Have Been."

For that—and for a pair of cat-green eyes that gazed at her with a love put on for the occasion. But hers had not been—and wasn't now.

The Earl of Malhythe was not a man accustomed to being kept waiting—especially by "Miss No One, daughter of Sir Nothing." But in this case he acknowledged that the chit had some right to accommodation from his family, whether she knew it yet or not.

When Severn had taken himself off to India—and not a moment too soon, from the tales of his conduct that had surfaced afterward—the Earl had interested himself in the Greetwell family. The girl was in some sense his responsibility, and the child, if there were to be one, certainly was.

But there had been no child, and Miss Greetwell had not been driven from the family hearth, so Malhythe had let the matter rest. He had retained enough interest to note that an announcement of her marriage had never appeared in the *Gazette*, and when he had conceived his plan he had set his man of business to confirm that Miss Primula Greetwell remained unwed.

But with all his careful research, Malhythe had never seen the girl with whom his son had so disgraced himself, and so it was something of a surprise to confront the young woman who opened the door to the room where Malhythe had been set to wait.

She was twenty-five years of age and neither stunningly beautiful nor shatteringly plain. The intractable set of her mouth was something for which he had not been at all prepared; Malhythe revised his plans.

"Miss Greetwell, how good of you to see me. I trust your father is well?"

Her father was well, her mother was well; her aunt's rheumatism, the weather, and the foreign visitors attending the victory celebrations were thoroughly exhausted as topics of conversation. By the time she had helped her visitor to a second glass of malmsey and offered him a selection of little sugared cakes, Primula had become convinced that he was laughing at her.

"But I must be boring you with my silly female chatter, Lord Malhythe," she said with great determination. "Are you quite certain that you wish to see me and not my father? I am certain he could be of more use to you than I."

The Earl smiled. "I doubt that very much, Miss Greetwell. Sir Rowland may be in all things an admirable servant to the Crown, but what I am seeking is a bride for my son, and I very much doubt that your father could be of more use to me than you will be."

Primula gazed at Lord Malhythe for an instant before jerking herself to her feet. "Then I shall ring for Badgley to show you out, my lord—and I trust your visit has been as amusing as you hoped!" Spots of angry color flamed in her cheeks as she strode toward the door.

"Miss Greetwell."

The sheer dispassion of his voice stopped her. Unwillingly she turned and looked back at the Earl. He had not stirred from his position in the chair before the fire.

"That was certainly ill-done of me, but I am an old man with few pleasures—"

And one of them is telling lies! thought Primula stormily.

"—and it was a matter of intense curiosity with me to discover just how long this veneer of politeness could be made to last. Now I have had my fun, so be a good girl and sit down, and we will discuss Severn. I see, from your manner, that you know him."

"And if, my lord Malhythe, I do not choose to discuss Viscount Severn?" It was foolhardy of her to attempt to cross swords with so notorious a person as the Earl of Malhythe, but there was something about the man that made her ache to slap him, even if he was old enough to be her father.

"And if, my Miss Greetwell, you do not choose to discuss my son, who knows? I might very well choose to make public your previous connection with him. He is coming home, you know, if both you and he behave yourselves."

On lifeless marionette legs Primula recrossed the room and seated herself again. So she was finished with Severn, was she? Now there was a joke. She was still poisoned with love for him, a malignity that had leached away her happy respectable future, and only the knowledge that she had no chance at all of attaching him had kept her from boarding the next ship to the East any time in these last nine years.

"So Severn is coming home," Primula said with wooden politeness.

"If he fulfills my requirements. Pray indulge my curiosity, Miss Greetwell; how did you ascertain the identity of your ravisher? He told me he had been discreet."

If the Earl had hoped for tears he was disappointed; Primula's eyes were dry. "It was not entirely difficult. Of course no one knew why Lord Severn had been sent away—there was talk that it might have involved an affair of honor. But he left at the right time, and someone described him to me. There are not so very many tall, green-eyed gentlemen in the world who have been banished from London for misconduct."

"You exhibit admirable powers of deduction, Miss Greetwell. And yet you told no one?"

"Whom should I have told? I do not think you would have brought Severn back to England, even if Papa asked you very nicely. And then I should have had to spend the rest of my life apologizing."

"And you did not wish to do so?"

"Frankly, my lord, I hardly feel that it was my fault."

Malhythe laughed. "You are a most remarkable girl, Miss Greetwell. You remind me of . . . Well, never mind. Talking pays no toll, as they say. What I have come to set before you is this:

"Severn wishes to come home from India. He knows that I have it in my power to make his return exceedingly unpleasant; thus, he wishes to return with my permission. I am prepared to give it, on the condition that he marry, sight unseen, a bride of my choosing and live with her in quiet amity for one year. I propose that this bride be you, Miss Greetwell."

"For all my sterling qualities?" Primula said acidly. She hardly thought it worth her while to expend common politeness on a man as dreadfully rude as Malhythe.

"For the hope that you will cause him great remorse," the Earl said. In an entirely new tone he added, "I do not know my son, Miss Greetwell, and the little I know of him is bad. Yet on my death a great deal in the way of money and position will pass irrevocably into his control. I will not give the power of great wealth into the hands of a reckless libertine and bully. If he has changed, you are the instrument that will reveal it."

Such absolute self-interest was a thing worth seeing at least once, Primula decided a little breathlessly.

"So I am to marry Severn for your convenience, my lord?" She was absurdly proud to be able to match his tone of detachment.

"And yours. Viscountess Severn . . . Countess of Malhythe . . . Your own establishment, the freedom of matronhood, a secret that will remain a secret—and certainly Severn is the last person to whom you need apologize about your past. Your dowry is a matter of supreme indifference to me, and no matter what provision I make for—or *against*—my son, I will see to it that you are well provided for."

"And in exchange for this you get what?"

"The acid test of my son and heir's reformation . . . and your promise that you will not reveal that you are aware of the previous part he played in your life until the first anniversary of your marriage."

"But . . . why?"

The Earl smiled thinly. "Because it will be so much more unpleasant for him that way, my dear. And because if he is aware that you already know, it would eliminate all need for him to confess."

Chapter 2

DECEMBER 1815

PRIMULA HAD PROMISED Lord Malhythe his answer in a week; the last several years had taught her enough caution to be wary of committing herself to anything she had not thoroughly reasoned out. But what answer would she give?

Malhythe had all but promised to make the *ton* a present of her childish folly if she did not fall in with his mad scheme, and certainly the consequences of that would be most unpleasant. But she was old enough to know that they would not be fatal. Not quite.

Mama and Papa would support her decision—and Papa would very likely praise her for refusing to truckle to a blackmailer.

So, thought Primula carefully, she could refuse. But what if she accepted?

If she accepted, she would have a smart address and nearly unlimited freedom—and she would have Severn, of course, who would cold-bloodedly have agreed to marry "a bride of his father's choosing" in order to come home.

And there was the crux of the matter. What would it be like to be married to John Rudwell, Viscount Severn?

* * *

Sir Rowland Greetwell's study was a long narrow room that ran the width of the house. Through a multitude of tall narrow windows it overlooked the stables and garden, and a long oak table was pulled up to the windows to catch every ray of the brief daylight. Upon the table was a small press for preserving botanical specimens and a much larger one for flattening damp watercolors. A bundle of mistletoe lay on the table in the middle of the litter of pens and brushes; its golden greenness was startling in the winter gloom.

"Papa, are you busy?" Primula peered hesitantly around the study door.

"If you wish to hide Christmas presents here, I am. I will not have your mother tidying me out of existence on the basis of her suspicions."

Lady Greetwell was both organized and inquisitive. It was the combination of those two character traits that gave rise to the "tidying mania" that was a standing joke in the Greetwell household. It was not that she was vulgarly prying or odiously insistent; merely that when Lady Greetwell wished to know something she dogged the maids' steps with a dustrag of her own; if there was physical evidence she unearthed it. Christmas was especially taxing to the ingenuity of her loved ones, though one could not deny that the house *was* clean.

"No, Papa, of course not. Mama's present is—" Out of habit Primula stopped and looked around.

"Oh, we are quite safe; your Mama is paying a call upon Lady Hawkchurch and won't be back for quite some time."

"Oh, dear—how very difficult for her," Primula said. Lady Hawkchurch was in deepest mourning; she had lost two sons on the field of Waterloo, and of a large and hopeful family of nine possessed only one remaining child. Lady Greetwell would certainly find no lively welcome. "Still, I suppose Lady

Hawkchurch will be grateful for the company," she added.

"And one must always do one's duty," Sir Rowland agreed. "But that is hardly why you came to see me."

"No, Papa. I came to ask you something." She came and seated herself beside him at the broad worktable placed in front of the uncurtained window.

As befit a man who had christened his daughter Primula—Latin for *primrose*—Sir Rowland Greetwell's passion was botany. He had published a folio of watercolor studies of the wildflowers of England and Scotland, and discovered to his chagrin that the prints were being framed rather than studied.

But there was another side to Sir Rowland's studies—one that had led him to cross the Channel many times when Primula was a little girl to sketch quite another kind of flower entirely: the fortifications that bloomed along the Calais coast as Bonaparte made plans to invade England. But all that was long past, and England now was safe—as safe as Miss Primula Greetwell wasn't.

"Papa, Lord Malhythe came to see me today."

"So Badgley gave me to understand, before I had so much as removed my coat. I trust you made his lordship comfortable?"

"Yes, Papa. I gave him the malmsey." She plucked one of Sir Rowland's watercolor brushes from the vase on the table and twirled it idly between her fingers.

"Well, then, he can have had nothing to complain of; I was most satisfied with that particular shipment. And having so encouraged him I trust he soon disclosed the nature of his most singular visitation?" Sir Rowland frowned down her misuse of the brush, and she replaced it in its jasperware container.

"Yes, Papa. He came to ask me if I would agree to marry his son."

At this Sir Rowland removed his spectacles and smoothed his mousey brown hair back over his temples.

" 'To marry his son.' Ah . . . Viscount Severn, the one packed off to India after he killed his man, or some such nonsense? Yes, of course; Malhythe has only the one son. And four girls; it is enough to cause a man to wonder . . . but perhaps you can enlighten me, Primula, as to why he would make such an astonishing suggestion to you. He can't mean that you should go to India; does he mean to bring Severn home?"

"He has said, Papa, that Lord Severn may return to England if he is to wed," said Primula carefully. "Lord Malhythe expressed his belief that I would be a suitable bride."

Sir Rowland polished his spectacles and replaced them on his nose, then peered at his daughter doubtfully, as the action did nothing to make matters clearer.

"Suitable for what, I wonder. Did he tell you that?"

"He wished the marriage to induce a condition of remorse in his heir," Primula explained gravely, and Sir Rowland laughed.

"Well, I don't know if he has settled upon quite the right female, if that is his intention. . . . And what did you say, lass, when Malhythe came to offer you his heir?"

"I told him he might call for his answer in one week's time—Oh, Papa, what shall I tell him?" Primula burst out. Now that she was well and truly tangled in Malhythe's plans, the way out seemed less and less attainable.

"It all depends on whether you think you will be

happy as the Viscountess Severn, Prim. If you will be, then nothing else signifies, of course."

Primula stared at her hands.

"Of course, the offer—and the fashion in which it was tendered—are peculiar enough to induce caution in even the most reckless bosom," Sir Rowland continued. "Why cannot Severn choose his own bride? Will he hold himself bound to his father's taste in daughters-in-law? If Malhythe is asking you to bind yourself to such an agreement without the chance to form any notion of your betrothed's character before the ceremony, it argues, rather, that he hasn't got one. There's no denying that—on balance—one wouldn't expect to be happy with a man like that."

"But Papa—we do not know that! He has been in India such a very long time—he might be anyone now! That is—" Primula said hesitantly, "I am not at all certain what we are to think of Lord Severn."

Sir Rowland patted her hand with rough affection. "Very well, daughter. Who am I to hold an opinion of a man where his possible bride refrains? I will speak to Lord Malhythe myself and attempt to satisfy my objections—and if I do so, I will not withhold my consent to the match. Whether you give yours, now, will be up to you."

"So Malhythe's cub is to wed, eh?" Mary Naismith delivered herself of her most burning *on-dit* even before handing her bonnet to Mrs. Clutterbuck, though that most worthy domestic had followed her all the way into her mistress's bedroom in constant hope of receiving it.

Once divested of rose-trimmed poke and rose silk pelisse, Mrs. Naismith dropped down upon the ornate gilded bed carved with swans that dominated the room to continue her assault.

"Oh, come, now, 'Spasia, don't keep everyone in

suspense! What has *your* gentleman said? Is it true?"

"Is what true? For all of that, is it morning yet? Oh, Mary, my head—! Do be an angel and ring for Mrs. Clutterbuck. There must be tea somewhere in the world," Aspasia added plaintively.

"I'm right here, duck," the housekeeper said.

Aspasia pushed herself upright in the lacy mass of pillows and lifted her aerophane mobcap up to peer suspiciously out from beneath the edge. "Oh, so you are. Do be a positive lamb, Cutty, and make us up a nice pot of that China Black my lord sent—and some scones. One must have something, rising with the dawn."

Aspasia regarded her friend with narrowed eyes only partially accounted for by her protests of sleepiness. Since no one knew under whose protection Aspasia lived, Mary's coming here with tales of Severn's wedding was coincidence, nothing more.

"Oh, bosh! Don't try to gammon me, 'Spasia—you've been up for hours!"

"I *was* going back to sleep," her hostess pointed out with great dignity, opposing herself to a threatened avalanche of pillows. "But now that you are here I probably shan't. Probably," she added, yawning.

Mary Naismith was several years younger than Aspasia, though not so many years as Mary's self-told biography insisted. Her guinea-bright hair owed more than a little to the assistance of hair washes, and her complexion to the cochineal in the French Salve she liberally applied. Her dress was of a cherry kerseymere that disagreed feebly with the garnet bracelets she wore on each wrist and above each elbow. Unable to be still for very long, Mary leapt to her feet and critically inspected each corner of the room she had seen so many times, chattering all the while as she did so.

"Well, I must say you missed a great to-do last night—or was it this morning? Lord Drewmore took over a whole tavern, down on Ratcliff Highway—threw everyone out but his party and held an inquest on the death of innocence, so *he* said. And Barham was there, and young Gressingham, and—oh, everyone. The owner was too green even to cheep, when Drewmore was done flashing gold and threats, and when some cit came along to complain of our noise, why, didn't my lord offer to draw his cork for him? Ah, it was a lovely bit of a brawl, that was." Mary Naismith sighed reminiscently and settled herself on the blue and gold sopha.

"Yes; I thought that was blood on your dress. Oh, Mary, when will you learn to be sensible? A tavern on the Highway—that's the place for penny whores the fine gentlemen pick up in the Garden along with a bunch of violets."

"Aspasia!" gasped her friend, shocked.

"What's wrong, Mary, didn't you think I knew the words? But it's true enough. Your Jeremy shouldn't take you on routs like those; it isn't proper."

"Proper! What's propriety to the likes of us?" Mary pouted.

Much as she loved her friend, Aspasia wanted to shake her. Propriety was everything; to act cheap was to be held cheaply. Or not to be held at all. She drew breath to attempt to impart some of this to Mary, but at that moment Mrs. Clutterbuck returned with the tea and Mrs. Naismith made her conversational escape.

"Oh, but don't scold me, 'Spasia! You know how Jemmy likes the flash kens—and if I don't go in with him, it's someone else who'll leave with him, and that's certain! But you are very bad to tease me this way, when I have come to hear all your gossip." Smiling, she helped herself to tea and poured a cup for her hostess.

"I never gossip," said Aspasia piously, accepting the tea and drawing her swansdown cape closer around her. "But I will promise not to tease you any more if you will tell me who is putting about such a shocking tale about the Earl of Malhythe's son."

"Oh, but how can it be shocking, 'Spasia, when it is probably absolutely true?"

Mary Naismith had heard, from her very good friend Doll Lambeth, who had had it in strictest confidence from her young gentleman, whose valet was walking out with a maid of the Malhythe household, that the Earl of Malhythe's personal secretary had absolutely, positively, been instructed to definitely recall Severn from India.

"—and why else, except to marry him safe out of the way?" Mrs. Naismith demanded. "Or murder him—though like as not he could safely have left him in that perishing place and let the heathens do it, or so I hear. Now, what have you heard?"

"Well, I have not heard the date the boat is to dock, anyway—really, Mary, what fustian! Everyone knows that Doll's Peter plunges so deep that he can't remember his own name, let alone his gossip! So Severn is to return home and marry, is he? Well, where's the girl?"

"You haven't heard, then?" Mrs. Naismith asked hopefully.

"Nothing about a girl," said Aspasia with reasonable truthfulness. "If a man wants someone to gossip about him, he has only to look in at the Wilsons', and 'The Queen of Hearts' will be delighted to do it. She says she will publish her diary one day, and bring Europe to its knees, I don't think. I daresay she can't even read, let alone write. And besides—if Malhythe *were* bringing the boy home to set up his nursery, what is that to do with us?"

Mary Naismith regarded her with an assumption of superior experience. "Everything's to do with us, 'Spasia—isn't that what you're always telling me? Suppose Severn takes you up, and your Lord *Inconnu* comes to pistols over it. Now suppose—"

"Now suppose I were the Queen of the Cats! Really, Mary!"

"They say that Lord Severn's a wild 'un," Mary said obliviously.

Aspasia bit her lip. That chance remark struck too close to home. If Severn were wild— If Severn hadn't changed—

"I'm sure that Severn coming back won't make the least bit of difference," Aspasia said hopefully.

"And is he coming home, then? Severn, I mean."

Aspasia flung a pillow at her, narrowly missing the teapot. "Wretch! And after I've told you I do *not* know? Very well—but in strictest confidence, mind you—I *have* heard that Severn *is* coming home to wed. And nothing you can possibly say will induce me to disclose the name of the bride!"

One week to the day from the last occasion on which he had called, the Earl of Malhythe ascended the steps of Sir Rowland's neat London house in its spacious square. Upon sending in his card to Miss Greetwell he was informed that Sir Rowland would see him; with a meekness belying his reputation, Lord Malhythe suffered himself to be conducted into Sir Rowland's study.

"Sir Rowland, how kind of you to receive me."

"Lord Malhythe, an unexpected pleasure." Both men smiled with identical formality. "But come, I do not intend that so illustrious a guest should stand upon ceremony. Perhaps you will be so kind as to give me your opinion on a sherry I am thinking of purchasing, and then we will touch upon the business of why you have come."

The sherry was tasted and approved; the news from France discussed. Lord Malhythe was a canny cardplayer, and in years past his had been the will that wagered such men as Sir Rowland in the Great Game played against the Continental Tyranny; Malhythe was willing to wait, if waiting would serve him.

"Primula tells me that Severn wishes to offer for her," Sir Rowland said at last.

"In a manner of speaking. I confess I had hoped to hear her answer today. News of his engagement would gladden the hearts of his sisters in this joyous holiday season." Lord Malhythe set his sherry glass precisely down upon the table at his side. "Are you so certain she will accept him?"

"My dear sir, if I were certain of any such thing I should already have sent the announcement to the *Gazette*. Allow me to proceed to assuage a parent's feelings."

Sir Rowland settled himself amiably in his seat and prepared to allow himself to be assuaged.

"I shall expect my bankers to meet with yours to draw up a marriage contract that meets with your approval. Though Severn's financial future remains uncertain, I do not intend that Miss Greetwell's should be. I shall make over one of my London properties to her as a wedding present, and tie that and her settlements up neatly so Severn can't get his hands on them. Whatever should eventuate, she and any children will be provided for. I imagine she may continue to look to you and your wife for emotional support?"

"She may."

"If at any time Severn does anything to disparage his wife's reputation and good name, he will be most severely dealt with. It will be made clear to the *ton* that his behavior has proceeded from the promptings of insanity, and has no grounding in truth. I do not propose that Miss Greetwell should suffer appreciably through accepting this match."

"Though you do, it seems clear, propose Lord Severn to suffer."

The Earl permitted himself a small cold smile. "If I do, it is my affair. You need only concern yourself with your daughter's comfort. Should you consent to the marriage, the engagement will be announced immediately. I shall support any story you care to put about in the line of secret betrothals, or you may allow the facts to speak for themselves. It will take Severn about a year to receive my letter and reach England; the marriage will take place as soon as he arrives. If these assurances are not sufficient, pray tell me what will content you."

Sir Rowland studied Lord Malhythe for a long moment. "It would content me very much indeed to know how it was you settled on my daughter for your son, and why it is you think she'll make him so unhappy."

"If I *knew* the match would make Severn unhappy there would be no need for it to occur," said the Earl sharply. "As for the other, I do not choose to share that information with you; make of that what you wish. I commend to you, however, a concern for your daughter's future."

Sir Rowland rose. "You will be surprised to find my concern exceeds your own, Lord Malhythe. With your permission I will ask Primula to join us, so that she may give you her answer herself."

Over the last seven days Primula had wrestled with the problem, taking it with her to breakfast and luncheon, shopping and driving, Sunday Service and evening prayers. The only thing she had discovered was that it was not susceptible to logical resolution. Of her decidedly mixed feelings for "Mr. Cunningham," sometime Viscount Severn, the chiefest at the moment was irritation.

Why could not the man and his sordid ideas of fun vanish safely into the past? She was honest enough to admit that if he were a part of her present, it was she who had kept him there, but beyond that she could not go.

"He does not love me, I do not know him, he does not know me, I do not love him . . ." Primula murmured under her breath as she arranged the forcing-house roses sent by one of Papa's friends in a bowl for the table beside the window.

"I beg your pardon, dear; I did not hear that." Lady Greetwell looked up inquiringly from the newspaper she was perusing.

"It was nothing, Mama," Primula said hastily.

"Well, I don't wonder you are upset," said Lady Greetwell, laying aside her paper and removing the grey suede gloves she wore for the purpose of reading it. "What a peculiar sort of offer for Lord Malhythe to make, after all. If his intention was to revert to the last century and make an arranged marriage for his heir he would more properly have gone to your father with the matter, and not to you at all. Then you could have been informed of the *fait accompli*, fled to your room in a storm of tears, and had the marriage ceremony read over you as you stood before the priest bound, gagged, and—who knows?—drugged."

"Mama!" said Primula, startled into laughter.

"Now that's better," said her mother approvingly as Primula's eyes danced with mirth. "Come sit by me, and we will tell the Earl of Malhythe to go to Jericho if he crosses us—and your papa too, if he dares to object. But really," she added, unwilling to abandon this conversational puzzle, "marriages like that were out-of-fashion in Malhythe's father's time—and even assuming they weren't, don't you suppose he could make a better match for Severn than you?"

"Oh, much," Primula agreed with mock seriousness. She settled herself on the sopha beside her mother, and Lady Greetwell put an arm about her shoulders.

"Well, I ask you!" said Lady Greetwell encouragingly. "There's any number of titled misses with more hair than wit willing to marry a Viscount's coronet and never mind what comes beneath it."

"I hope I have better sense than that, Mama," said Primula, who wondered if she did.

"Than to marry for an empty title? Of course you do. But since you have never met Lord Severn it would be wonderful indeed if you had any more idea of his character than you may find in the Peerage. And this is why your papa is speaking to Lord Malhythe at this very moment, to see if Severn is a rainbow you may safely chase."

Primula glanced sideways at her mother, stirred by the seriousness of her tone.

"When we are young, my darling—and we must include you in that company, even though you are five-and-twenty, because of the so very sheltered life you have led—we want a great many things. And because we are young, we can not-at-all imagine what it would be like if we had them. Certainly we assume that to have what we want will make us happy, but it is sometimes not an assumption a person older and wiser would make in the same circumstances. In fact, most of the things we want make us unhappy when we get them."

"Yes, Mama," said Primula. She wondered a little apprehensively if the point of this kindly lecture was that she should reject Severn even if Sir Rowland approved the match, and was surprised at how strong her disinclination was to do so.

"But there are degrees and degrees of unhappiness, you know. Some are mild, and some are inevitable, and some—a very few—are so dreadful that there is no going back from them. It is that last sort that we hope to preserve you from, dearest, and if that is the sort that Severn is, your Papa will certainly tell Lord Malhythe 'no.' "

"An unhappiness that there is no going back from," said Primula musingly. Certainly it sounded very grand, and perhaps even romantic. "It sounds very Gothic, Mama."

"You are so good and sensible, Primula; my own dear mother always said that young people should always appear sensible since they certainly could not be so, but I imagine it was because she had not met you. For my part, I am not convinced that the young should be sensible."

"If they are not, then they will always regret it—and it is never themselves alone they hurt, but everyone around them!" Primula flung herself away from her mother.

"Primula, darling—" Lady Greetwell began in surprise. Primula felt her cheeks burn with sheer uncontrolled emotion and wished that Lord Malhythe had never been born. She started for the door, but Badgley forestalled her.

"Sir Rowland wishes you to come to him in his study, Miss." The butler had opened the door nearly in her face to deliver himself of this intelligence; he gazed upon her in mild reproach.

"I— Yes. Of course. I shall be right here. Mama, I am very much afraid I am all to pieces today—do you forgive me?"

"Of course, darling. How could you not be? So Papa approves. . . . Shall I come with you?"

"Oh, dear, no. I have decided what I must say to Lord Malhythe."

"Thank you, my lord; I will be pleased to marry Lord Severn." There, it was done, and the secret buried forever. And not only Primula was saved, but Sir Rowland and Lady Greetwell, too.

"Here, Prim, sit down and drink to the health of the groom. Don't want you falling on your face in front of my lord," Sir Rowland added in an aside.

Primula sank gratefully into a chair beside her father and took the glass he held out to her. Using both hands she managed to get it to her lips without spilling any, and after a few sips of wine she felt steadier.

"And to your health as well, Miss Greetwell," Lord Malhythe said, raising his own glass. "I shall send the announcement to the *Gazette* at once, and perhaps you will do me the honor of making up a family party at Rudbek in the new year. It is the custom of my daughters to flock to my side at this time with their various progeny and pendant husbands in order to reassure me of their continued existence; I know they will be delighted to learn that you exist as well. Perhaps you will like to invite a few other agreeable young people to round out the party," the Earl added.

"Thank you, my lord," Primula said numbly. Lord Malhythe rose to his feet.

"I congratulate you on your very good sense and I look forward to my son's making the acquaintance of his bride. Now, there is just one thing more. Hold out your hand . . . no, the other one."

Primula extended her left hand. Lord Malhythe reached into his pocket and withdrew something that flashed.

"Opals are said to be unlucky unless given as

gifts; accept this one in token of Severn's pledge to you," he said, placing the ring on her finger.

The milky hemisphere flashed its separate sparks of blue and green and pink from the center of a circle of tiny diamonds. The wide gold of the band looked very old, and the ring felt awkward on her finger. Primula looked up at the Earl.

"Welcome to the Rudwell family, Miss Greetwell."

Chapter 3

ONE YEAR LATER, DECEMBER 1816

CHRISTMAS OF 1816 was an uncharacteristically festive affair.

"Only think, Prim! The bridegroom will be home in the spring—and then we may all put on our mourning blacks!" Mrs. Lionel Lambton clasped her hands before her in mock ecstasy at the prospect.

"Addie, pray do not talk in that fashion. I shall think you mean it, and then I will be utterly cast down," Primula answered with equally assumed mournfulness.

"Oh, but I do mean it—after all, I have known Severn all my life, the wretched creature. At least you have had fun this year to console you, for when he comes home he will cut up your peace entirely!" Mrs. Lambton, or, as she was equally entitled to be known, Lady Adeline, peaceably retrieved a button from the mouth of one of her young nephews.

"Well, I shan't let him. Oh, bother Severn anyway—where are those invitations?"

"I believe Margie has them," the Earl of Malhythe's eldest daughter observed, and Primula swooped to seize them from the chubby fist of an angelic child of two.

"Naughty Margie! Mama would not like you to cause us all this trouble—and neither do I!" The child's face crumpled in a mask of disappointment, and Primula forestalled tears by offering her a warm gingerbread in place of the small vellum cards.

"Well, you *would* write out cards in the nursery. I only said that with their nurse 'peening for the healens,' or whatever it is that the incomprehensible Scots do, I would take the chance to visit my favorite relations. Isn't that so, my Rob-Roy?" Adeline Rudwell-Lambton said, dandling the very little boy on her knee.

"But you know perfectly well that they are my favorite relations too—excepting Catherine and Frances and Margaret, and of course Jane Emwilton, Mama's goddaughter, and—"

"Enough, pray!—or you will be listing half the families in the county! I am sorry that Miss Emwilton cannot be here, but with the General, her papa, being carried off only two months ago I suppose she and her mama would not think of accepting an invitation to a house party."

"And very proper of her, but Mrs. Emwilton did not answer Mama's last letter, and we are a little concerned—but I warrant it is only the condition of the roads, and does not signify! As for you, Addie Lambton, you may stop looking at Robbie as if you never saw a child before and may never see one again, when you know perfectly well that your own Georgie will be presenting you with a quiverful of grandchildren quick as a cat can lick her ear."

"Not, I hope, before he has presented me with a daughter-in-law. Oh, Prim, what am I to do with Georgie?"

But even if Primula had any answer to the vexed question of what to do with a gay young spark of two-and-twenty who fancied himself a dangerous rake about town, she was destined not to deliver it, for at that moment the rest of her soon-to-be-sisters swept into the room.

The Earl of Malhythe begat four girls—Adeline, Catherine, Frances, and Margaret—before the arrival of the vitally necessary heir. Adeline, the eldest, had been ten when her brother was born and (to hear her tell it) after spending eight years under the baby tyrant's sway had married Mr. Lionel Lambton pretty smartly thereafter. Her son George was only a few years younger than Primula herself.

Lamb's chiefest charm, as Adeline had confided to Primula dotingly, was that he could never on any account be persuaded to do anything at all. It was an article of faith with Mr. Lambton that his health was delicate; the Lambtons resided, for his health, in a comfortable small house near Tilling.

Catherine, the second eldest, had cast her net wider. Lord Malhythe had been pleased to bestow her hand upon the Laird of Rannoch, who lived upon his Scots possessions in the far north. She produced offspring with what her sisters told her was alarming regularity and doted on them fiercely, to the extent that her annual pilgrimage to Rudbek Hall was conducted with various ghillies, nannies, and other uncouth northern servants to see to the care of what Catherine insisted on calling "the bonnie wee bairns," who also accompanied her.

Frances, who had married a Sir Geoffrey Appleby who dwelt in Suffolk, was more restrained in her embracing of motherhood. Her two boys and a girl often remained behind while she spent her holiday at Rudbek, and sometimes her husband bore them company. Sir Geoffrey was a mild man of still milder habits; he had severed the connections with the East India Company that had so enriched and ennobled an already excellent lineage, and devoted himself to keeping bees and writing a history of the Roman invasion of Britain.

Margaret, the youngest, was still some years Severn's senior. By the time their father had tired of their brother's rigs, Margaret had been married six years to a Mr. Trevose of Cornwall, a consequential man in his home county, with connections to the influential Pengethlys. In fact, all the Rudwell daughters were happily married—happily married and far away from Rudbek Hall.

Primula's sisters-in-law-to-be had received the news of her betrothal and Primula herself with the delicate dismay suitable to the welcome of a great warrior who has not long to live. Though deploring the insanity, bad taste, or desperation that caused her to espouse their brother Severn, they made her warmly welcome, sweeping her firmly into society in a fashion that would admit of no demur.

For the past twelve months Primula Greetwell had been Important—the betrothed of Viscount Severn, son of the Earl of Malhythe. All doors were opened to her, all *congés* extended. With Adeline to act as her sponsor she danced at Almack's, ate ices at Gunther's, saw the illuminations at Vauxhall Pleasure Gardens, and had agreeable young men without number sighing with love of her. Her marriage settlements were paid out from the moment the betrothal ring was on her finger; she did not lack money for the wardrobe and the incidentals that went with her new position. Primula now owned a phaeton and matched bays of her very own, and when Miss Greetwell drove in Green Park (suitably accompanied, of course) she could be serenely assured of acknowledgments from everyone who mattered in town. It was all very agreeable.

And this year, just as last, she had come to Rudbek Hall with the family for the Christmas holiday—only this year the party was longer, the guests more dazzling, and the entertainment more lavish, because very soon indeed would come Settling Day, and Primula would marry Lord Severn.

"Oh, there you are—naughty things, to be hiding from us! St. George had wanted you to come out walking with us most particularly, Prim—"

Catherine, Frances, and Margaret—Lady Rannoch, Lady Appleby, and Mrs. Trevose, respectively—swirled into the day-nursery bright in velvets and fur trim.

"—as he says the snowdrops are made brighter for your smile," finished Lady Appleby fulsomely. A nephew beckoned and she swooped him up into her arms.

"They'd have to be made pretty bright indeed, as they won't be out for another six weeks at least," said her sister tartly. "Really, Fanny, try to make up a *convincing* tale." Baby Margie, tired of trying to see if the passementerie trim on her aunt's gown was edible, abandoned that project to toddle over toward her mother.

"Well, he *did* miss her," Frances countered. "After all, I told him she would come walking out with us—"

"Aha!" said Lady Rannoch. "The truth is out." Margie reached her goal, and Lady Rannoch knelt to receive a rather ink-stained kiss.

"But how could I," Primula protested, "when I have all these invitations to write out?"

Margaret, the Earl's youngest daughter, pounced upon the pile of cards and snatched them from Primula's hands. "*Addie!* You know you should be doing these yourself! You are Papa's hostess while we are at Rudbeck, after all—and since the New Year's ball is in Prim's honor I don't see why she should have to do any of the work."

"Because if Prim does them their recipients have

a fair hope of being able to read what party they have been invited for and when it is to be held—you know my wretched scribbles, Maggie! Besides, I am only attempting to bring her life of gaiety and ease to its natural close. It will not do for her to find life *too* enjoyable, after all. Severn will be here by May, Papa thinks, and then Prim will have to marry him."

"Oh!" said Margaret Rudwell-Trevose. It was obvious, from her expression, that until that moment she had forgotten the entire matter. Primula burst out laughing.

"Oh, Margaret! Anyone would think I was going to the Tower instead of to the altar. Severn is your brother, as well as my husband-to-be! Surely one of you has a kind word for him?"

"Well!" said Frances briskly, gathering in her sisters with a speaking glance. "We can't all be sitting about here all day—even in such agreeable company," she added, relinquishing little Robert into the arms of a nurserymaid who had come to see what all the fuss was about. "It is far and away time to dress for dinner—oh, leave those, Prim, Bredon can do them. Coming?"

Chapter 4

RIO DE JANEIRO, EARLY JANUARY 1817

THE GREEN ON the mountains surrounding the harbor was almost indecent, Severn thought from his vantage point at the rail of the *Surety*. The buildings of the town the Portuguese had built on the shores of the River January were small white appendices to a rather strenuous amount of natural grandeur, and Lord Malhythe's son was glad, at the moment, that his health on the voyage home had been so uncertain. For him there would be no balls and fetes such as the captain and other passengers were forced to undergo. He could take his ease here for the week or so the Indiaman lay at anchor, and know that when she filled her sails again he would be within six weeks of home.

Severn had arrived in Calcutta in 1807 a cross, rebellious, and thoroughly self-pitying young man. After six months at sea he was certain it would have been better to have stayed in England and outfaced his father, and only the prospect of another six months aboard the noisy, stinking tub of an Indiaman that had delivered him dissuaded him from instantly going home again.

Determined to thwart Malhythe's plans for his future, Severn soon discovered that he had only three choices for his life in India: join the Army, the Government, or the Company. As the Army was a scandal and the Government a joke, Severn had, in the end, no choice but to fall in with his father's wishes. The East India Company was the real power in India. It bought and sold native princes, set up local governments to suit its mercantile interests, and had its own army—mercenaries drawn from every corner of Europe and the New World.

It took him about a year to run through—and survive—the dissipations that killed men in this unfamiliar climate, and once he had finished with drink and drugs and petty cruelty he was no longer the man Lord Malhythe had banished from England. The man that was left was very useful to the Company.

And so for the next eight years Viscount Severn ranged the frontiers of the East India Company's domain, conducting the Company's business while living in the palaces of the native princes. His rank was an asset, as was the fact that he simply did not care what his fellow countrymen thought of him. To be seen abroad in aigrette and turban and ruby earrings, gorgeously costumed and richly perfumed and seated cross-legged on the back of an elephant was something the stiff-necked merchants of the Company would rather die than do; the Earl's son laughed and went off to shoot tigers in the company of princes whom he found far more agreeable than his countrymen.

But the life he built was not a real life. It was a place to wait until he was summoned back to the world—to London, to the society of his own kind.

He only wished he was still sure they were his own kind.

The letter permitting his return had been dated December 1815. He had received it in June of the following year, and might as easily not have gotten it until that September, as his mail was not forwarded and few of the English in India cared to risk Calcutta in summer. But as it happened he had been called to the Company offices for an urgent consultation and so had received the letter within six weeks of its arrival—and had proceeded to annoy his masters by abandoning all their plans in favor of plans of his own. He dispatched his letter of acceptance to Lord Malhythe that very day, and less than a month later had loaded himself, his servant, and his possessions aboard a westbound Indiaman.

Three months after that he was at Capetown, and hoped his letter was still ahead of him. It was quite possible, of course, that a letter dispatched one month before he sailed would arrive after he did, or not at all. At least the worst of the journey was past; the probability of pirates was much diminished in Western waters and, with good fortune, the ship would never again be more than a month away from land.

The Atlantic crossing had been smooth, and now the *Surety* stood at anchor in Rio Harbor—the last stop but one before England. Soon he would walk the streets of London—to freeze in her foulest weather, of course, but at least he would do so in his own land.

In the company of his wife.

The wind off the water made him shiver, and he hunched his shoulders against the chill. Home and England, England and Home. Somehow, for all his longing, he could not make the two ideas fit together. Home was a house shockingly white against a deep-blue tropical sky, noisy with the chatter of Indian servants and the shriek of monkeys. Home was a tent in the *ruqh*, with the musty smell of the elephants thick on the air and the disappointed commentary of brush-hidden leopards carried audibly to his ears. Now, when it was far too late to change his mind, he wondered if he could readjust to a land that in his absence had grown unimaginably strange.

The swift summer night was falling over the Rio de Janeiro harbor. As the green hills turned to black in the white dusk he could see the lights bloom in the windows of the Governor-General's residence, high on the hill overlooking the city. A ball was being held there tonight, and Lord Severn was not among the glittering dancers. Once he would have clamored for admittance. Later he would have rejected such an entertainment in a fine Byronic passion. Now he was simply grateful his health excused him from a social duty he had no energy for. He turned and headed for his cabin.

When he arrived he found, to his pleasure, that Loach had lit the small brazier that served to heat the room and a large can of water was keeping warm over a spirit lamp next to a half-full copper bath.

"And will'ee be wanting anything more, Your Grace?" The bent and gnarled figure of his servant shambled forward.

"I—" About to call for brandy, Severn stopped himself. "Tea, I think. Is there any supper?"

"Oh, aye, we don't be wanting sperruts, Your Grace. Sperruts just burns a man up, she does. A good hot bath and a good cold curry, here's what Your Grace will be needing." The little man shuffled out, still conversing with himself.

Severn had never been able to convince Loach that he wasn't a duke—or, indeed, of anything else Loach did not wish to hear. He had bought him at the price of a gold repeating pocket watch from his host in Sherabad, who had wished to see his tigers devour the raggedy scarecrow man for the amusement of the thing. Fortunately a chiming pocket watch was equally amusing, and so Severn found himself undisputed suzerain of a seamed, scarred, bandy-legged enigma of indeterminate age whose remaining teeth were alarmingly red from chewing betel nut, and who babbled his thanks in good round Midlands vowels while raising Severn several grades in the peerage at the same time. Loach was missing an ear and an eye and a finger or two, and the whole of his left leg below the knee had been replaced with good Indian teak. The clothes he had on were less than rags, and the block-printed native cotton gave no clue to his origin. Loach had firmly attached himself to Severn, declaring himself indispensable to "Your Grace's" comfort—and perhaps, thought Severn, sliding into his bath, he was.

Severn closed his eyes and listened to the groaning of the ship and the sounds Loach made as he moved about the room brewing tea and laying the solitary cover for Severn's meal. He had never gotten any answer to his questions about his servant's past, whether he placed them in English, French, or good strong Hindi. The old man's manners were farcical, but he had seen service in some great house or other, Severn was sure. For years he had thought Loach a deserter from a naval ship, one of those poor wretches press-ganged from the shores of England, but had tentatively discarded the idea when Loach had chosen to sail for England with him. He had never before thought of what Loach would do when they reached England; some provision would certainly have to be made. Perhaps the little man's several skills included those of valet.

To be perfectly honest, he had never thought of what either of them would do when they reached England. When the letter came setting forth the conditions under which he might return he had never considered refusing them. He had prospered in India, and by the standards of the world Severn was a rich man. His father's threat to leave him penniless was an empty one, but the threat to shut him out of all society was as intolerable as it had been so many years before. To regain what he had so thoughtlessly lost he would pay any price, including wedding some ambitious unknown dazzled by a Viscount's coronet and the prospect of an Earldom at her beck.

"And will Your Grace care to dine, or will he set there in his copper bucket until he shrivels up like a raisin?"

"Yes, yes; I'm coming. I swear, old man, I had no notion that I'd purchased the finest *ayah* in all India," Severn grumbled affectionately. He stood and toweled himself off and shrugged into his dressing gown. The silk was Chinese, a legacy from one of his private trading ventures; it was lined in hill-squirrel. He was grateful for its solid warmth and oblivious to its opulence as he padded over to the table.

The cabin of an Indiaman had not changed in ten years. Even the furniture, purchased from an arriving voyager, was much the same as that which had accompanied him to India. Save for the presence of Loach, and a few minor mementos of his own, the last decade might simply not have happened.

And one more thing was the same. When he left this ship at the end of its voyage, his life would be wrenched once more from a semblance of normalcy and sent spinning off on some unforeseeable tangent.

The letter was waiting for him when the ship stopped in Madeira; a curt acknowledgment of his letter of 16 June inst. and the adviso that the *Surety* would be met at Gravesend by Lord Malhythe's private secretary. Lord Malhythe reminded Severn that disobedience to Mr. Bredon would be considered equivalent to disobedience to himself.

Now that the moment was fast approaching, Severn's blythe self-promises that marriage could be no more bizarre or unfamiliar than many other things he had done were giving way to uncertainty. He discovered that he very much wished this unknown wife to approve of him—while stoutly rejecting her right to judge him. His nerves were not improved at all by Mr. Bredon's demeanor, nor by the information he received from him.

"What do you mean, you don't know who she is?" Severn's temper was nothing soothed by the quiet excellence of the country inn to which he had been conveyed. Outside, the raw February weather blustered hesitantly at the diamond-shaped panes of the coffee room window. Inside, Severn paced like a caged panther. Loach, who had accompanied him from the ship, sat on his heel by the fireside silently drawing long white curls from a piece of wood with a wicked-bladed knife.

"If your lordship will recollect, I did not say that I was not aware of the identity of the young woman; I said I would not tell you," Mr. Bredon said.

"Well, why not?" Certainly he had not expected to be welcomed with open arms—but to be shunted off and buried this way like a disgraceful secret . . . !

Mr. Bredon sighed. "It is his lordship's wish that her identity remain a secret—at least to you—until the wedding is solemnized." He thrust his hands deep into his coat pockets and said nothing more.

"Well then, do I know her at least?" Severn demanded, with the air of one grasping at straws.

"As to that, my lord, I could not hazard a guess." With Malhythe for a master, however, it was far more likely that Bredon *would* not.

There was a long pause as Severn wrestled with his temper and his good intentions. Prudence won;

it was difficult to be irate when you were freezing. He had forgotten England was so damned cold.

"Build up the fire, would you, Bredon?" Severn shivered and poured himself another glass of punch, but even that was strange. He had grown out of the habit of heavy drinking in the East; the brandy burned on his tongue and did nothing to warm him. His father's secretary poked up the fire and Severn pulled his chair closer to it.

"Very well; I shall meekly wed the fair *incognita*. Afterward, I understand, my time is my own. . . . Has the date for the wedding been set?"

"Yes, my lord. The banns are being called, and the wedding is fixed for the seventeenth of March. His lordship trusts that you will remain in town for the Season, as he has taken the liberty of procuring you a most superior residence."

"*Most* superior," Severn murmured ironically.

"His lordship expects that you will occupy the time until your wedding with repairs and additions to your wardrobe. For such things as you may require from London, he has empowered me to act as your agent. For the time being, my lord, you are not to leave these rooms." Mr. Bredon spared hardly a glance for Lord Severn's bizarre manservant; the omission was eloquent.

"And am I also to be conveyed to my wedding blindfold and in a closed coach? My lord father once accused me of living in the last century—how odd that he should choose to emulate me." Severn rapped out the words in his old style, but his heart was not in them. There was something about the date his father had chosen for the wedding that made small bells of warning chime in Severn's mind.

"That is as may be, my lord—but surely three weeks is not so much time to humor him? Once you are wed, as you say, your time is your own."

"Livened chiefly by the spectacle of my lord of Malhythe rewriting his will on a daily basis. My God, Bredon, does he think I need the Rudwell money?"

"I could not say, my lord. Naturally you will wish to meet with your bankers at your earliest convenience—"

"—which will, I take it, be *after* the wedding?"

"—and for the present, the items which you have brought back with you have been conveyed to your new home. Suitable provision will also be made for your—ahem!—suite."

"Means me, does'ee?" Loach spoke at last.

"I don't give a damn *who* he means!" Frustration—and fear—boiled over; Severn's roar of fury was enough to make Bredon fall back a step. "My lord father may order my life as he likes—and suit his macabre notions of fun without my slightest protest—but those in *my* employ are *my* responsibility. His meddling starts—and stops—with me! Is that clear?"

"My lord—!" Mr. Bredon said faintly. "I only meant . . ."

"Aye, tiger in the pit do roar gradely," agreed Loach, not looking up from his whittling.

Severn laughed; his ill-temper seemed to have vanished. He clapped Bredon on the back. "Loach is right; the trapped tiger makes the most noise—and me without even a tethered kid to show for my foolishness. Tell Father I'll keep my manservant with me; I'll stand surety that he'll keep to the inn as well. Now let us see what dinner this place has to offer—and since we are going to be much in each other's company, Bredon, I hope you thought to bring a pack of cards."

Chapter 5

MONDAY, MARCH 17, 1817

MONDAY, MARCH 17, 1817, dawned bright and clear. The bride was being dressed at Colworth House. She would then be conveyed to St. George's Church in Hanover Square, there to be wedded to her affianced groom.

Miss Primula Greetwell could not imagine how she had ever gotten into such a mess.

"Oh, Addie—I can't!" she moaned. With no particular success she attempted to remove the trailing veil of aerophane crepe from her hair and sank down upon the bed. "I can't possibly marry Severn!"

"Well, this is a fine time to discover that," Severn's sister said.

Adeline Lambton had abandoned every principle—as she expressed it—to make an extended stay in town in support of the bride-to-be. And while it was no wonder that, faced with the grim reality of Severn in the too solid flesh, Primula's nerves should give way, there was no denying that this was the worst possible time for them to do so. Adeline Rudwell-Lambton strongly suspected that should the bride not appear at the wedding the consequences would exceed even the power of her imagination to devise. Lord Malhythe was set on this marriage for Severn, and none of his daughters had been able to find out why.

"Better now than in half-an-hour's time." Lady Greetwell moved toward her daughter, and Primula flung herself into her mother's arms. Adeline looked beseechingly at Lady Greetwell, but that formidable matron had no time for the Rudwell family's problems.

"I have had my doubts about the wisdom—and, in fact, the sanity—of this betrothal from the first. I will not go so far as to say that Primula has come to her senses—"

"I think I'll ring for some brandy. *Someone* is going to need some," Adeline announced desperately.

Her gesture in that direction was interrupted by the return of Claggett, Primula's dresser, who had been sent to fetch the last items of the bride's toilette. Claggett set down the chaplet of white forcing-house roses on Primula's dressing table and took in the pretty tableau—Primula in silver and white, Lady Greetwell in shades of blue, both ladies in a state of agitation—and headed for Primula purposefully.

"Bride's nerves, my lady, and the best cure for that is marriage. Come along, Miss Primula! It's nearly nine of the clock now, and you're being married at ten-thirty sharp. It won't do to keep Lord Severn waiting."

Primula looked up at this call to duty and reluctantly released her hold on her mother. "Addie, there's something I have to explain to you," she began, taking a deep breath. "It's about Severn—"

"Oh, Prim, *no*! I know he is dreadful, but how will it look if you cry off now, with Severn already on his way to the church? Papa will not be pleased—and surely Severn is no worse now than he was six months ago? It is only nerves, dearest; no more than that."

"You don't understand!" wailed Primula, frustrated to tears. She had been so certain when all this began that it would be a simple matter to marry Lord Severn—but after the wedding they would be alone together, and what could she possibly say to him?

Adeline took Primula's hands in hers to draw her closer to the mirror and the waiting maid. Primula could feel the warmth of Addie's hands even through the thin glazed kid of the short gloves that completed Primula's bridal costume.

"Now you just stand up here, Miss, and let me fix these flowers in your hair," Claggett said firmly, taking Primula by the shoulders and maneuvering her into position. In the mirror she could see the bridal *grande toilette* in all its glory: the tiny cap sleeves in white satin slashed with silver, the long sweep of silver lace over satin of the skirt, and the Rudwell pearls everywhere.

"They're laying the covers for the breakfast downstairs right now—and all your guests are waiting for you at the church. You can't want to disappoint them, now, can you?"

"I say Primula should do as she pleases," Lady Greetwell said sharply. "And if she's decided that she doesn't want Severn, then that's the end of it."

Adeline, having received the revivifying spirits from the footman who had been standing ready for her call—for Mrs. Lambton remembered her own wedding day well—swooped down upon Primula with a large glass and a ferocious air of cheerfulness.

"Now, Prim, dearest, I don't wish to influence you by telling you that if you cry off you'll be ruined for life"—Lady Greetwell glared at Mrs. Lambton, who rushed on—"but marrying Severn cannot be *all* bad. And then we shall truly be sisters, only think! Do drink this, dearest, it will make you feel better.

Papa will see to it that he does nothing you do not like—and you need not see much of him, after all."

"I cannot cry off now!" muttered Primula distractedly, pressing her hands to her cheeks. Adeline held a glass to her lips, and she choked as the burning taste of neat brandy filled her mouth. A jumbled vision of her father—Lord Malhythe—Severn—disgrace—flashed through her mind like reflections from a shattered mirror. "I cannot cry off now," she repeated. "Oh, why am I doing this? I must have been mad."

"I must have been mad," said Lord Severn, in awe.

"My lord?" said Mr. Bredon.

"I cannot believe that I am marrying, sight unseen, some chit of a girl proposed by my father—my *father*!—of whom you will tell me nothing at all! It is not possible."

Mr. Bredon digested this conversational offering in silence for a moment. "Are you proposing to reject the match, my lord?" he said at last.

"No," growled Severn in disgust.

Viscount Severn had been roused at six o'clock in the morning to dress in his finest new-bought plumage and descend to his father's crested traveling coach to begin the two-and-a-half-hour drive to the church. Lord Malhythe had taken the precaution of having the rose brocade curtains nailed shut over the coach windows, as if Severn were in danger of finding his bride's likeness and lineage blazoned on handbills all around the town.

But in a few minutes more the secret would be secret no longer. The sound of the coachwheels on the paving suggested that they were approaching the church, and Severn pulled his soft grey gloves more snugly over his fingers for the dozenth time. Any man who had hunted tigers afoot was surely capable of standing through a brief ceremony—after which he need never see the new Lady Severn again.

"We have arrived, Lord Severn," Bredon said.

The inside of St. George's remained much as Severn had seen it on his infrequent church appearances in what now seemed another lifetime. His father nodded to him imperturbably from the family box as Severn took his place at the altar. Mr. Bredon stood right beside him, acting as groomsman—in case he should bolt, Severn thought sourly.

It seemed an interminable period until the bride appeared, trudging resolutely up the aisle on the arm of her father with Adeline Lambton walking ahead. The bride was no one he knew—not surprising, as Severn's acquaintance of respectable women had been limited—and much younger than he'd expected. He had been convinced, somehow, that the Fair Unknown of his espousal would be older. As she approached he saw that she had brown eyes, brown hair, and an expression of panic-stricken determination that he suspected matched his own.

Severn smiled at her encouragingly, and was nettled to see her eyes widen with something very like horror at the gesture. What had his revered father been telling her? From the look of her she was too young to have been Out the last time he'd been in London, and he very much doubted he'd remained a topic of conversation among the *ton* these last ten years. Irritated, he turned his attention back to the bishop, who was regarding the wedding party with the expression of one who expects an outbreak of high drama.

"The ring, my lord," Bredon murmured, passing it to Severn.

* * *

Lord Severn's serene conviction that things could not possibly get any worse lasted until they had reached nearly the end of the wedding ceremony.

"Do you, Primula Miranda Greetwell, take this man to be your lawfully wedded husband?" If there were conditions to her acceptance Severn did not hear them. Primula Greetwell was a name he was never likely to forget.

"—and now, my sweet, we part." Severn smiled down at the tear-streaked face before him. "It was a famous lark, to be sure, but larks go to bed with the sun and so must I." He opened the door, and the chill light of mid-March—March seventeenth, to be exact—bled into the hired carriage. "Get out."

"Do you, John Clerebold Acelet Rudwell—"

"No," Severn muttered.

Primula felt herself go ice cold. He did not seem to know where he was, but he knew *her*—knew her and would not have her.

Lord Malhythe had constantly assured her that she had the power to make or mar the match. He had been so convinced of it that she had driven any thought of Lord Severn's rebellion straight from her mind. Marriage was the price of Severn's return to England. He would not refuse her.

But he was.

She had not recognized him when she first saw him—if she had not known beforehand that it was Lord Severn, the tall rangy stranger would have possessed an elusive familiarity, nothing more.

His skin was dark brown, and above it the hair was startlingly light. The chestnut curls she remembered so vividly were gone—this man's hair was bleached to the color of tarnished brass, and when she stood beside him she could see that it was liberally streaked with grey. The face was older, too—the random mockery turned inward, the cold wit warmed with compassion. But the green eyes were the same, and when he had smiled at her in rueful acknowledgment of their mutual plight, she had been convinced in that instant that all the rest was a bad dream. The intervening decade had vanished like smoke. She had been sure the two of them could put things right.

Until now.

"Lord Severn?" In a lesser man the note in the bishop's voice might have been panic. "Do you take—"

Recalled to himself, Severn looked down at the pinched white face and staring dark eyes of his bride. Primula Miranda Greetwell—his greatest triumph, most notorious escapade, the cause of his banishment. The innocent and undeserving victim of the cruelest act of his life.

He had wallowed in self-pity and the injustice of his exile and forgotten her completely. But Lord Malhythe had not forgotten. Ten years ago today Severn had thrown Primula back on her parents' doorstep. He doubted the date of his wedding was a coincidence. His father meant it to remind him, and it had.

What sort of a woman would marry Viscount Severn sight unseen? Now he knew.

Severn looked at the bishop. "I will," he said firmly.

Beside him Primula swayed, eyes fluttering closed. Severn reached out to steady her, but Primula had turned to his sister Adeline for support. When he tried to kiss her as the ceremony required, Mrs. Lambton glared at him in fury.

"So you are Lord Severn." Sir Rowland gazed affably at his new son-in-law across the width of the rocking coach. Severn's bride had been spirited away from him at the church door, and before he had quite recovered from learning the identity of the bride he was confronted with the bride's father. He hoped, cravenly, that the coach would negotiate the few minutes' ride to Colworth House in far more instantaneous a fashion than was at all likely.

"I must say, you are not at all what we expected," Sir Rowland went on.

"And what was that, sir?" Severn said cautiously.

"Well, you must agree, when a man's father makes an offer on his behalf to a girl he's never met, the impression is given that if she knew him she wouldn't have him—"

"Never met!" began Severn hoarsely, then stopped. He had assumed Primula knew who he was; but if she had, she would surely have told her father—who would be challenging him to a duel instead of making polite conversation.

But Primula had met "John Cunningham" all those years ago, not Viscount Severn. He knew his father—it would have amused Lord Malhythe to engineer the match without telling Primula the true identity of the man she was to marry. And then, of course Severn would reveal himself, and she would be trapped, helpless, wedded to the one man on earth she must hate more than any other.

No wonder Malhythe had kept the bride's identity such a dark secret! Severn had been given no chance to warn her off.

A cold chill settled in his stomach. He had ruined her. He must make amends. But if she did not know him as her ravisher, she would surely make some shift to explain her "disgrace." How could he explain that no explanation was necessary without explaining why?

Severn's general feeling of malaise settled down to a good pounding headache.

"No, sir, I never met your daughter before. But I repose complete confidence in my father's ability to choose a bride in all respects suitable to my situation in life, and I am certain she and I shall deal extremely together. Primula is a fine girl—a charming girl," Severn said vehemently.

"Her mother and I have always thought so," said Sir Rowland noncommittally. Severn glared.

Malhythe's byzantine plots be damned. Ignorant he had come to the altar, and ignorant he would stay, by God. If Primula did not know him, he would not enlighten her. Let her save what pitiful dignity she still possessed. If the Viscountcy would make her happy, then she would have it, by all means.

"A fine girl," Severn repeated stubbornly.

Lord Malhythe had caused all the doors to the salons to be thrown open, the furniture to be removed, and tables laid to welcome the several-score persons invited to celebrate Severn's nuptials. Most of London seemed to have risen to the challenge, if Severn was any judge. The new-wed lord could see the tables stretching off to white-damasked infinity, and the glittering horde of society milling about them—like goats, Severn thought uncharitably.

He didn't know any of them, but his bride did not seem to share his ignorance. Primula seemed to know quite a number of people. From across the room he could see her engaged by a circle of women in diamonds and plumes. Adeline should be among them, and, next to Lord Malhythe himself, she was the person Severn wanted to talk to most. He started forward.

"*There* you are, Johnny," Adeline said with venomous sweetness, linking her arm through his and dragging him to a stop. "How we have all been dying for a word with you." She was bright and neat in the elaborate modern fashion that jarred so strangely on Severn's unaccustomed eye, and her color was the sparkling deep pink of a sister about to do battle.

Severn looked at his sister for a long moment. "I have been rusticating in a country inn for the last three weeks, Adeline, and in India for almost ten years before that. I do not see what I can possibly have done to annoy you in all that time."

"Oh, you haven't done anything—yet. I don't know why Papa was so insistent that Prim marry you—and I certainly don't know why she agreed!—but I do know that if you ever—*ever*, Johnny!—do anything to make her unhappy—"

But he could make his bride miserable simply by telling her who he was. Oh, Malhythe was a clever devil, and in coming home his son had put himself well and neatly into the trap.

"Listen, Addie"—he turned and took his sister firmly by the shoulders—"hard as it is to credit, I don't mean my wife any harm. I—look here, does she know why I married her?"

"Because Papa told you to, I expect," said Adeline coolly.

"Do you know why she married me?"

Something in the urgency in his voice reached her. The martial fire died from Adeline Lambton's eyes and she looked at her brother in puzzlement. "No, Johnny. I don't think anyone does. Papa spoke to her father and she agreed to have you. Do you know why?"

"Yes. No. I— Look, Addie, I'm freezing to death and my head is splitting. Can you get me a cup of tea?"

"Tea?" said Mrs. Lambton in amusement. "You wait right here and stay out of trouble and I'll bring you something to drink."

* * *

Adeline didn't know. Sir Rowland didn't know. And that meant Primula didn't know who he "really" was. Which meant she'd agreed to marry him. . . . Why?

Bribery. Blackmail. But for whatever reason, Primula had consented—and was now faced with explaining or concealing her past from a stranger who was no stranger.

"My . . . lord?"

Severn turned around and stared straight into the face of his wife.

The rest of the ceremony had passed for Primula in a dizzy blur—he did not know who she was, after all—and it had only been as the carriage pulled away from the church that Primula realized that her husband wasn't in the coach with her.

"He is the most dreadful man alive!" Adeline said vehemently.

"Severn?" said Primula blankly. Her mother patted her hand. "Where is he? Oughtn't he be here?"

"I believe he is going in Lord Malhythe's coach, with your Papa and that nice young man—Lord Malhythe's secretary, I believe? But we will see them all directly. You must compose yourself now, my love. Everything went off just as it ought, except—"

"Except when Severn decided to pretend to jilt her, just for a lark! Lady Greetwell, I apologize most sincerely for the very fact of my brother's existence!"

"Now, Mrs. Lambton, there is not quite any need for you to do that," said Lady Greetwell.

"I do not think he is at all well," said Primula in a rush. "His color was not good, you know."

"Oh, Prim, you are too good to live! Making excuses for him—when he is brown as a savage and healthy as a horse. And has not changed one iota,"

Adeline added acidly. "Saying 'no' to the bishop. Really!"

"His hair has gone very grey," Primula began, and blushed violently at her self-betrayal. No one must know she had seen Severn before!

"I grant you, he does not look at all like the portrait Mme. Vigée-Lebrun painted of him at eighteen," Adeline agreed, "but he is not above five-and-thirty, Prim; surely you cannot think his hair is going grey."

"It *is* grey," Severn's bride insisted. "Perhaps he has caught one of those wasting fevers. They are common in the East, so I have read."

"Well, if he did, he did not waste away far enough—and you know, Prim, that I do *not* say that simply because my Georgie would have been the next Earl."

Lady Greetwell regarded her daughter's sister-in-law with some surprise at this plain speaking.

"Can you actually have wished my daughter to contract a marriage with such a desperate character, Mrs. Lambton? Or do I hear natural sororal affection in your voice?"

"Oh, affection, of course, Lady Greetwell. Lord Severn's not a bad lot for. . . ." But whatever comparison Adeline was thinking of making was apparently too hideous to utter; she made a helpless motion with her hands and sighed. "And I am quite certain he will be very good to Prim—oh, it is so wonderful that you are to be one of us now, dearest! I shall be quite reconciled to staying in town."

"Staying in town?" Primula said, startled. "But I understood. . . . Of course, I am delighted you will remain—but is not Mr. Lambton looking for you to return?"

"Oh, Lamb can manage for himself a few weeks longer—and Georgie cannot. He informed me this morning—informed his Mama, if you please!—that he intended to remain fixed in town for the Season as he was quite old enough to 'welcome Uncle Severn home properly' as he put it. Well, what could I do but agree to remain with him?—not that he asked me, I assure you. At least while I may keep my eye upon him he cannot get into too much trouble. Not like—"

"Like Primula's husband," finished Lady Greetwell equitably. "My dear Mrs. Lambton, marriage is generally considered to wash a groom's sins whiter than snow. Even though he is your brother, you might be a good deal happier were you to espouse this charming delusion."

"I am sorry we did not see Sarah Jane at the wedding—aren't you, Mama?" Primula said quickly. "I know you have heard from Mrs. Emwilton, who said—oh, I do not remember what, precisely! But even if Sarah Jane did not wish to attend, with her Papa so recently taken from her, she might have paid us a visit." Primula did not care what conversational hare she started, so long as it led the topic of conversation far from one upon which her Mama and Mrs. Lambton seemed so prepared to disagree.

"Perhaps she felt you would have no time for her, being newly married . . . but it is most odd. Sarah wrote me a very short note, hardly more than a line or two, and all she said was that she was removing to Bath. I do hope Sarah Jane is all right."

"I am sure she is, Mama," said Primula, wondering why the words sounded so much like a lie. Her nerve-storm was over, and having had more than a year to prepare for this day, she was becoming used to the idea of marriage. After all, the worst that could happen to her already had. "And I will write her again in a few days. Surely she will not despise the opportunity to keep me company for the Season."

* * *

The carriage had pulled up at Colworth House, and footmen in the severe Malhythe livery assisted Primula to descend. The ladies swept into the house, which was transformed into a veritable Arcadia. Wide silk ribbands and hothouse flowers decked the rooms that Malhythe had thrown open to the party, and a number of Primula's friends seized upon her instantly to offer their congratulations and demand her opinion of the groom.

"So tell us, Primula—now that you've seen him, do you wish you'd cried off? I vow, it must be beyond anything strange to marry a man you've never seen before! What do you think of him?" Lydia Mainwaring leaned closer, eyes sparkling with vicarious excitement. Mrs. Mainwaring was a matron of Primula's own age—having been widowed at Waterloo she was just long enough out of mourning to find other people's marriages exciting.

"Oh, he is—well enough, I suppose. Really, Lydia—I only married the man; I should have learned more of his character standing up with him at Almack's!"

General laughter greeted Primula's cross-grained wit, but the bride did not join in the merriment. Strange, Lydia said, to marry a man she had never seen before. But Primula *had* seen him before—seen him and fallen in love, then, with the man she had thought he was. That man must exist somewhere in Severn, or he could not have made her believe in him.

"Almack's! He'll never get vouchers to Almack's! I daresay, Lady Severn, you shall have to get used to sitting home Wednesday nights—or do you plan on going without him?" Mrs. Mainwaring asked.

"I shall bet you five guineas that you will see us both there, Lydia!" Primula said recklessly.

"A wager? If I put *that* about, neither of you will

be seen in 'Seventh Heaven,' " said Miss Alice Cakeborne, wagging a minatory finger.

" 'A matron may do what a maiden may not,' " Primula parroted primly, quoting a popular tag. "How now, Lydia, afraid you'll lose? And when I have had more than that off you in an afternoon of cards!" Lydia's worldly airs had been a source of vexation to Primula for some months, and her airy assumption that Severn could not make his way in society had been the last straw.

Mrs. Mainwaring, who did not like to be reminded of her poor cardplay, jerked her chin angrily. "I won't lose—but if you're so confident, my dear Prim, why not make it more interesting? A hundred guineas that Viscount Severn has not attended an Assembly by the end of the Season!"

"Oh, Lydia, *no*!" gasped Miss Cakeborne.

"Done!" said Primula, regretting it as she spoke. A matron might do what a maiden could not, but this matron had been married less than an hour and did not think her consequence was great enough to pass such a wager off as mere eccentricity. She had vowed to be a model of propriety at her wedding, and forgotten that a model is only a non-working imitation of the real thing.

"I—I think I see my husband—pray excuse me!"

Lord Severn was easy enough to spot; he was the only person in Colworth House who looked as though he could imagine neither how he had gotten here nor wished to be here in the first place. Primula had no idea at all of what she would say to him when she reached him; granting that marriage was held to be the equivalent of a formal introduction, what did they have to talk about?

It was not simply her promise to the Earl of Malhythe that kept her silent. Malhythe might say what he chose about her past; once the wedding ring was on Primula's finger Severn had made the reparation Society demanded, and the scandal would pass. More than fear of scandal, it was the feeling that she should walk carefully around her new husband, lest an incautious word shatter matters beyond her capability of mending.

And that, thought the ever-sensible Primula, was sheerest nonsense. Of course he knew who she was—and even if he didn't, to reveal herself as the girl he'd mocked and ruined, the cause of his banishment, would. . . .

Do what?

What would Severn think of any woman who'd agreed to marry him after he'd done *that* to her?

Abruptly confused, Primula stopped a few feet away from Severn. He hadn't noticed her, and she had suddenly decided that any other time would be a better time for him to start. She had taken one step backward when Severn swung around to face her.

"My . . . lord?"

His eyes, she noted with detachment, were still that unlikely shade of green. Too vivid for normal eye color, they gave Severn an air of unreality, as though he were an actor and all the events surrounding him a play. Now they focused on her, and Primula felt herself drawn into the performance.

"Lady Severn." The words sounded very final; she saw him realize it at the same moment and sketch a smile. "I am . . . pleased to make your acquaintance."

"They tell me you've been in India." Rattled, Primula gave tongue to the first thing that entered her head.

"And you wish me back there? I assure you that I will contrive to be very little trouble to you. You will hardly know that you are married."

"Except for the title."

"Except for that, of course."

This was not going at all the way she wished—and urgent and unbidden came the thought that a husband who would be very little trouble to her was a husband who was unlikely to appear at Almack's any time this Season.

"But surely you will not just *disappear*, my lord? After all, you have been so long away from England; you will wish to renew old acquaintances. I'm sure you will find London very much changed—I thought we might give a small rout-party in a few weeks. Or—attend the theater?" Primula said breathlessly.

"Or present my wife at Court?" Severn asked. That was it, of course. Lady Severn did not wish to be done out of the perquisites of her new rank—one of which was a Court presentation as Viscountess Severn. Having acquired her trophy she would wish to display it as well. "I shall be delighted to behave precisely as required. You need only make clear to me the extent of my obligations to your . . . rank . . . and I shall fulfill them with dispatch."

"Your obligations? I should be surprised, my lord, to hear that you knew what an obligation was," his bride said tartly.

The headache receded a pace, and to his own surprise, Severn laughed. "If you have been listening to my sisters, Lady Severn, I am surprised that you are talking to me now."

"But not surprised I married you," Primula said flatly.

A Viscountcy is worth such small sacrifice, don't you think? The words ran through Severn's mind, but he found he could not say them. Though she had no reason to marry him except his title, he clung to the slender hope that Primula Greetwell had found some other reason to wed.

"Tell me, if you would be so kind, have you seen, ah, 'our' new and would-be happy home? I have not been much in town since my return, and Lord Malhythe tells me that I have presented my bride with a fashionable town residence."

He saw her brown eyes widen a bit at the non-sequitur, then narrow speculatively. A sudden impulse seized him—he would ask her why she had married him, and from her answer he would—

"Here you are, Johnny," Adeline said, holding out a cup. "And I see that Prim has found you. I hope you are keeping her tolerably amused."

"I have been on my best behavior, sister dear." He looked at the dark liquid in the punch cup, caught the scent of alcohol, and decided that nothing could make him feel worse than he did at the moment. With a flick of the wrist he tossed back the cup's contents, and cleared his throat briskly to cover the reflexive choke.

"Lord Severn says—" Primula began, but just then the gong sounded to summon the guests in to breakfast.

"You can take me in, Johnny," his sister said amiably as she threaded her arm through his. "After all, you won't wish to be seen dangling after your wife like the husband in a French farce, will you?"

Chapter 6

MONDAY, MARCH 17, 1817, 4:00 P.M.

SHE'D BEEN RIGHT after all, Primula told herself with grim satisfaction. He *was* ill.

By the end of the first course it was obvious that the groom was much the worse for wear, but for some reason Primula wasn't able to fathom, no one else could see anything amiss in Severn's behavior. It was as if all the rest of the party had some predetermined image of Viscount Severn that the man before them fit well enough for use, and only Primula saw him clearly. But the few glasses of wine Lord Severn had taken in answer to various toasts were not enough to explain the flushed cheeks and glittering eyes—why did no one else see that?

On the face of things he was the perfect host—jovial, witty, and if his remarks were just this side of improper, the occasion excused all. The company was scandalized, titillated, and well prepared to believe that Severn had not changed at all in the ten years of his exile. Stories to cap his—suitably laundered for the ladies—were offered, and Primula received more than one sidelong look of spurious sympathy. The meal was lengthy and elaborate, with dozens of removes, and when Severn gracefully resigned pride of place in the conversation to others, only his bride saw that it was necessity more than manners that dictated the relinquishment.

Fortunately the company rose from the table soon thereafter and Primula made her way to her husband's side.

"We must get you away from here, my lord. You are not well."

The green gaze leveled upon her was opaque with fever. "I can manage," he said shortly.

"You are ill. You will take a chill standing about here like this. No one will think it odd if we wish to be the first to leave," she said coaxingly.

"Are you sure?" he said, as if the customs of this land were alien to him.

"Yes, my lord, I am sure." Primula said firmly. She tucked her arm through his and went in search of Lord Malhythe.

The Earl of Malhythe held court in one of the small salons that adjoined the main rooms. Windowless since the passing of the Window Tax some years before, these rooms enjoyed something of the air of a niche designed for the repose of a holy relic.

"Young man, it hardly matters what airs of the valet's son you ape. You are too tall to be a man of fashion. Your only hope is to excel in the Corinthian line."

"But, Lord Malhythe," returned the gentleman so addressed, "I hardly dare to mention that I find the Corinthian pose tedious beyond belief. If one must impersonate, why not one's betters? And if one is presented with handicaps by circumstance, it is one's duty to attempt to surmount them, however inadequately."

Mr. Bartholomew Rainford gazed gently down from his imposing six-foot-two upon the Earl of Malhythe and allowed his sky-blue gaze to wander.

"Why, it is Lady Severn. Allow me to extend the felicities of the day to you and to Lord Severn."

"Thank you, Mr. Rainford," Primula answered. Since King Brummel's flight to the Continent in May of 1816, the post of *arbiter elegantiarum* to the *ton* had gone unfilled. But though that make-or-break recognition was a thing of the past, there were still members of the Polite World who were acknowledged to have an importance out of all proportion to their earthly rank. In Brummel's absence, Mr. Rainford's star was on the rise, and Primula had been fortunate enough to bask in his good fellowship from the first moment of her social career.

"And here is Lord Severn. Tell me, my lord, how does married life find you? This may be your only chance to offer up an answer that is both honest and favorable, you know." It was an article of faith with Mr. Rainford that the pursuit of good form absolutely precluded thoughts of matrimony.

"I hope, sir, that I will never have to refine upon honesty in my dealings with you," Severn said noncommittally. "I was hoping for a private word with my father, if it does not inconvenience you."

"Not at all," returned Mr. Rainford, bowing from his imposing height. "You will have much to occupy you after your long separation." With another bow to Primula and Lord Malhythe, Mr. Rainford took himself off.

A number of most unfilial similes occupied Severn's thoughts as he gazed upon his parent. The Earl of Malhythe had not, to all appearances, changed at all in the last ten years. The wig that he wore made the barest concession to fashion by its unpowdered state, and the heavy-lidded yellow-green eyes were fixed upon his only son with an unwavering serpentine intensity.

Comparisons to serpents and most of the lower reptiles came easily, though whether they were for Malhythe or himself Severn couldn't quite remember at the moment. All of the remarks he had been rehearsing crowded his throat, unsayable in the presence of his wife. His carefully chosen wife.

"Father," Severn said tightly.

"My congratulations to you, Severn, on what must be the happiest day of any man's life," Malhythe said blandly. "And to you, my dear, although in your case I must wish you felicity and not triumph, must I not?"

"Thank you for your good wishes, Lord Malhythe. I shall cherish them just as I ought," Primula said dryly. Severn looked at her in surprise. The little churchmouse he remembered would not have faced the Earl of Malhythe with such assurance.

"But it has been a long day for you both, and by custom the bridal couple is the first to leave, so I collect that you have come to tender your farewells," the Earl continued with unwonted amiability.

"I will be happy to remove my bride to her new home, sir, if you will do me the kindness of telling me where it is," Severn said crossly. A great weariness dragged at his every limb, and even the seductions of a proper jeremiad seemed far too much effort.

"Far more to the point, I have told your coachman," Lord Malhythe said. He lifted a small silver bell on the table beside him and rang sharply. A servant who, from his celerity, seemed to have been hovering outside the door, entered at once.

"Have Lord Severn's coach brought at once, Naseby. I trust you will find Kitmatgar House to your satisfaction, Severn," he added when the servant departed. "I have kept you constantly in mind as I readied it."

"You've kept everything in mind, haven't you?" Severn said dangerously. *Kitmatgar* was Urdu for *servant*; Malhythe had made the very name of the house into an insult.

Normally Primula enjoyed her verbal fencing with Lord Malhythe—never more so than now, when she was invulnerable to him at last. But the depth of the feeling between father and son made her feel as if she had been wading along a country brook and stepped suddenly into quicksand, sinking slowly and helplessly while chill currents buffeted her.

It was nothing as simple as hatred. If Malhythe had hated his son he would simply not have allowed him to return to England. If Severn had hated his father he would surely have ignored the prohibition and been home long ago.

Her parents' feelings for each other were simple and clear. Her own feelings for Severn were more tangled, but even they did not approach the passionate obscurity of the feelings Severn and his father held for each other. Their confrontation gave her the frightening sense of impending doom that being alone in an open field during a lightning storm might.

"Please, Lord Severn—may we go? I—I have the head-ache, and will be glad to see home," Primula blurted desperately.

There was a pause, and a sense of disengagement in the fencing that was much more than verbal.

"Of course. My son and I have both been lacking in courtesy, my dear Lady Severn. I am sure your carriage is waiting, and I trust you will soon recover your health."

Primula curtsied, head down and eyes averted.

"And I will hope to call upon you at your earliest convenience, my lord father, to discuss all of the *arrangements* you have made for me in my absence."

"No doubt Bredon will know the best time for you to call," Malhythe said imperturbably.

The Earl had never meant for her to keep his secret, Primula realized in shock. The swift March day was already drawing to its close; the late afternoon sun painted long shadows on the streets she saw through her coach windows. Her husband had wedged himself into the opposite corner of the vehicle and sprawled more than sat, eyes closed and breathing stertorous, and Primula herself felt rather as if she had escaped the cage of a large and hungry tiger.

A tiger who had meant her to break her promise. A tiny line formed between her winged brows as Primula tried to puzzle out what seemed to be a labyrinthine plot indeed. She only wished she could ask her father's opinion of the whole—there was no one so good at unraveling puzzles as Sir Rowland.

"First, my dear, we must organize our holdings," his voice said in her memory. Item: the Earl of Malhythe wished her to marry his son because she was the girl Severn had ruined. Item: Lord Malhythe did not wish her to admit to Severn that she knew that he and "John Cunningham" were one and the same. Item:—

But there her store of hard information stopped. *She* had not been using a false name ten years before, but—here her mouth firmed in rueful acknowledgment—it was highly unlikely that she had impressed herself upon Severn's memory. With the scandals told of him, she had been only fortunate to have claimed an entire fortnight of his time in what must have been an exceedingly busy schedule of debauchery. He did not know who she was.

But then again, she did not know for certain that

he didn't. And he'd be almost certain to guess who she was if she told him the story of her disgrace, which would lead to—

What? She didn't know. It would take an Act of Parliament for Lord Severn to rid himself of the wife his father had chosen for him.

At the wedding breakfast she had been almost ready to reveal all, despite Malhythe's prohibition. Now she thought that very thing might have been the Earl's plan. But in all this shifting web of uncertainty there was one thing she was certain of. She would hold her secrets until she—*she*, and nobody else—decided it was time to tell them.

Between Oxford Street and Piccadilly, west of Regent Street and east of Grosvenor Square, lay Kitmatgar House. It was situated in one of the new squares of townhouses that had grown up in London's West End over the last decade, and like its fellows it had a Palladian facade, iron gates with brass knobs, an imposing front door with gleaming brightwork and a quizzical knocker, a kitchen in its basement and servants' rooms in its attic, and—wonder of opulence—a stables and carriage house tucked carefully behind the tiny garden that marched in regimented magnificence around three sides of the house. It had a pocket-sized ballroom, a conservatory, a music room, and a library, in addition to a host of more mundane chambers dedicated to Lord and Lady Severn's comfort and divertissement.

All of these elegancies were currently of supreme irrelevance to the occupants of the carriage that pulled up before them.

"Severn?" Primula felt the carriage rock as the footman descended from his post, and heard the rattle of the steps as they were placed in position. Most of the square was already in shadow. The cressets in their iron baskets flanking the townhouse door had been lit, and in the wan light that spilled into the carriage Primula could see that her husband lay silent and unmoving against the plush upholstery of the bench seat.

"Severn?" she said again, leaning forward.

Primula had not bolted the coach door for such a brief journey, and now the footman swung it open. A wave of colder air rolled in, and with it Severn roused and muttered a few words in a language Primula did not know.

"My lord?" the footman said, and Severn stared about himself blankly. His face was unwholesomely pale and sheened with perspiration.

"We are home, my lord," Primula prompted.

"Of . . . course." With an effort he roused himself and climbed from the carriage. Primula thought lustfully of hot bricks and hotter tea as she saw him shiver, then scooped her skirts and pelisse around her to follow.

If she had relied on her husband's support to descend the carriage she would have fallen, but her kid-gloved fingertips on his sleeve were for show only. Far more in earnest was her grip upon his arm as she led him up the steps and into their new home.

The new Lady Severn spared hardly a glance for the servants clustered in the entry hall.

"Badgley, Lord Severn has been taken ill. Please have his bedroom made ready at once—a large fire, and—"

"Ah, t'is sperruts. Very worritsome, is sperruts to his Grace."

"Loach?" There was no mistaking the relief in Severn's voice.

A small, scarred, nut-brown, bandy-legged apparition approached Lord and Lady Severn.

It was evident that some attempt had been made to garb him in the style of the day. It was equally evident that no hammertailed coat, silk stockings, and satin waistcoat ever stitched could cope with the exigencies of Loach's physiognomy. The left leg of the knee-breeches flapped open above a teak peg-leg that thudded harshly upon the marble as its owner moved, and the right glove sat oddly on a hand without enough fingers to fill it. But above the inappropriate magnificence of the costume, Loach's remaining eye shone bright and merry in the dark, seamed face.

Primula stepped back, both fascinated and disturbed. Two years after Waterloo no Englishwoman could be a stranger to physical deformity, but this was somehow different.

"Ah, and tha' do be her new Grace. There's nowt to trouble 'un here, lass, only the sperruts."

"My God," said Severn in admiration. "You look like a nautch-girl's pander gone to war." He began to laugh and was racked by a violent spasm of coughing. Primula reached for him, and he clutched at her for support.

"Aye, laugh, your Grace—the more when tha's clapped up in a fine white tomb with the drink and the fever just like any Johnny Newcome. It's a fine wide bed and a fine hot brick as his Grace is to be wanting now, and not any of your maudling truck," he added to Primula. Stepping smartly forward with a thump and a click, he gathered Severn's arm over his shoulder. Severn leaned heavily on him and turned to look at Primula.

"I'm very sorry, Lady Severn. I'm not foxed, I think, it's this cursed—" Another spasm of coughing wracked him.

"Oh for heaven's sake, Severn—go to bed!" Primula cried. Loach favored her with a small approving smile and started off, delivering a scold in his peculiar patois all the while.

"Ah, her knows what's to be done, does her. His Grace goes to rollick and roister like a Tom Raw with never a thought to megrim waiting to settle on 'un's chest, but her knows hawk from handsaw. Most particular are megrims, and lies in wait for him as has been took by sperruts—" The muttering died away as Loach began managing Severn up the stairs.

Primula turned away and found Badgley regarding her with the well-bred look of shock that is every English servant's birthright. Mama and Papa had hoped to ease her transition to great ladyship by loaning her Badgley while they vacationed in the Scottish Highlands, but Primula secretly wished they hadn't.

"See to it that Lord Severn's manservant has everything that he requires," she said firmly.

"As you wish, my lady."

Half an hour later, rested, refreshed, and garbed in a gown more comfortable and less elaborate than her wedding dress, Primula went in search of her husband.

She saw room upon room furnished in the blandest and most unexceptionable of high style, until she began to wish for something freakish, or at least interesting. Instead—or possibly therefore—the next door she opened was into a room that held nothing of the milk-and-water convenability of the rest of Kitmatgar House.

She pushed the door wider and took a cautious step inside. This was the room of an Indian prince, as fantastic as a fairy tale.

Inlaid sandalwood screens were ranged about the walls, their inset ivory panels tinted in dawnpearl colors. Tiger skins made bright splashes of tawny savagery against jewel-dark Chinese rugs, and in place of familiar chairs there were huge hassocks of tooled and gilded leather. She saw a carved and gilded elephant tusk standing on its end like some uncanny plant cheek by jowl with a squat golden statue with a leering grin. The room was bewildering in its variety, as overly ornate as a shopkeeper's display. But then Severn *had* been in trade, of a sort.

Coals were heaped on the bedroom grate, making the air dance and shimmer as they burned, and a full scuttle of coals stood ready to be added. There was an odd, sweetish smell in the air, and Primula could see the languid smoke curling up from pastilles burning on a silver dish at the bedside. The walnut bedstead was a startingly English note in all this foreign opulence. Another step, and she saw the bed was occupied. Severn's tarnished hair curled damply against the pillow, and his face was turned away from her. She turned to push the door shut against the draft.

"Aye, we don't be wanting cold when the megrim is sitting on un," Loach said sagely. He had removed his coat and stood in shirt-sleeves and vest, methodically brushing out Severn's clothes.

"Is he all right?" Primula asked, automatically lowering her voice.

"Right as may be," Loach said dourly.

She walked over to the side of the bed. Her clothes were already beginning to cling to her in the room's tropical heat. Severn lay beneath a mound of blankets, a fever flush on his cheek. In a daring gesture, Primula placed her hand on his forehead. It felt cool because the room was so hot, but there was a healthy dew of sweat on his skin. Severn didn't stir.

The scent of the burning pastilles made her dizzy, and Primula turned away. Severn had a fever, nothing worse. With luck he would be free of the sickroom in a week or less. She glanced back at his peculiar manservant.

"You must tell me if there is anything else that Lord Severn requires. If he is worse tomorrow I shall send to Harley Street for Sir Henry Halford to attend him."

"Oh? Never to mind that, your Grace. It's me as had the doctoring of his Grace time out o' mind. Never worrit yourself, your Grace." Loach returned to his brushing.

And so much for the start of her marital career, Primula thought a few hours later. Claggett had been certain that Primula would want someone near by on her first night in a strange house, and now she was glad she had given in. Everything was strange, from the shapes the bed curtains made against the posts to the shadows the moon cast through her windows.

It would have been stranger still to have her husband asleep beside her, and Primula was profoundly grateful to have been spared that. What explanation she could possibly have rendered up to Severn that did not compromise her vow to reveal nothing of either her history or his father's meddlings she could not imagine. At least she would have a few days to settle matters in her own mind before being called to account.

As she drifted off to sleep, the last thing her mind tossed up to her was Lydia Mainwaring's wager. There must be some way to get Severn into Almack's. . . .

Chapter 7

MARCH 20, 1817

"I SHALL MISS this," Lord Malhythe said, setting down his teacup.

The morning light slanted through the eggshell-thin Sèvres porcelain and sparkled on the silver and crystal of the breakfast things laid out before the fire in Aspasia's parlor. The lady herself was as exquisite as the table, in a combing-coat of azure silk trimmed with bands and bands of swansdown.

"Miss it?" she said silkily, eyebrows arched. "Why, Colley? Where is it going?"

" 'It,' as you so ingenuously put it, my love, is going nowhere. I, on the other hand. . . ." Fabulous and imperturbable in a dressing gown of blue velvet and ermine, the Earl took a piece of toast from the rack.

"Ah! You are leaving me for another!" Aspasia cried, clasping her hands in mock delight. "I knew it must be something of the sort," she added, and reached for her own tea.

The vexing Viscount Severn had been home nearly a month, and had married three days previously. Demi-monde gossip had him fled to France, dead in a duel, or a hundred other things to account for his absence from Society. She had not dared to press Malhythe on it, but he had volunteered the information that his tiresome heir had turned his nuptial couch into a sickbed, and that Lady Severn had canceled all of her engagements on that account. "The course of true love is tedious, is it not, my dear?" Malhythe had said.

If this were true love, Aspasia wished Severn might choke upon it. Confined to his bed he was unlikely to be irritating Malhythe, but he'd be sure to be out of it sooner or later, loving wife or no.

"Leaving you, yes, but not for the reason you are attempting to persuade me of. Business interests compel my presence on the Continent. I have put them off too long while concentrating on settling Severn's affairs. Now that his wife has him well in hand it is time I turned *my* hand to other things."

And the moment he was out of sight Severn would be back at his old tricks! "But surely you needn't go yourself, my lord?"

Malhythe smiled. "At my advanced age, you mean? I have not quite yet reached my threescore and ten, you know. Or were you going to say that you would miss me?"

Aspasia set down her teacup, carefully centering it upon its fragile saucer. Of course Malhythe could send anyone else to France—his secretary, or one of his monstrously dull sons-in-law, or any of the dozens of caretakers of the Rudwell fortune.

"Would you like me to say that I would miss you?" she drawled challengingly.

But no, he was going himself, and though France was pacified and she had never thought of him as old, she did not want him to go. It was arrant provocation, that's what it was, and she would not let him see how it galled her.

"I have never been overfond of deceit, my dear Aspasia. I expect you will find quiet ways of amusing yourself; you always do. You might, for example, ask the Marquess of Barham to call."

"Ask Barham? We'll call that a joke on your part, my lord of Malhythe. I'd as soon take up with one of the Drewmores as Bad Jack and his set. There isn't a scandal in London but he has his part in it, as I make no doubt you know. Everyone says he's doing his best to go to the devil—"

"And yet Owlsthorne refuses to see him. One should never despise the path of reconciliation, my child. Filial devotion is a rare and cherishable commodity, and one should value it," Malhythe said mockingly.

"At least for what it's worth."

"Rare things are often costly, child."

But the conversation had moved to deeper waters than Aspasia was willing to hazard. "So you're staying in town to keep me from boredom?" she said.

"So I am going to Paris for at least a month. It is a pity Bredon is such a poor storyteller—the spectacle Severn will present when he rises from his sickbed to confront me and finds me gone is one I reluctantly forgo. You should really see something of young Barham while I am gone, my dear, it might prove educational."

"If I want my furniture broken, my cellar drained, and my gown ruined I shall certainly take your advice. Otherwise I shall devote my time to church-going and good works for . . . how long?"

"I trust that my business will be concluded by May. Perhaps I will send for you then, and foist you upon Paris society as a titled refugee from the Terror."

"I doubt it," Aspasia said placidly. "Shall I see you again before you go?" At least it did not seem that he was suggesting she attach herself to the Marquess of Barham, ludicrous notion as that was. But perhaps he was going to France to choose a suitable bride. Aspasia told herself firmly that it did not matter. Her investments were sound. She had the money to retire.

But oh, she did not wish to be retired by Malhythe's plans to marry! And nothing could ensure that faster than any threats she might make.

"Perhaps. I have a few visits to make—there are those of my acquaintance who might not still be alive when I return, and I must cherish them while I may. With Severn safely abed, I need have no fear of a public accosting. My bank has instructions to supply you with sufficient funds to maintain this establishment while I am gone, but I shall expect to hear, upon my return, that you have contrived a small flirtation to wile the hours of my absence. Dangling out for news of Severn's marriage can hardly be a full-time occupation."

Aspasia directed a demure and downcast gaze in the direction of her gilded fingernails. Fond as she was of Malhythe, there were times that she wished his perceptions were less acute.

"Perhaps not . . . but meddling is, you know. Perhaps I shall occupy myself with that."

Malhythe reached across the table and caught her hand in a grip more martial than loverlike. "I should be very displeased, my dear, to find you stooping to the level of the French dramatists," he said softly. "Cast your nets anywhere else you choose, but leave the ordering of my son's life to me."

Chapter 8

MARCH 1817

THE OLD MAN had outlived his time and all his contemporaries. When he was born, Royal France extended webs of power and unshakable privilege across half a continent, England was rich in her American possessions, and the first German usurper was only a handful of years upon his English throne. In those days it was unthinkable to true-born Englishmen that any but a Stuart King should rule them, and he had dedicated the first sixty years of his life to returning that family to its rightful place.

In vain. Now the last of the Stuart line was ten years dead, and still the old man remained—a peaceful spectator at last in the world he had not been able to change.

In his time Christian Warltawk had comitted both murder and treason; had escaped the Hanoverian betrayal that claimed the life of the twenty-sixth Baron Hanford and others of even higher rank; had suffered honorable exile and ignominious recall to live sheltered beneath the wing of a nephew who had, in the end, predeceased him. The most dangerous man of his time had lived long enough to be less than a nuisance to the worldlings who followed him. Not even an embarrassment; forgotten.

His contempt for the world was great enough that poverty did not weigh heavily on him now. The great estate in Northumberland was gone long since; the fabulous treasures all squandered or attainted. He had been loved once, in what now seemed his youth, but the woman had died and showed him the futility of trusting in the future. The revolution in France had taken nearly all the rest, but hell-born luck and supreme indifference had brought him to this safe harbor for his dotage; a cockatrice at bay.

Yet some remembered him.

"You will forgive me, Malhythe, if I do not rise."

A manservant nearly as ancient as his master ushered the Earl of Malhythe into Warltawk's Albany rooms.

"Of course, my lord. I pray you will be at your ease." Malhythe set hat, gloves, and cane down upon the narrow Italian table by the fire and regarded the frail old man in the invalid's chair with respect.

Here is what my son wished to be—and what many say that I am. Malhythe found detached amusement in knowing that the thought disturbed him enough to have kept him from Severn all the weeks his heir had been in England. If the wish had become truth, better not to know just yet. Malhythe turned his energies to offering Lord Warltawk the forms and courtesies of his vanished age.

In defiance of time Warltawk wore his head uncovered. The naked scalp thus exposed was the bluish-white of age, mottled by liver spots. The rich red of the fox fur coach robe thrown over his legs only emphasized his frailty, but the pouched and rheumy eyes, faded with age, were as yellow as an animal's. Evil.

"I have come to pay my respects, my lord, on the eve of embarking upon an extended journey."

"Very proper in you, Malhythe. Mason, a glass of wine for my guest." The manservant, hovering nearby, bowed and withdrew.

"I am surprised that you are willing to leave the boy to his own devices in town," Warltawk said. "Or are you hoping he will kill himself, fresh out of a sickroom as he is?"

"I thank you for your concern, Lord Warltawk. I regret that the urgency of my business in France prevents me from paying as much attention to Viscount Severn as he properly deserves. But it is good of you to take an interest in him."

"The last man I 'took an interest in,' my so-dear Earl, is dead because of it. Even at my advanced age I could hardly bear to concern myself with your damp and untidy relationships. Such a disappointment—both to you and your proud heritage. No, Lord Malhythe, the Viscount is merely a topic upon the town, and I find myself a fad among the young who are engrossed in him."

There were few men from whom Malhythe would tolerate such insolence; perhaps only one. In Lord Warltawk's presence the Earl of Malhythe held his temper.

"I rejoice that your lordship's health admits of visitors," Malhythe began as Mason returned bearing a silver tray with a decanter and a single glass. Malhythe poured and sipped.

"This is excellent, my lord; are you sure you will not join me? You must allow me to send you a few bottles of a rather tolerable little claret I've found. I am most interested to have your opinion of it."

Warltawk inclined his head, and Mason shuffled

off again. Malhythe glanced around the room as surreptitiously as possible.

Lord Warltawk was nearly destitute; Malhythe's own money paid for these rooms. But everywhere were the unmistakable signs of new wealth, from the beautiful enamel clock on the mantelpiece to the massive jeweled rings that glinted with regal style upon the twisted hands. Though Warltawk had nearly attained the fantastic age of fivescore years, he was still closely watched by those who made it their business to assure England's safety, and now it seemed he had a patron.

"But you must not permit me to tax your patience with a recitation of my own affairs, Lord Malhythe," Warltawk said. His laughter had a dry, unpleasant sound. "We were discussing your boy . . . and your heir."

"I think I have the matter well in hand, my lord."

"He is alive, is he not? I despair of your ingenuity, my dear Earl. Mortality is such an ever-present companion, even for the young." Warltawk gestured carefully, and the rings flashed: garnet, peridot, topaz, ringed in diamonds and pearls and lesser stones. A glass was brought for Warltawk and he drank. "It would be a simple matter to have him murdered. A band of Mohocks, a fever, a maddened horse. It is simple enough to put a man out of the world. But you find me wandering, my dear boy; it is an old man's failing. Of course I mean nothing of what I say."

"Not at all, my lord; you are, as always, an education. But I am tiring you, and I meant only to call for your good wishes to accompany me on my journey," Malhythe said, rising. "I hope to give myself the felicity of calling upon you again upon my return."

"I will look forward to it, my lord. And do bring

your pretty slut with you. I may take her up myself when you marry, who knows?"

Malhythe stiffened in the act of bowing to his host. So Warltawk still had his little ways of gaining information not generally known—Malhythe would have given a good deal to know who had provided him with Aspasia's name. He met Warltawk's gaze and saw the bleached yellow eyes kindle with malice. He bowed again, more deeply.

When he had reached the doorway Warltawk's voice stopped him once more.

"Shall I take an interest in the Viscount Severn, Lord Malhythe? I would be remiss if I did not acknowledge our . . . common bond."

Malhythe regarded his host a moment before replying.

"You must certainly follow your own inclinations, my lord Warltawk. And so shall I."

Chapter 9

APRIL 1817

MARCH GAVE WAY to April. Lord Malhythe departed for Paris, and Lord Severn, rising from his sickbed, discovered the fact. Lady Severn, her feelings relieved of the possibility of her husband's imminent demise by the freedom with which he expressed himself upon that occasion, took up again the duties of her busy social schedule.

The new bride was expected to be "at-home" to callers for at least a month. Invitations poured in as more and more of her circle returned to town, but all of the engagements were for the middle of April or later. To fill this void in her calendar Primula threw all manner of afternoon entertainments: teas and musicales and even a small dancing-party. The pattern of life she had grown accustomed to during her betrothal year resumed its sway.

Her husband was the very pattern-card of virtue—and if virtue was conspicuous by its absence in Society, why, then so was Lord Severn. He was rarely to be found at home—she had not dared to promise his presence at any of the entertainments she had accepted invitations to—and he had not yet crossed the threshold of her bedroom floor.

The matter was exceedingly vexing. In reply to

her discreet and indirect inquiries he swore he was knocked-up with fever, and. . . . She could hardly call her own husband a liar, could she, after being married less than a month?

On this particular April morning Primula was in her boudoir, enscribing invitations to a theater party that she was giving in a last-ditch attempt to solicit her husband's interest in the game of Society. She had Severn's opera box to command and had borrowed those of two others who owed her favors. They would be twelve couples to dinner, and if she could not interest Severn she was at least half-convinced that Mr. Rainford would be willing to bear her escort. With an energy all out of proportion to its subject, Lady Severn scribbled names and directions on the stiff vellum cards.

Primula's rooms did not enjoy the dubious advantage of an eastern exposure, but even at this hour they were far from dark. The walls had been covered with silk in her signature color of primrose yellow, and the glass chimneys of her lamps had been hand-blown in the same xanthic hue. It was, said Claggett, like living in a loaf of buttered toast.

Primula was musing upon this happy comparison, and wondering if she might ring for a little mid-morning restorative, when her sister-in-law came sailing into the room like a full-rigged ship borne before the gale.

"Prim!" she burst out. "How *can* you be so *calm* on such a day as this?" Mrs. Lambton flung herself down upon Primula's yellow brocade sopha and took up one of the invitations to fan herself energetically.

"It is a very nice day, Addie . . . at least it *was*," said Primula warily.

Her sister-in-law regarded the morning outside Primula's windows with distaste. "It is a wretched day. A truly vile and hideous day. Black—and made a good deal blacker by the most truly unfilial serpent's tooth who ever—"

"Has something happened to Severn?" asked Primula quickly.

"Severn?" said Mrs. Lambton blankly, focusing at last on the card she held. "A theater party; very nice, my dear, but you will never get him to attend. Nor me."

"Addie, pray do make sense this instant, or I shall be quite distracted. You rush in saying the world has come to an end because of a serpent's tooth, which I collect to mean my husband, and—"

Mrs. Lambton tossed the card back onto the table and laughed. "Oh, Prim, Severn isn't the only serpent's tooth in creation—and while I do not match my Georgie against him, I have the most dreadful feeling that blood will out. Ever since I brought him up to town—against my better judgment, but he *is* two-and-twenty, after all—he has pursued the most ruinous course, and I am quite certain that I do not know the half of his activities."

"All young men are inclined to be a bit wild, I believe," said Primula as sweepingly as if George Lambton were not within a few years of her own age. "And he will not dare to be too bad while he must account to you and his grandfather for his comings and goings."

"That is precisely the trouble," said Mrs. Lambton mournfully. "Papa is most disobligingly in France, and not to be expected home for weeks yet, and in a very few days I shall not be here either!"

It had always been an article of faith with both Mr. Lambton and his wife that he was of delicate health. Oddly enough, this assertion was being borne out; Mr. Lambton, solitary in Tilling due to his wife's sojourn in town, had taken a chill, which had inarguably become a nasty cold. It was unthinkable that Mrs. Lambton should do anything but rush to his side—but George refused to accompany her.

"And while it is true, of course, that he could only be a vexation to his Papa—it is so fortunate that Georgie has inherited my constitution and not Lamb's—the thought of him 'cutting a dash,' as he would have it, without anyone at all about him to make him feel ashamed of himself. . . ."

"I have the perfect solution," said Primula.

"Severn, I have invited George Lambton to make his home with us while his mother is away."

Lord Severn set down his morning paper and regarded his wife with a betrayed expression.

"I promised Addie that you would take an interest in him."

In actuality Primula had promised Mrs. Lambton just the opposite, but she saw no reason to burden her husband with this intelligence. Chaperoning a high-spirited young man some years his junior around the metropolis seemed to Primula an ideal way both to keep George Lambton under control and to establish Severn's credit in the eyes of the *ton*.

"You did what?" Severn asked in disbelief. His wife obligingly repeated the information.

"And since you are both strangers to London—you returning from a long absence and Georgie newly arrived—I am certain you will deal extremely together. Which reminds me, Severn; I am giving a small theater party next week and—"

"Have you run mad?"

"No, Lord Severn, I do not think so," Primula said.

"I beg your pardon, Lady Severn. I spoke out of turn. But surely you must see that it does not answer at all."

Positively her new husband's most maddening

quality—and one which, logically, she had not looked for in him at all—was his reasonableness. Primula was quite irrationally certain that if she should choose to parade naked down St. James Street Severn would be reasonable about it.

"I see no such thing. George Lambton is your nephew. Addie says he is grown quite wild, and since she must go home and he will not go with her, and since Lord Malhythe is not here to moderate the excesses of his behavior—"

Lord Severn emitted a sharp bark of laughter but declined further comment.

"—then surely the only reasonable course is for him to abide beneath our roof. I am sure that you could only be a moderating influence on his conduct."

"You are certain of no such thing!" her husband told her roundly. "In the first place, he is far too young to be on his own—he should be in the schoolroom, not on the town. In the second place, dear wife, my sponsorship of their brat would mortify the solid and respectable Lambtons beyond speech."

"Which is why I thought it best not to mention it to Addie," Primula said agreeably. "But once she sees what a good effect you have upon him—and you know, Lord Severn, your nephew may not be quite as young as you conceive—I am certain she will approve the notion. For instance, this theater party—"

"I am certain that she will not. Lady Severn, my father cannot have made a secret of my past conduct, and I *know* that my sisters have not—"

"But a reformed rake, Lord Severn, must be ever so much more convincing than someone who has never had any need at all to reform," Primula urged cordially.

"Ah," said Severn softly. "I am to be the bad example used to terrify the young into submission."

Thinking over the conversation carefully, Primula was certain she had said nothing from which any sane person could gather such an impression. "For heaven's sake, Severn, I am quite certain that no one thinks anything at all of your—"

"Childish peccadillos?" suggested her husband sweetly.

Primula bit her lip. "The past, Lord Severn, is as uncomfortable as the future as a place to live. You may very well have been notorious once—"

"Thank you."

"—but that was a long time ago, and I am afraid we have all had a great deal to think about since then. After all, you did not turn pirate like Conrad Pengethly, or murder your mother like the Marquess of Barham—"

"What do you know about the Marquess of Barham?" demanded her spouse.

"Oh, only what everyone knows. Well, he did not *precisely* murder his mother, of course, and so he is still received. But Severn, about the theater—"

"You gladden my heart extremely, but you will not invite Barham to this house, *if* you please. Nor do I intend that you should turn it into a pirate den, or a gaming hall, or any other such interesting location on the theory that it will make me look respectable by comparison."

"Respectable?" said Primula, in a voice dripping with scorn. "How are you to look respectable if no one ever sees you at all? Now, I had hoped you would take up Georgie, but if you shan't, then I imagine it is fruitless to attempt to persuade you. Regardless of that, he is coming this afternoon—Adeline is quite correct that it would be ruinous to leave him alone in Colworth House, though I imagine it impossible to shock Lord Malhythe's servants."

"Impossible," commented Severn, amused despite himself.

"And I hope that even if you utterly despise Georgie you will give some thought to *establishing* yourself in town. You cannot imagine you are still known, of course, but if you will put yourself in my hands I imagine that we can establish you creditably. I am holding a theater party next week—quite the most respectable people, very few pirates or murderers, and I hope that you will wish to attend."

Lord Severn was staring at her with a decidedly odd expression on his face.

"There will be nothing in it to distress anyone," said Primula plaintively. "It will be very quiet."

Severn shook his head, more in wonderment than as an actual act of negation.

"Please?" said his wife.

It wasn't the same girl after all, Severn decided. He had retreated after breakfast to his library, where, since his recovery, he had made desultory attempts to organize the tale of his time in India into some sort of readable memoir. But today his attempts were even more hopeless than usual.

Obviously he had mistaken the name of his long-ago victim. Greenleaf, or Ghibelline, or some such—certainly not Greetwell. Primula Miranda Greetwell Rudwell had obviously never been blighted in her life.

And the worst of it was, he had promised to attend her damned soiree.

Lord Severn had thought himself inured by his sojourn in the East to every possible combination of misery and boredom that could be had for ready money. When he had thought of London, as he did rarely, it was as a paradise of ease and comfort, where tedium could be banished with a wave of a hand.

This pleasant view of events survived quite until he found himself, hale, married, and unencumbered by his father's presence anywhere in the British dominions, at liberty upon the town.

His clubs—White's, Brooks, Boodle's—had accepted him back, and in any of them he could drink, or game, or quarrel—providing he could find anyone to do it with. Of his contemporaries, many now were dead. A number were worse than dead—married, and with no desire to resume an acquaintance with the companion of their wilder days. Those of his peers who had escaped both chain-shot and parson's mousetrap were of two kinds: sober and dignified and headed for careers of public service—and the other kind.

The "other kind" were happy enough to welcome Severn to their inner circles. Theirs was the life he had used to lead, after all, and though he suspected that it no longer suited him he did his best to deny the fact. At its worst it was better than the alternative—the respectable society of genteel people.

Severn could not remember precisely when the conviction that he scorned the gentle company of his peers had been replaced by the notion that they rejected him, but it was now a tenet of long standing. The thought of socializing with them at the party to be given by his wife, if not precisely anathema, was nothing from which he derived any degree of comfort.

He was bored, he was irritated, he had neither friendship nor its illusion, and in addition to all of these things he had witlessly given his pledge to attend a party at which he would be ogled by mothers intent on convincing themselves on behalf of their daughters that his wife had made no very desirable match. His temper was such that it was perhaps fortunate that Mr. George Lambton chose that moment to make his appearance.

George Tiberius Daggerwood Lambton had been twelve years old when his wicked uncle—whose exploits had been spoken of in whispers and in corners all his young life—was banished to the East for an unknown crime. Unknown it might be, but his mother and his aunts had impressed upon the young boy that it was something pluperfectly dreadful nonetheless, and from that moment George Lambton's worship of his uncle was assured.

As young George grew older, the vanished uncle took on all the attributes of myth and legend—a giant of mirth and irreverence, with a strength of will sufficient to allow him to scorn convention and mock the empty codes and cowardly observances that characterized lesser men. His bravery was that of the lion, his fashion sense unerring, and his capacity in any sphere of human endeavour unquestioned.

Having spent his youth creating this god of his idolatry, it was only natural that Georgie should wish to make himself worthy of the great man. And since the mild coast of Suffolk afforded him little satisfaction for such ambition, he was both delighted to be brought to London and determined not to leave it.

"My lord?" Severn's sulphurous reverie was interrupted by the approach of the butler. "A Mr. George Lambton to see you, my lord."

"Send him to the devil," Severn growled, before remembering who Mr. Lambton was. "No, on second thought, show him to the devil. Send him in."

Mr. Lambton aspired to the Corinthian graces without having the least aptitude for them, and so to Severn's untutored eye his nephew appeared both slovenly dressed and untidily informal. Had Mr. Lambton the least inkling that his snowy-white buckskins, gleaming oxblood Hessians, dark blue superfine coat, and softly curled beaver hat exposed him to such ill-will, he would have sunk instantly from sight, but since in all his twenty-two years of life Mr. Lambton had never yet met anyone who did not think he was a very fine fellow indeed, and since (furthermore) this very turn-out had been approved by those to whom he had learned to look as the new gods of his circumscribed cosmos, his mind was at rest.

It must be noted that Mr. Lambton's mind was not a very active organ even at the best of times.

"Lord Severn! I say, what a very great— It's perfectly splendid of you to see me, my lord!" Mr. Lambton lunged forward, extending his hand.

"I trust your horse is well?" said Severn, without rising. Mr. Lambton lowered his hand.

"My horse, Lord Severn?" The look of bewilderment on Mr. Lambton's face would have wrung a harder heart than Severn's. The boy was his nephew, after all, and damnably young to boot. It was hardly his fault that the current fashion demanded the wearing of stable clothes in the parlor.

"I beg your pardon. I was thinking of something else. Do sit down and tell me how I can be of service to you. My—Lady Severn tells me you are to be a guest beneath our roof."

"Oh. Er. That's dev'lish awkward, Uncle—I mean my lord."

" 'Uncle' will do, Georgie. I am, for my sins, your mother's brother, after all."

Mr. Lambton perched himself gingerly upon the edge of a chair. " 'For your sins'! Oh, I say, Lord—Uncle. That's very good! 'For your sins.' May I quote you?"

"Perhaps you had better call me Severn, just as if we were on terms," Lord Severn said. He had the vexing conviction that if Primula were here she would be laughing at him. He cudgeled his memory for previous meetings with Mr. Lambton and dredged forth shadowy reminiscences of some Christmas at Rudbek House when Addie had brought her boy. Georgie had been —six? —ten?

"But I don't mean to take up too much of your time, Uncle Severn. Aunt Prim said that you would want me, but I daresay she is only saying that to please Mama. You know how women get—she will not believe that I'm no longer in leading strings, and— But I don't mean to bore you, sir."

"No, do go on. I am quite spellbound." Mr. Lambton was ready to believe this, or at least to believe that no one would say it if it wasn't true. "At any rate, my lord, Mama seems to think I can't get through a few weeks in London by myself, which is utter rot! Haven't I got all Colworth House to rattle around in? And Grandfather won't mind—he'd just say it gives the servants something to do. I thought I might invite a few of the fellows to come and help me drink up the cellar. Lord Drewmore's a ripping chap, don't you think? And, oh, Gressingham and St. George—men like that."

"You seem to be admirably popular," Severn said noncommittally.

"Oh, nothing I daresay to what you are used to, sir, but—say, Bobs has invited me to a little 'do' he's going to this evening—says it's pretty wild, and of course if Mama found out I'd gone she'd have my head—and Aunt Prim would tell her, she knows everything—but if you were to go with me, sir, well, then neither of them could say anything at all, could they?"

Severn had a better idea than Mr. Lambton might guess of the sort of "pretty wild" party he would be attending—and, further, thought it would be damned dull. But undoubtedly Primula, when she heard of it, would not think it dull and would realize that he was far too dangerous a guest for her musicale evenings. It was upon this cheering and half-baked rationale that he promised George Lambton his attendance at the promised party this very evening, and released him from all obligation to reside beneath the Kitmatgar House rooftree.

Chapter 10

THE SAME DAY, APRIL 17, 1817

IT WAS OBVIOUSLY some other Viscount Severn, Primula thought. Certainly the thought of being married to an unscrupulous rake was not terribly attractive, but on the other hand, she had no desire to be leg-shackled to a Lob-lie-by-the-fire either.

It would be a difficult feat to manage to live in fear of someone you had nursed through the catarrh, and Primula had not managed it. The man she had been led to expect through his sisters' tales and her own experiences did not exist, and it had not at all required Primula's intervention to turn the Beast into a. . . .

Rabbit. Primula sighed. A very nice rabbit, certainly, and even a rabbit she suspected herself of being halfway in love with. But there was no triumph to being loved by a rabbit—and Severn showed no inclination to fall in love with her, in any event.

Viscount Severn kept early hours, abstemious habits, and showed no inclination to enter Society, let alone resume his career as a rake. He certainly showed no sign of holding himself back from crushing her to his manly bosom and forcing his burning kisses upon her swooning lips, and might be said, by a small-minded person, to be avoiding her as much as was humanly possible—which, in Kitmatgar House, was a very great deal. Primula did not think of herself as a small-minded person, but during the year of her engagement she had become quite used to being feted, courted, and sought after. Now Severn seemed to find it a strain even to look at her.

And that was vexing. It was nearly as vexing, in fact, as Lydia Mainwaring's sly inquiry a few days before as to the date upon which they could hope to see Lord Severn gracing Almack's. At least she had managed to secure his agreement to attend her theater party next week, and that would keep the hounds at bay for a little while.

Hounds made her think of rabbits again, and Primula roundly wished Society, her husband, and her own heart at the devil.

"Dear Prim, how well you are looking! I can hardly stay an instant—Bobs Gressingham is taking me round to the bazaar and *swears* he will not keep the horses standing above ten minutes but I just had to call and tell you how absolutely delighted I am by this charming entertainment you are having for us. Town is so *flat* this time of year, and I was just telling dear Alice how grateful we all must be to you for lifting us all out of the mopes—" Despite the exertions necessitated by the delivery of this nonstop verbal barrage, Lydia Mainwaring managed to remove both the dazzlingly high-poke bonnet trimmed with curled scarlet plumes and the matching *pelisse à la hussar* without interrupting the torrent of chat.

"And you must not keep us in suspense a moment longer; Claire Rushton positively would not let me leave her house yesterday until I swore faithfully that I would insist that you tell us that Severn is to be there. It's hardly my place to tell you these things, dear Prim, but when Bobs heard that I was actually to make up a party of which Severn was to be a member—I told him in strictest confidence, of course, as I was *not* certain you would want it known just yet—he was *quite* concerned. Quite! So really, dear, you must tell me—"

"If Severn were that notorious, he would hardly be eligible for vouchers, Lydia, now, would he?" snapped Primula.

The moment the words had left her mouth Primula realized that they could be taken as an assertion that Severn *had* received vouchers to Almack's, and that all her careful overtures to Lady Hawkchurch and Lady Lockridge to intercede on his behalf would be dust and ashes the moment the mendacious tale came to the ears of one of the Patronesses.

And it would. There were three great gossips in society—since Mr. Bartholomew Rainford heard more than he told—but Lydia's companion, Mr. Robert Gressingham, was fast aspiring to the tutelary seat now held by his sister. Of any item retailed by the younger Gressingham offshoot, you could be certain that it was designed not to convey truth, but to shock its hearer.

"Oh, Prim, you are not saying that you Have Them?" breathed Lydia, much diverted.

At that moment the footman announced another caller.

"Oh, yes, please, Briggs, send her in. And—oh, dear, look at the time." Primula sprang to her feet and reached for Lydia's bonnet. "Of course you are always welcome here, but you must scurry, dear Lydia, or Mr. Gressingham will force you to walk to the bazaar."

There was a scrabbling as of eldritch beings heard upon the stairs leading to Lady Severn's morning room; a wet snuffling low to the ground; Lady Pamela Lockridge burst into the room.

That beloved wife of the most indulgent of husbands, Sir Gerald Lockridge, entered in the midst of a covey of tiny panting Maltese dogs. Lydia squealed as one of them scampered forward and pressed its wet black nose against her silk-stockinged ankle.

"Oh, do stop that, dear," said Lady Lockridge, but not as if she expected to be attended. The desultory tug she gave to the small white bundle of fluff's leading string only removed the ribbon from the dog's neck and caused it to hang limply along the other ribbons that she held. "Mrs. Mainwaring, how lovely to see you again. Don't mind Ratafia; she is just going through a phase, you know, and Gerry says she is just like me."

Lady Lockridge regarded Lydia Mainwaring, standing rigid in stark horror as the busy investigative presence nosed about her ankles. "Well, perhaps not exactly like me—she *is* a dog, you know."

Lady Lockridge could not be expected to be conversant with Mrs. Mainwaring's distaste for the canine community. On the other hand, it was not a particularly well-kept secret. Neither was Mrs. Mainwaring's much-quoted description of Lady Lockridge as "a woman who would make wallpaper look intellectual."

Primula regretted both her friend's hasty tongue and the possibility that Lydia's remark had come to Lady Lockridge's attention, because although it was witty, it certainly wasn't true. Though her mild blue eyes and soft brown curls—and gently meandering conversation—might give a listener the opinion that her character bordered on the feebleminded, Primula had always found Lady Lockridge's advice to be both well-meant and sound.

Of course, she had never done anything to annoy her, either.

"Oh, get it *off*!" wailed Lydia desperately. Primula foraged among Lydia's skirts for the dog.

"*Nice* Ratafia," she said encouragingly, pouncing on her prey. The wiggling Maltese licked her face. Lady Lockridge had released the ribbons of the rest of her pack and they were wandering industriously about the room, following smells.

"Oh, do give her here, Lady Severn. Naughty Ratafia!—although I can hardly blame her, can I, when it was my fault her ribbon came undone? Oh, are you leaving us?" she asked of Mrs. Mainwaring, who was fastening the closures of her pelisse with angry jabs. "I do hope it was not your coachman in the street—but how could it have been? It wasn't a coach at all, but a chaise—so decorative, with those yellow wheels!" Lady Lockridge's budget of information about the yellow-wheeled chaise apparently ended there, and Primula firmly restrained herself from asking after it.

"Do come back soon, Lydia, and we shall have a comfortable coze," suggested Primula to her friend. Almost in the same breath she added, "Lady Lockridge, it is always lovely to see you. How fortunate that you caught me at home. Shall I ring for tea?"

Lady Lockridge seated herself upon the exquisite Hepplewhite sopha upholstered in primrose and cream and spread her celadon skirts with a practiced hand. Primula rang for the footman as Lady Lockridge gazed about the room with an expression of vague alarm, Ratafia cradled in her arms.

"I confess I had not expected to find your drawing room so thin of company, Lady Severn, even so early in the Season. It *is* Wednesdays that you are at-home, is it not? Oh, dear, that hardly sounds at all well, does it? I don't know what I am saying; Gerry says I am sadly shatterbrained, but I ask you—how is one to know these days what one is obliged to ignore? I know that I am *not* supposed to notice that no one at all has seen Lord Severn since his return, since surely you will not wish to refine upon it, but how am I to pretend that an empty room is full of people? Or shall I pretend that it *ought* to be empty, do you think? That doesn't seem at all friendly. Perhaps we should try again from the beginning?" Lady Lockridge said mournfully.

"Pray, do not give yourself the slightest concern, Lady Lockridge—in fact, the room seems quite full to me," Primula said. She lifted the puppy at her feet and settled it on her lap, where it collapsed with a happy sigh. "And I was hoping you had come to congratulate me on my soon-to-be triumph." She was not quite certain how to break the news to her guest that while she was, indeed, at-home to callers Wednesday mornings and found her rooms pleasantly filled, this was Thursday.

"A triumph? Or ought we say, another one? How lovely—but don't tell me, I shall guess. Is it about Lord Severn?"

"Who else? He is finally recovered from his illness—these Indian fevers, you know!—and Lydia was just calling to say how pleased she was that he would be at the theater next Wednesday." So much for Lydia's attempts to worm the news out of her—now Robert Gressingham would hear it after everyone else, for Lightfoot Bobby was not the sort to circulate at the elegant heights attained by Lady Lockridge's salons.

"*Wednesday!* I knew there was something. . . . It isn't Wednesday at all, is it, Lady Severn?"

Primula was forced to agree.

"Oh, dear. I was supposed to be at Madame Francine's on Wednesday—she is so very strict; she told me that if I missed one more fitting she would fling the dress into the gutter. I don't suppose she will, though, do you?"

Even the most fashionable modiste could hardly afford to offend one of the reigning social lionesses. "I don't think so, Lady Lockridge."

"And besides, now that I recollect it, my appointment with her was for *last* Wednesday, so it will hardly do me any good at all to go now," Lady Lockridge said, brightening. "Perhaps you will go for a drive with me instead—or perhaps it had better be tomorrow—I called on Lady Sefton just the other day and she was wondering if the Assembly Rooms might not need a new touch. But she hardly likes to mention it for fear we shall all suddenly find ourselves all over *mode oriental.*

"So Lord Severn is coming out at last!" Lady Lockridge swept on with barely a pause for breath. "Gerry will be so pleased—I imagine that he had a bet on about it; everyone does, it's such a dull Season, at least so far. Don't you find it so? But I am being quite silly; of course you aren't bored; not with a hundred guineas riding on him. Not Gerry, or course. There is nothing quite like being a nine-day's wonder on the tenth day, is there, Lady Severn? People do what they can; to be sure, but warmed-over scandal-broth never boils, does it? It's so hard to believe that one has become uninteresting—but I'm certain he will manage. Oh, not to *be* uninteresting, you understand, or . . . dear me, I'm *sure* I had a point when I started. . . . " Lady Lockridge looked at Primula hopefully.

Pointless or not, Lady Lockridge's conversation already held enough content to make Primula's blood run cold. "One hundred guineas riding on Lord Severn? Oh, dear, it makes him sound a bit like a horse, doesn't it?"

"But betting on horses would be rude—at least, I *think* that's what Gerry says. Rude for us, I mean;

the gentlemen may follow the turf just as they like. It's much better to bet on one's own husband—and *safer*, too, don't you think? Because really, it would be perfectly horrid if you *lost*, Lady Severn, wouldn't it? If the Earl of Malhythe's son can't get vouchers to Almack's, who can?—so everyone would think that it was because you couldn't bring him around your thumb. And such a *trifling* matter, really. Even if one does not precisely *care* for Almack's, one must go once, mustn't one? I mean, it's almost like a Royal Drawing Room, except of course so very many more Personages. . . . "

"Of course," said Primula numbly. Of course she had known that Lydia Mainwaring could not possibly keep such an exciting bit of gossip to herself—but she would not have expected it to come back to her in the person of Lady Lockridge, repeating it as innocently as if no breath of opprobrium could possibly attach to such a stunt.

Or was she? Wasn't it far more likely that she was warning Primula of how far the tale had spread?

"Well, there you are, then. I shall positively remember to mention to Lady Sefton that you'll be wanting two subscriptions this year instead of one, shall I? And now I really must dash. I will call for you tomorrow morning at ten—providing it does not rain—and we can talk then."

After Lady Lockridge had left—returning only twice to retrieve dogs that had evaded her first ingathering—Primula made her way upstairs. The day had already been unduly full, and it was barely noon. Fortunately Georgie would be here tomorrow, and keeping an eye on him was bound to be diverting.

She was debating the rival merits of a drive in the Park or a good brisk gallop when a motion glimpsed out of the corner of her eye turned out to be Severn, slinking cat-footed out of his study and down the back stairs.

"Lord Severn, a word with you, if I may?" Primula tried very hard to keep any tone of accusation out of her voice.

"I am, as always, your devoted servant, Lady Severn."

A month's care had banished all trace of fever from Severn's appearance. His hair was still that bleached-bronze color, but traces of its natural auburn were beginning to show, and his face had lost its thin and hollow look. But the jewel-green eyes no longer danced with reckless life. That fire was banked.

But not extinguished. When he bowed punctiliously over her hand Primula had a sense of a wild thing desperate to be gone.

Was she so undesirable that her own husband couldn't bear the sight of her? Common sense and recent experience told her that this was not so—but then, what did Severn know that made him avoid her?

"It is nothing to trouble you, I assure you, my lord." She spoke hurriedly to cover her trepidation. "I will be speaking to Cook in a few hours and I only wished to know how many covers to lay this evening. Georgie is to come to us this afternoon, so I imagine he will dine with us as well."

"Imagination is a wonderful thing," Severn said, as if to himself. "But I'm afraid I must tell you that young George has expressed it as his desire to remain beneath his grandfather's roof indefinitely. I imagine that goes for dinner, too. And as I will be dining out as well, I'm afraid that leaves you. . . ."

"Alone as usual?" Primula interjected. Severn bowed. "But surely you aren't serious?"

"About dinner, Lady Severn? I assure you: I have plans to dine at my club, and then—"

"*Must* you try to drive me mad by deliberately misunderstanding me?" cried Primula, pressing her hands to her head. There was a wrongness to the gesture that she instantly perceived; she and Severn were hardly on such terms of intimacy as to allow such freedom of expression.

"Very well," said Severn. "The meat of the matter is this: Mr. George Lambton feels that he is old enough to be free of parental or avuncular supervision and chooses to remain at Colworth House. He brought the matter to me, and as I too could see no reason for him to remain in leading strings—"

"But Lord Severn, surely you of all people can see why a—a *boy* like Georgie shouldn't be left to rattle around the town by himself! Only think of what might happen to him; he is far too young to be sensible, and he might very well—"

"—Fall into bad companionship?" Severn supplied silkily. "Among ivory-turners and gull-gropers; rakes and seducers . . . ?"

He *did* know about her past! Or at least, Primula admonished herself sternly, he knew something.

"Yes, Lord Severn," Primula said coolly. "Georgie might be drawn into the company of persons of bad character who did not care about the pain they inflicted on their victims so long as their own pleasure was served. Surely you have heard of such persons, in your own wide experience?"

Severn checked as if he had been slapped, and Primula was instantly sorry for what she had said, even though it had achieved the desired effect. He stared at her for a long moment, casting the illusion that in a moment he would speak and dissolve all the trouble between them.

But it was only an illusion.

"I assure you, Lady Severn, you have nothing to

fear. George Lambton will have his bear-leader. No matter what den of iniquity he chooses to enter, I shall be with him." He smiled a brilliant terrible smile and bowed again. At the head of the stairs he stopped and turned back.

"So you see, you may as well call for a tray in your room."

There was no point after that in anything but a sick head-ache; Primula retired to her rooms, dosed herself with cordial, and lay upon her chaise.

Well the cat was among the pigeons now. She would have to go to Georgie tomorrow and make one last attempt to persuade him to come and live with her; after that, there was nothing for it but a letter to Addie in hopes that maternal terrorism would succeed where sweet reason would not.

And meanwhile, there was Severn. Primula forced herself to think logically, just as Papa had taught her.

Her husband Severn seemed to have an active aversion to her. It might be that he did not care to be married, but he had agreed to that by coming home. There was no way Severn could know that his wife was the woman he had ruined a decade before. But what if he had guessed—or even worse, had discovered she was ruined without knowing who her ravisher was?

Chapter 11

FLASHBACK—
1816 THRU APRIL 1817

MISS SARAH JANE Emwilton was the daughter of General the Honorable Horatio Emwilton, who, despite sharing his given name with England's great naval hero, had meandered quite unregarded through a military career neither infamous nor heroic until he was carried off by a stroke two months after Waterloo from a chair in his favorite club. His death was mourned by all his peers as unexpected, and his wife and her daughter had ample cause to realize its unexpectedness when the time came for the reading of the will. If General Emwilton had expected to die, he would surely have made better provision for his wife and only daughter.

As matters stood, by the summer of 1816 a combination of delicacy and economy had reduced them to a set of furnished rooms in Bath.

"I do not see, Mama, why you do not accept Lady Greetwell's invitation," Sarah Jane said, continuing to take tiny stitches in the dress she was remaking. The dove-grey lutestring was fine fabric, glossy and rich; but the dress planned for it would be too severe to make the most of either its natural beauty or that of its wearer. "She is your bosom-bow, and my godmama. I can hardly count all the times she has written you since Papa died that you or I must come to visit her at once—and now that Primula is to be married. . . ."

Mrs. Emwilton smiled gently, but did not look up as she replied. "Now that Primula is to be married nothing could induce me to cast a shadow over Jane's happiness. When you are older, Sarah Jane, you will understand. Once Jane saw how matters stand, you may depend upon it that she would do all in her power to aid us—but as we could do nothing in return, it would be an act of charity pure and simple, and nothing is more invidious." The General's widow was a woman of erect carriage, firm principles, and great stubbornness.

"That's hardly what they tell us in church," grumbled her daughter, who had inherited many of these traits.

"Ah, but in church they also tell us that it is more blessed to give than to receive—and that is especially true of charity. Jane Greetwell is my friend. I could not wish to become her suppliant. Nor, I must observe, do you."

"But Mama, that is entirely different," said Sarah Jane, continuing to stitch at her traveling wardrobe. "I am young and strong and perfectly equipped to go for a governess—and I shall! You'll see: not only shall I have a post within *days* of reaching London, I shall marry the scion of the house (who will be frightfully handsome) and you will come to live with us and dispense charity, not receive it!"

But that had been nearly a year ago. Now Sarah Jane was two-and-twenty; she knew how foolish all her air-dreams had been, and how very unlikely it was that her circumstances would ever rise above what they were now.

The coach jarred her against its side as it wallowed through the spring mud, and Sarah Jane hoped they would reach London soon. Even the scantling attic room with its grudging fire that had been hers on her employer's last sojourn to town would be preferable to this endless stuffy jouncing.

She had known that both youth and looks were against her even before she had gone to London and placed her advertisement in the paper. No one wanted a governess under her roof who would tempt a son, or, worse, a husband, into indiscretion—but to Sarah Jane's surprise and relief she had found a place almost at once, and had lived the gay romantic life of a governess for nearly eight months now. Her duties were not onerous, but by no stretch of the imagination could she conjure a future of luxury and ease.

Sarah Jane's charges were three girls, the eldest within six years of her own age, and part of the reason the family had engaged her was to be "a companion to them." Since it had gained her the post she could not grudge the circumstance, but even she could see that the need for companionship would not last forever.

But while it did, Mrs. Courtenay was more than kind. She had given Sarah Jane a number of her dresses to make over for her own use, saying that while she had tired of them they were far too good for the maid. In fact, if there was one enduring flaw in the entire situation, it was Mr. Courtenay's elder brother, Lord Drewmore.

The coach jolted again. The head-ache that had been hovering over her all day began in earnest. Sarah Jane sighed, knowing that relief was nearly an hour away. She hoped that at least there would be a warm fire awaiting her. She could hardly imagine what calamity had bred her frantic summons, nor what domestic trial the services of a very young governess could ease.

* * *

The coach's breakneck speed slowed, and over the racket of the wheels and the hollow clop of horses' hooves on cobbles Sarah Jane could hear the brawling noise that meant they had reached London. In a few minutes more the vehicle pulled to a rocking stop.

The inn-yard was busy and crowded in the predawn hustle. The sky was just beginning to lighten, and dawn was gilding the weathercocks on the church steeples as Sarah Jane was lifted down from the coach to stand unsteadily upon the paving. Fortunately she had traveled by coach once before and knew what to do; she took hurried possession of her carpet bag, ignoring all offers of help, and made her way quickly to the hackney stand, where the last of her borrowed funds served to buy her transport to the Courtenay home.

The window shutters were still securely fastened on the big Palladian brownstone when the hired carriage deposited Sarah Jane Emwilton on her employer's doorstep. The cab rattled off, and she looked around herself in growing bewilderment. The summons from Mrs. Courtenay had been so urgent that she had spent her meager savings on the Mail rather than wait the four days it would take to reach London with one team in her employer's coach, yet the knocker was not yet on the door, and there was no sign of habitation. Her knuckles were quite sore by the time the door was opened in response to her battering.

"And what would yourself be wanting?" demanded the man who stood there. Five o'clock in the morning was time and enough for servants to be up and about their business, and so he was already dressed for the day, but he had not shaved, nor did he look as if he intended to.

"I am Sarah Jane Emwilton. Mrs. Courtenay sent for me."

The caretaker considered this, rubbing his bristled chin. "Did she now? Then you'll be wanting to come in," he decided, and swung the door wider.

The hall was barren of the kickshaws and folderols it contained when the Courtenays were in residence, and through an open doorway Sarah Jane could see furniture still shrouded in drifts of white Hollands cloth.

"Is Mrs. Courtenay here?" she asked, bewildered. The man turned on her in exasperation.

"Now why in all the great world should she be, I'm asking? It's himself that's here, and himself you've come to see, by the look of you, my fine great lady." The irate servant flung the street door shut with a crash, rousing ghostly echoes from the rooms around. "In there," he added, jerking his chin toward the library doors.

"But why . . . ?" Sarah Jane began, only to find that she was standing alone in an empty hall.

She was not a stupid girl. She had a strong suspicion of who "himself" might be. She hoped she was wrong, but she would not know until she had seen who was waiting in the library. She had no choice but to do that. She did not have the money to pay her coachfare back to the Courtenay's country home, and there was nowhere else in London that she could go.

She went up to her room and took off her pelisse and bonnet. She made such repairs to her appearance as could be managed without water to wash in, and saw in the small cracked glass the image of a small frightened mouselike girl. Surely no one would wish to bother with someone so obviously unimportant?

The cook at Oakley's had packed a luncheon for

her that she had been unable to bring herself to eat on the road. Now she drank cold coffee and ate most of a macaroon, hoping the food would give her courage. Then she brushed her hands clean, and smoothed her hair and her skirts once more, and went down the stairs.

About ten o'clock last night the library of the Courtenays' London home had been splendid with candles. Now the empty sconces and candlesticks were webbed with melted wax that had dripped and spilled over tables and floor before it hardened. The remains of a cold supper were strewn on the sideboard, and the aftermath of a game of whist lay discarded on a small table, a few stray gold guineas gleaming softly amid the scattered cards.

One single candle still burned in a solitary candleholder on the small table beside the chair near the fireplace. There was a brandy decanter on the table also, and a glass, and an untidy pile of gold coins.

"Good morning, Lord Drewmore," Sarah Jane said steadily.

"Ah, it's little . . . Jane," the chair's occupant said, remembering her name with an obvious effort. "So prompt." He levered himself unsteadily to his feet and smiled engagingly at her. "Promptness is a wonderful quality in the young. So . . . prompt."

She had always thought him handsome, and distrusted him all the more for it.

"You sent that letter telling me to come here, not Mrs. Courtenay." His handsome face and winning ways were the coin he traded in, trusting it to pay for all.

"Dull Simon's duller Cynthia. Why is it that one's sisters-in-law always resemble cows? No, sheep. Fat, fluffy, stupid, little—"

"I came because I thought Mrs. Courtenay had

sent for me. Since she has not, I will go back to Oakleys."

"How?"

Perhaps Lord Drewmore was not as drunk as he appeared, or perhaps he had a great deal of experience in being drunk. His wits, at least, were fully functional. "I don't imagine you have a great deal of money left. Travel costs money, you know. Do sit down." He indicated the sopha with a sweeping gesture more suited to the stage.

"I prefer to stand," Sarah Jane said, trying to ignore the tight knot of fear in her stomach. He was quite right. She had perhaps half a shilling in her reticule upstairs, and six copper pennies would not even take her back to the coaching station.

"The better to flee? You wrong me. Yes, you do indeed. Here I am, a mag—a magna—an *open*-handed fellow who has taken pity on a pretty little country mouse. Pretty little mouse," he repeated, and splashed brandy into his glass.

The drink seemed to sober rather than further intoxicate him. "So I thought I would take you to Paris, my dear. Some friends and I are going to pleasure ourselves where so many of England's gallant laddies gave up the ghost. Good food, good drink, deep play and gentle company. A fitting memorial, don't you say? And better fun than playing nursery-maid to Simon's stinking brats. I'll buy you a diamond necklace and a grass-green gown, my little dove, and sleep upon your soft—"

"Don't!" Sarah Jane cried in disgust. "I will not hear it! If my father were alive he would have you horsewhipped for saying such things to me—how could you possibly think I wished to hear them? Leave this house at once, and we—and we will say no more about it, if you please."

Lord Drewmore laughed until one carelessly outflung hand swept the brandy decanter and the candle to the floor, and the gloomy room was plunged into darkness.

"Little dove, little dove, where have you gone?" he declaimed.

Her heart was fluttering just like the mouse-heart she knew she possessed, and frantic tears made her eyes ache. Rather than sit in darkness Sarah Jane groped her way over to the window and threw open the drapes. Pale morning light crept into the room.

"*There* you are," said Lord Drewmore with satisfaction. His hands gripped hard on her shoulders as he grabbed her and swung her around.

Seen in the cold daylight the illusion of youth and beauty was gone. Lord Drewmore's face had a pale waxworks softness that spoke of decades of dissipation. He reeked of brandy, and beneath that smell was a faint sweet scent that Sarah Jane's panic-stricken mind associated with decay. Terror gave her the strength to push him away with a shove that sent him sprawling against the table, into the spilled wine and broken glass.

"You ungrateful little sow," Lord Drewmore said flatly. Sarah Jane shrank back against the window. There was nowhere to run.

Laboriously Drewmore pulled himself to his feet. "You've ruined my coat—and my shirt. You'll pay for this, you precious high-instepped little guttersnipe, and before I'm through you'll thank me for the lesson." He strode over to the window and grabbed Sarah Jane's chin in a painful grip.

"Cynthia won't protect you. She's a silly little chit, none too bright, and likes her comfort too well to make a fuss. Further, she likes her gaming debts paid without having to bother Stuffy Simon, and I am more than willing to oblige her in that trifling matter—in exchange for a little quiet compliance. If there were anyone else on earth who cared whether you live or die you'd be with them now instead of scraping and bowing to other people's children for a few shillings a year. And since no one will hire you even for that once word of this morning gets around, I think you had better start being very, very sorry that you weren't nicer to me."

"Nice to *you*?" The disbelieving scorn in her voice brought a rush of dark blood to Drewmore's face. He raised his hand to strike her and Sarah Jane twisted out of his grip.

She ran from the library and down the hall, thinking only of escape. The front door was heavy, and she heaved at it fruitlessly for some seconds before she realized it was on the latch. Finally she released it and the door swung open.

"I take it this means that you don't wish to go to Paris with me?" Lord Drewmore asked from the hall.

"Never!"

"Then, my dove, you may go to the devil." He walked briskly toward her and she scampered backward onto the step. Then he shut the door in her face.

Chapter 12

APRIL 1817

"DO YOU KNOW, Mary, this is not nearly as much fun as I was promised it would be," Aspasia said to her friend.

"But 'Spasia, I never promised you that—never!" Mary Naismith was honestly outraged. "I only came for tea, and you said you were perishing for a sight of Bad Jack, and I said that wasn't what you said last month, and you said—"

"I know, Mary," Aspasia said soothingly. "I did ask you to bring me." *Heaven above knows why*, she added silently.

Margaret Leacock—known in the trade as Cocky Peg and also by several less repeatable names—ran what she called a "nice respectable place" close enough to Covent Garden to be liable to the title of Covent Garden Abbess. At Cocky Peg's you could get Blue Ruin that had never seen an excise stamp and subtler forms of ruin above. Peg rented respectable rooms to gentlemen—if not rooms to respectable gentlemen—for their parties, and for a price could arrange introductions between the Fashionable Impure and any number of smitten swains.

Aspasia had a certain fondness for Cocky Peg's establishment. After all, she had met Malhythe here. But tonight any suggestion of genteel elegance was long vanished; the open-handed young rakes of the *ton* had taken over the upper rooms of the Peacock for the usual sort of entertainment.

To which Aspasia had asked to come.

The walls were hung with drapes of red and black damask, and there were torches instead of candles lighting the room, making a smoky, flickering light. An immense, round, and very sturdy table occupied the center of the room beneath a bullion-fringed black velvet drape, and the only seating to be had was upon low couches beside even lower tables. Aspasia, who had been hoping for a species of decadence including whist, thought this did not look at all encouraging. The presence of the table seemed to imply dancing upon its surface, later, and though her lack of character could certainly support such dancing, she was not certain that her nerves could. People who danced upon tables were likely to be similarly uninhibited in other directions, as well.

A lavish cold supper had been laid on, and champagne and punch flowed freely. One could even fill one's cup with wine from the spouting paps of a bronze Venus, were one so inclined. Aspasia was not.

She had known that what she wore would be noted, reported on, and—more than likely—ruined by the evening's fun, so she had dressed accordingly. Aspasia wore a crisp blue-and-gold striped gown with bullion fringe about the hem and a shawl of gold tissue. Since the evening seemed to require it she had sprinkled gold spangles among her dark curls; the touch would have amused Malhythe, had he been here.

And many of her friends and acquaintance *were* here. Without moving from her prudently chosen seat in an alcove near the window, Aspasia could see Doll Lambeth and The Phoenix and Kitty Blakely and half a dozen others whose appearance in any London drawing room would cause its hostess to faint dead away.

It was one of life's small injustices that the men who dallied with these despised barques of frailty would be welcomed by those same hostesses with eager arms. Robert Gressingham, Viscount St. George, Lord Hawkchurch—all were here, and would be welcome tomorrow in homes Aspasia and her friends would never be invited to enter.

Even their host, Bad Jack Barham of the black sins and golden eyes, was undoubtedly dangled after by sighing maidens and shrewd mamas—after all, what son of a Duke wouldn't be? The party this evening was to celebrate his recent streak of luck at the tables—and most of his winnings would go to pay for the lavish refreshments here.

All the fast and disenchanted younger set were here, though at this hour things were relatively decorous, and Aspasia resolved to leave before things got really wild. Why in heaven's name had Malhythe so particularly wished her to come to something like this? Well, she would write a detailed account tomorrow—and post it to him, if she could discover his direction!

Mary's Jeremy was here, casting a roving eye upon some *artistes* that Barham had, apparently, engaged. Aspasia glanced in their direction, and then snapped her fan open to cover her face so she could stare in shocked fascination. She could hardly believe it. Why, they were—

Mr. George Lambton was a mature man of considered taste and discrimination—or, at least, so he wished the world at large to believe. The gathering was very dashing, and Bobs Gressingham had explained to him most kindly when he extended the invitation that it would be "quite in the *Corsair* style" and that such style was the crack, the mode, and certainly the only way to go on that persons of fashion and taste could not affect to despise. Thus Georgie was prepared to greet any manifestation of vice, decadence, and perversion with cool dispassionate disinterest.

He was certainly not to be drawn by the stale stratagem of a flesh-colored net gown sewn with black ribbons over pink tights to impersonate nudity, he told himself while gazing at a woman who was almost certainly a member of the muslin company. To notice such a shabby thing would be to mark himself as a greenhorn of the most verdant hue. He raised his quizzing glass and gazed through it at the lady, to signify that his ennui was complete.

Then she turned, and he discovered that the body in question wore neither net nor tights. The not-quite-lady wore red silk stockings gartered below the knee, which could be plainly seen because her entire costume consisted of black ribbons with nothing whatever sewn between them.

Georgie swallowed hard. "I say, Severn, isn't this ripping?" he said hopefully.

Lord Severn swept the room with a basilisk gaze that ought, by rights, have reduced the room and its occupants to ashes. "If you care for this sort of thing, I suppose it must be," he said wearily.

And to think, he had chosen to come here of his own free will. Severn looked around at the lurid pseudo-Gothic drapings and the naked painted statues that passed for decoration, at the young and not-so-young men who were victims of the cutting edge of fashion, and at the "ladies" of the demimonde who were trying to evince a lively interest in something that obviously bored them silly. He remembered these parties well: how they began, how they ended, and how entertaining he had once thought them. In his day they had called them

Medmenham routs; he wondered what the current trope was. The parties had not changed.

Had he changed so much, then?

Georgie was looking at him anxiously; Severn forced a smile. Of course, part of the fun in those long-ago days had come from imagining how shocked others would be if they only knew where he was and what he was doing, and at five-and-thirty Lord Severn had no one left to shock, including himself.

"It may be dull, Georgie, but then all parties are, aren't they? The ability to survive boredom is one of the great assets in—"

"Ah, Lambton, there you are! And Lord Severn—I say, you do us much too much honor indeed. I trust your wife is well?"

Mr. Robert Gressingham, Severn thought critically, was rather too young for that air of oleaginous bonhomie he cultivated. Never mind. The boy would grow into it, if somebody didn't shoot him first.

"My wife, Mr. Gressingham, is just as you might expect," he answered, wondering why he was making this futile attempt to depress Mr. Gressingham's pretensions. It might be because it was the height of bad form to inquire after a man's wife at an orgy. On the other hand, it might be because his joints ached. *Old man*, Severn jeered at himself.

"Oh, ripping—we shall see some fun tonight, I promise you, Lord Severn. Bad Barham has the reputation for driving to the inch, as it were—it will be almost like old times, for you, eh, my lord?"

Lord Severn skewered Mr. Gressingham with a look that could by no stretch of the imagination be described as friendly.

"But it was actually the Lamb I was hoping to catch out," Mr. Gressingham added hurriedly. "Remember that matter we were speaking of, Lambton? You'll excuse us, Lord Severn, surely."

Severn bowed with exact politeness; Mr. Gressingham took Georgie by the elbow and hurried him off.

"That matter" was either dice or women, from the look on Georgie's face. Either way it was no concern of Georgie's uncle. George Lambton was a man grown; let him make his own mistakes. Lord Severn turned away and set himself to find amusement in what everyone said was a quite amusing party.

Aspasia had been at the party only an hour and thought that at that it was fifty-nine minutes too long. Mary's Jeremy had sought them out just as he had promised Mary he would do. Mary was delighted at such particular attention, but she signified her joy by asking Jeremy to come back to her rooms with her. A nasty little spat ensued, and Mary's Jeremy flung himself off.

"Here, Mary," Aspasia said, proffering her handkerchief, "you will want this."

Mary was not pretty when she wept. "Oh, why is he so hateful?" she wailed, pressing the soft cambric of the handkerchief to swollen red eyes.

Because you love him, and he knows it, and he does not love you, Aspasia thought sadly. Aloud she said, "And when will you learn not to tease a gentleman when he is feeling important, my angel? He will not wish to go off with you, Mary, when he can stay here and strut and preen. Now dry your eyes; if he sees he has made you cry he will be even more impossible."

"It is easy for you! You have never loved!"

The rush of fury Aspasia felt quite surprised her, ridiculous though it was. She did not wish to wear her heart on her sleeve, so why object when she succeeded? "Perhaps you are right—but Mary, even if it is hard, you must still do it. Do you want him to laugh at you?"

The tonic worked; Mary dried her eyes and sat up and drank off a revivifying glass of champagne, leaving Aspasia to nurse her own sore heart in peace.

Colworth Rudwell, Earl of Malhythe. She could have him, but never marry him, and the day he married, he was lost to her forever. And such a day seemed frighteningly near.

She smiled meaninglessly and plied her fan. What was it Malhythe wanted her to learn from Barham? How very tedious it was to be a rake? Or how to tell when Lord Severn returned to that self-same path?

Someone came and struck up a conversation with Mary. She glanced after the absent Jeremy and then slanted her eyes at the newcomer, laughing and tossing her head. A few minutes more of low talk and she allowed herself to be persuaded to take the air on the balcony. Aspasia watched them go, hopefully. Perhaps Mary's Jeremy would see, and be jealous.

It was probably time for her to see and be seen as well, and then she could call her carriage and leave. Mary had rooms in town and could find her own way home, but Aspasia had come a farther distance.

She adjusted her shawl, folded her fan, and stood, and as she did she saw Lord Severn standing across the room, talking to the infamous Bad Barham.

There was no mistaking that face. Father and son shared a strong physical resemblance, and he matched in all other particulars the description she had of Severn: bronze hair, emerald eyes, wretched morals.

It was hardly an endorsement of virtue to be seen

at an affair such as this, after all, and Severn, with his age and history, might be presumed to know better than to attend . . . at least if he had any desire at all to be a reformed soul. Which obviously he did not.

And so Malhythe would marry, and she would be forced to leave him, and there was nothing, nothing that she could do.

Aspasia turned and walked quickly away.

It was incumbent upon a guest to be polite. Therefore Severn, with punctilio, sought out the Marquess of Barham.

He found Lord Barham surveying his wonderland with a pleased expression; like the chief devil at an *auto-da-fé*. Barham was well dressed, and his clothes had the matter-of-fact plainness that characterized the ex-military and others who patronized Weston, but the coat was dragged to shapelessness and its pockets bulged with the weight of coin they held. As Severn approached, Barham flipped a coin to one of the opera dancers standing nearby; it was gold, so she caught it and tucked it away and dropped him a mocking curtsey.

"Ah, the soothing power of money."

"Good evening, Lord Barham. I have come to pay my respects."

Barham turned toward him and tipped him a salute from a large shallow goblet. The stem and base were silver; the bowl was white bone, and there was little doubt that one was meant to think it a human skull. "Last respects? I warn you, sir, there is a good deal of life left in me." He drank, ostentatiously.

"Do show that to my little nephew," Severn urged cordially, nodding toward the goblet. "*He'll* be impressed."

Barham regarded him a moment through narrow

eyes, then laughed. "Say what you will, sir—but it holds a great deal." With a flourish, he offered the cup to Severn.

"Your servant." It seemed to hold nothing more lethal than a rather young burgundy; Severn tipped it back and drank.

"Who the devil are you, anyway? Did I invite you?" Barham asked.

Severn handed back the grisly relict. "As it happens, I am here by the invitation of another of your guests, a Mr. Lambton. I am Severn; you may throw me out if you like."

"And have you miss the fun? My lord, we are aiming at something truly unique here tonight, for the benefit of the children and stay-at-homes who were unable to attend the Late Unpleasantness on the Continent. It is sad that they should miss such a grand fireworks display as that, but I shall show them hell yet," Barham said with satisfaction. "I've heard a good deal of you, my lord. No doubt you've learned a few tricks in India that would make things even livelier—perhaps I can induce you to share them?"

"Of course. But it's no use my just telling them to you, Lord Barham. You haven't any elephants, you know, and without them. . . . " Severn shrugged apologetically.

"You're probably right. One must temper the wind to the shorn lamb, and after that nonsense last month about the bear, Peg'll throw me out if I bring any more livestock into the place. Small-minded wench." Barham looked about the room. "My God, we've been overrun by the infantry. I'm sure I don't know these people—and half of them look too young to be out without their nurses. It's a pity their money spends as well as any other's—I suppose I'll keep inviting them. And there will always be another party, eh, my lord?"

So I used to think. "Tell me, Lord Barham, what will you do when the money runs out for good?" Severn asked impulsively.

Barham looked startled, as if no one had ever asked him the question before. "Oh, the obvious thing, my dear Lord Severn—find myself a rich pretty heiress and marry her."

Barham bowed and turned away, fishing in his pockets for a suitable coin to toss.

There was something epicene about men with no other concern in life save their own amusement: their conversations revolved around their mistresses, their drinking, their gaming, and their clothes. It was a new generation and a harder brighter world. The demi-monde that Severn remembered was gone; or perhaps only the boy who thought it so new. There was no place for the Viscount Severn here.

But where, if not here? He had no estates to manage, nor did he have a calling to medicine or law. The Polite World would surely prove as boring as its subfusc counterpart, and then what was left?

His constitution would not withstand heavy drinking, cardplay was amusing but he had no taste for staking enormous sums just to lose them, and for all the joy afforded by a mannerly trot around Green Park, he might as well stay home.

The only trouble with that was that his wife was there.

The thought of his dear and monstrously suitable wife made Severn clench his fists. Everyone said she was a darling. Everyone was ready to take her part instead of his own. Everyone contrived to make him feel a perfect monster for having married her.

But if she was such a saint, and he such a sinner, why had *she* married *him*?

The answer, of course, was that Primula was no

saint. She was a fallen woman—he should know; he was the one who'd tripped her. Instead of sitting in pride of place at Kitmatgar House, lapped in luxury and surrounded by servants, she should be here, where—

But Severn didn't like that either. This was no place for his sweet, demanding, stubborn, arrogant little Lady Severn, who had no idea how long the fall from grace or how hard the landing. In her way she was still innocent; he did not want to change that. What he wanted was—

He didn't know what he wanted.

Yes he did. He wanted to come home.

Aspasia had fled precipitously from the odious sight of Severn returning to his rakish muttons and had collided with a wineglass full of burgundy, which promptly launched itself into space and landed on her dress, soaking it from the knees down.

"Oh, I say! I'm dreadfully sorry!"

The gentleman whose glass it had once been regarded her, stricken, and then fell upon hands and knees, swabbing seamanlike away at her dress with a large cotton handkerchief. The wine had soaked instantly into the soft surface of her dress, leaving a dark purple stain, and had already penetrated to the layers beneath.

"Oh, I pray you, don't distress yourself, my good sir. I imagine the dress is a dead loss, not to mention the slipper and stocking. Fortunately the leg is unharmed."

"And a lovely leg it is, too!" he said impulsively, and blushed. He was really quite young, Aspasia saw, and gave him one of her best smiles.

Her rescuer rose to his feet and gazed at his handkerchief in some bewilderment. "No, entirely my fault; ought to know better than to go around carrying things—they always wind up where they shouldn't." He looked at the ruined handkerchief once more, and then deposited it in a large Chinese vase. "I'm George Lambton—and if there's anything—"

"And you may call me Aspasia," she answered. Really, he was very nice.

Mr. George Lambton blinked. "Oh my; you're very well preserved, Mis Aspasia, but it's a dashed long chalk from Periclean Athens, isn't it?"

So the nice young man had a brain or two, as well. "Oh, one does what one can to keep amused. I was just about to leave, but now I feel that by rights I should drink a glass of wine with you before I go."

She linked her arm through Mr. Lambton's and led him off to the buffet. By the time he had procured them glasses of wine, Aspasia was in possession of Mr. Lambton's direction, expectations, hopes, and length of residence in town. He seemed intent on modeling his career on that of an unnamed uncle—who sounded to Aspasia, from Georgie's description, like the worst amalgam of idiot and bore.

And he'd manage it too, if he started out running with Bad Barham's set. Before the night was out one of the grand ladies here this evening would have rooked him into taking her into keeping; he'd receive a fine selection of debts and vices from her fast enough, as well as a dose of pox. Of course, he might just be ruined at the tables, set out for home well-foxed and end dead in the gutter. George Lambton did not strike Aspasia as someone with either the taste or aptitude for being bad.

"Will you sit with me a while, Georgie? I was hoping for a game of whist, but this doesn't seem quite the occasion for it. What a pity—all these court cards and not a playing card in sight!"

* * *

Finally Severn could withstand the nagging of his conscience no longer. Yes, George Lambton was a man grown—but a very young one, without the faintest idea of how to handle himself in this shark-infested sea. Addie and Primula both said he needed to be watched out for, after all.

Why in God's name must everything come back to Primula? He didn't want her. She didn't want him. He wanted a comfortable quiet establishment in the land of his birth without a wife burning like a slow match toward the sometime day that she would recognize his true identity.

But thanks to his loving father and his carefully selected bride he couldn't have that. At least he could stun Addie inexpressibly by looking out for his little nephew. Severn went in search of Georgie, wondering how best to break it to him that he, the wicked uncle, had turned his coat.

Since Severn did not waste his time in being shocked by the entertainment or apologizing to the couples he disturbed in his search, he found Georgie fairly quickly. Mr. Lambton was sitting in relative decorum next to a dasher of the first water—as out-of-place in this clichéd debauch as a respectable woman would have been, and judging from her clothes, nearly as expensive to know.

"You must come and see me in a day or so, Georgie," the woman said as Severn approached. "We will have that game of cards—and I promise you you will not be bored!"

"Ahem," said Severn, and both of them looked up.

The dasher had enormous blue eyes and a roses and cream skin that had undoubtedly made her fortune. She had gold spangles scattered in her hair, too, but not as if she meant it. And he would have sworn that she recognized him.

"Ah, Miss Aspasia; here's the man I wanted you to meet. My uncle, Lord Severn."

"Severn's *your* uncle?" the dasher called Aspasia said in shock.

"It would be more accurate to say that Mr. Lambton is my nephew—and has forgotten that he is promised to another party. So if you will excuse us, dear girl . . . ?"

The blue eyes were wide with alarm; she flipped open her fan and peeped over it at him. "Of course," came the slightly muffled reply, "if you will excuse *me*. I'm very nearly sure my carriage is waiting."

She stood, and the folds of her dress fell open to reveal a large purple blotch.

"You really must let me—" Georgie began.

"Not-at-all, Georgie; one must hazard to play. But don't forget about our assignation—and now I really must go. I don't want to keep you from your entirely specious party, after all."

She was gone before Severn had registered what she said, leaving a strong scent of amber and roses in her wake.

"There isn't any party, is there, Uncle?" Georgie said doubtfully.

"Not as such. But this is such a damned bore I thought we might look in at one of my clubs—and in the name of God, don't let one of *them* get her claws into you. Above your touch, my lad—did you see those sapphires?"

"She was nice," Georgie said defensively.

"Oh, aye, until she—"

There was a crash from the other room, a feminine squeal, and then a roar of male laughter. Georgie looked alarmed.

"Of course you can stay here, if you like—but I hoped you would bear me company," Severn said cannily.

Georgie looked relieved. "Oh, yes—of course, Uncle Severn."

Chapter 13

APRIL 17, 1817

SHE WAS COLD.

Sarah Jane had wandered the streets for hours after Lord Drewmore flung her out. Her bonnetless, cloakless state drew curious glances from the passersby; respectable people avoided her.

At last she had recovered enough to know that she had suffered a calamity beyond her management, and that she must have help. She recalled that she was not friendless in London, despite Lord Drewmore's taunts.

But the ladies she approached for directions drew their skirts aside and would not speak to her, and she could not bring herself to speak to any of the unaccompanied gentlemen. Some of them tried to speak to her; they thought she was a woman of the streets; when Sarah Jane realized that she ran from them.

It was difficult to thread the maze of London's West End without a map, but at last she managed to win through to the safety of her godmother's house.

The door was opened by an unfamiliar servant, who, seeing her, began to close the door in her face.

"No! Wait! I am Sarah Jane Emwilton—is Lady Greetwell here?"

The footman gazed at her, and Sarah Jane was suddenly painfully conscious of how she must look. Her gown was draggle-hemmed and spotted with mud by now, and her hair hung about her face. Her proper jean traveling boots were dusty and scraped. She did not look like someone Lady Greetwell would wish to see admitted to the house.

"Her ladyship's away," the footman said, and started to close the door again.

"Wait—*wait*! I am all alone in London; something terrible has happened—is Badgley here? He is Lady Greetwell's butler; he will vouch for me—" She was babbling and unable to stop; in another moment she would be weeping—cool, calm Sarah Jane, whom Papa had always called his little soldier!

The footman closed the door in her face. She pounded on the door, not caring what any onlookers might think. A moment later it opened again, to disclose another unfamiliar face.

"What's your business here, girl?" the man said.

"I want to see Badgley," Sarah Jane said in a small voice. "He will tell you. I am Lady Greetwell's goddaughter—oh, let me *in*—"

She stepped toward the door; the butler closed it warningly. "Mr. Badgley isn't here and neither is her ladyship—the Greetwells have gone to Scotland, as I make no doubt you know."

"But I must see her! Can I— Can I wait for her here? If I could just send a letter—"

"Be off with you!" the butler snapped. "We don't want any dirty gipsy thieves skulking about—if you've business with Lady Greetwell come back next month. Now hop it before I have you thrown in jig. *Go!*"

This time the door was slammed with great finality. Sarah Jane stared at it until she realized that it would not open—until a bucket of dirty water poured from an upper window fell on her, soaking her to the skin. Then she ran, shivering and crying.

Every time she stopped to rest that day there was someone to chivy her on—beadles and park guards and watchmen and footmen. Eventually she found herself in a part of town that she had never been in before; she only knew that when she collapsed in exhaustion on a doorstep people did not ask her to move on.

She slept that night in a doorway and drank water from a catch-trough. Every sound was a source of terror, and hunger made her light-headed. She could hardly believe this had happened to her. She was still Miss Sarah Jane Emwilton. How could she have been reduced so easily to a dirty scarecrow crouching in an alleyway? She had a place and a home and people who loved her.

If she could reach them. She had no money and no one in London to help her. She did not have so much as a pen and a sheet of paper to try to send a message. Lady Greetwell was gone—even if Primula were not gone as well Sarah Jane had no way of finding her; Prim had married, and Sarah Jane was not sure of her new direction. Her clothes, after the bucket of water and a day on the Mail and a day walking and a night of being slept in, marked her as a denizen of the streets. She had nothing to rely on but herself.

Very well, said General Emwilton's daughter. If that was all she had it would have to be enough. She would walk to Oakleys.

Aspasia had left Lord Barham's party rather later than she meant to. It was true that there were vanishingly few highwaymen now on the mile or so of Hounslow Heath she had to cross to reach her little house in St. John's Wood; on the other hand, she had no desire to meet even one.

She was thinking hopefully of her own bed and a warm brick to heat it when the hired carriage jolted to a stop as the horses shied. Aspasia clung to the strap as the carriage swayed, and the moment it had settled she flung open her window.

The moon was full and high and the sky a lovely deep blue velvet, spangled with stars. She could hear the jingle of bits as the outriders' animals danced nervily back and forth.

"What's there?" she heard her coachman call.

"Something in the road," answered the postilion.

Aspasia leaned out of the carriage, drawing her fur-lined hood closer about her face. One of the outriders had dismounted and was holding his pole-lantern close to what looked like a bundle of rags. He turned it with his foot and looked up, seeing the flash of her face at the window.

"Body, Miss." But the body stirred, and cried out, and raised a pale, fine-boned hand to shield its eyes from the light, and Aspasia cried out herself and scrambled out of the carriage.

She sent one of her outriders back to town for a doctor, and rode the rest of the way home with the revenant cradled in her arms. The girl had taken a little brandy, and her pulse was stronger now, but her lips were blue and her slender fingers were cold. Her lashes made damp dark stars on her cheek; try as she might, Aspasia had not been able to rouse her.

Who was she? And why was she lying in the middle of the road, when a sensible person would have chosen the ditch to do her dying in?

The clothing was of quality, though dirty and stained. The hands were not work-hardened, nor the face drink-coarsened, and she was young—barely out of her teens, if Aspasia was any judge.

"M-Mama?" the girl whispered without opening her eyes.

"Hush, my angel; it is all right," said Aspasia, and drew the coachrobe higher over the girl's thin shoulders. She thought she knew the answer to her riddle now; a good girl, ruined and turned out of doors by her parents when the sin was discovered. Aspasia had seen no sign of a child, but perhaps the discovery had been made another way. The little *inconnu* could tell her, if she lived.

At last there was a clatter of hooves on stone, and the motion of the well-sprung carriage changed to the staccato rocking that meant they were very near home.

The footmen carried the inert body up to Aspasia's sitting room, where her housekeeper stood in wrapper and mobcap, marveling at the disarray.

"Miss! Whatever's toward?"

The footmen laid the girl on the couch. Her head lolled limply, and Aspasia wondered for the first time what would happen if she died. Malhythe was not here to protect her.

"Oh, Cutty, I'm sure I'm in the most dreadful pickle! I've sent for Doctor Southland–build up the fire, put water on to heat and–"

"Hush yourself, Miss. Don't you think old Cutty knows her business by now? Poor little chuck, turned out of doors in this nasty April weather–and what are you looking at, you pair 'o country lummoxes?"

The footmen, thus addressed, retreated. Aspasia went after them to bestow upon each a sovereign for his efforts on her behalf, and when she returned, Mrs. Clutterbuck had already removed the girl's shoes and stockings, and had begun on the dress.

"These things will want a deal of tidying before

they're fit to be seen, but she's near enough of a size to you, Miss, that you might loan her a gown if you're of a mind."

"Something cut high to the neck," Aspasia said dryly. She built up the fire and set the watercan to heat. Idly she examined the growing pile of discarded clothes.

The cambric dress was grey with dirt, but the seams revealed that its color had once been blue. The underclothes were plain but good; the shift embroidered in careful whitework. Aspasia traced an *E* that was surrounded by a laurel garland.

"No—no—*no*—"

Aspasia turned back. The stranger was struggling against Mrs. Clutterbuck's attempts to slide a voluminous flannel nightgown over her head.

"Now, lamb, give over, do," the housekeeper coaxed. The girl's eyes opened very wide. They were blue, noted Aspasia irrelevantly.

"But I am Sarah Jane Emwilton," the stranger said with great distinctness, and fainted.

Chapter 14

APRIL 18, 1817

MUCH TO SEVERN'S surprise, he discovered in himself a genuine desire not to hurt his puppyish nephew's feelings. As a result, the evening progressed to an enjoyable tour of some of the more discreet hells before winding homeward. Severn had the satisfaction of knowing, when turning to his own longed-for bed, that he had achieved something like deification in Georgie's eyes—a small joy that went far toward making him forget that young George Lambton was still wild for to hold, at large upon the town, and under no one's governance save his own.

The morning of April eighteenth dawned bleak and raw, and Lord Severn lay abed watching the rain bead on the windows without the slightest desire to rise. It was as if some anchor-chain had snapped last night and cast him adrift. The old life was closed to him. He could not go back to what he had been.

But who was Lord Severn anyway? He looked around the bedroom heaped with India's gaudy pagan glories. Not a Company man, as he had been for the last ten years. Not a rake-about-town, as he had been the decade before that. But if neither of these, then . . . what? What should Lord Severn become?

He wracked his brain, trying to dredge up some boyhood conversation where Malhythe had spoken of his hopes for Severn's young manhood. But there was no template there. Perhaps Malhythe's own life was something he should base his upon—but Severn realized with a little shock that he had no idea how his father spent his days. He remembered vaguely that Malhythe was active in the Government, but beyond that, nothing.

He could not imagine his father placidly conserving his estates and listening to speeches in the House—it was equally impossible to imagine himself doing those things.

Why had he bothered to come home? What could he possibly have thought was waiting for him here?

"And good morning to Your Grace—no mind that it's halfway to noon, if un can call her daylight at all." Loach entered the room, apparently feeling that Severn had slept long enough. He held a silver shaving basin and a case of razors under one arm, and a copper piggin of water in his other hand. "No doubt Your Grace mistook the light and thought we be setting for the monsoon," he added sarcastically.

"I don't see why I should get out of bed at all," Severn announced. "I have considered the matter in great detail, my good man, and I have come to the inescapable conclusion that I am absolutely, completely, and utterly worthless."

"Aye, and there's reason to lie abed o'day? I'll shave 'ee there, if un's not careful." Loach set the steaming can of water on the hob and began shaving soap into the bowl. "Her doesn't think so," he added conversationally.

"Lady Severn's judgment is perhaps not quite sound," Severn said shortly. He toyed briefly with the idea of going to Primula and telling her the whole—their previous meeting, his scandalous past. What, after all, could she do?

"I'm a-coming with that-there soap, Your Grace," Loach warned. Severn hurriedly swung his legs over the side of the bed and reached for his dressing gown.

She could hate him.

And he didn't want that. God help him, he wanted his wife to love him.

Ridiculous. He strode to the fireside and seated himself in the chair that Loach held ready.

"Lady Severn's an . . . ordinary sort of person, wouldn't you say?" he suggested hopefully to Loach.

"Aye, if gold sovereigns grow on berry bushes," was the dour answer. "Her's quality, is Her Grace." Loach took up a soap-filled brush and liberally anointed Severn's jaw.

Any attempt to open his mouth now would result in a mouthful of soap; Severn was perforce silent.

Quality, was she? Was Loach's judgment any sounder than Primula's?

Yes, said his conscience.

Only suppose, for the instant, that he told her all. She would hate him, naturally, and demand that he avoid her. But she would certainly wish to avoid scandal, so she would not wish an open break. They would be much in one another's company; he could coax her around, make her fall in love with him. . . .

Would there be any more truth in his lovemaking now than there had been the last time?

Severn twitched and was instantly rewarded. Blood stained the lather pink and the soap burned in the nick.

"Move, and un cuts un's self—not me," Loach said placidly. Severn growled and subsided.

Who was Lord Severn, that he should want a wife to add to his misery? Would a course of true love render him any more able to deal with the world?

And besides, he had no idea what his feelings truly were—or hers. Perhaps he owed her the truth—but in that case didn't she owe him the same? And a full disclosure of her past had been suspiciously absent from their conversations so far.

She had, in fact, married him under pretenses as false as those he'd married her under—hadn't she? He knew the sins of *his* past—what were *hers*? And would it not be the gentlemanly thing not to care?

It would . . . if he knew *why* she had married him. He knew full well that her reputation was spotless, whether it had any right to be or not, but his father had blackmailed him into marrying this woman and no other, and he wanted to know why. Was she a further punishment for the sin of filial disobedience?

"Wants to look like the bramble-bush prince this morning, him does," Loach said as Severn collected another cut. "Bide ee for mercy's sake—time and enough to be doing when un's scraped."

Or had Malhythe forced *her* as well?

The thought was new, and it disturbed him. He knew nothing of his wife save that she had charmed the *ton* and all his sisters. She had never indicated that this marriage was unwelcome—but had he indicated that he wished to hear if it was?

Well, he wanted to hear it now. Primula's soiree was in less than a week, and he had promised to go. Before he was exhibited like a prize bull before the *ton*, he wanted to know why—and to the devil with maundering on about his future.

Loach lifted the razor and Severn irritably brushed the arm back. "Aren't you done yet?" he said, grabbing for the towel. "Have done—and find my coat. Don't just stand there gawping—I'm in a hurry, man!"

She would positively not take "no" for an answer today. Primula stood before the mirror in her room, putting the last touches on her toilette. She was going to Colworth House, routing Georgie out of bed, and bearing him back here with her.

She was conscious of a heaviness at her heart that all her wrathful animadverting did little to ease. She had hoped it was all a sham. She had hoped the time would come when Severn would throw off his poses and begin to court her as any young husband might court his bride.

It was time, Primula realized bleakly, to abandon hope. Severn did not want her. Perhaps he did not want any bride. But the warmth she thought she had seen in him at their bridal had been only an illusion.

So oughtn't they deal openly and honestly with one another? She did not know what Lord Malhythe's plan was, but she did know that Severn's heartstrings were unlikely to be pulled by the realization that they had met before.

Only . . . Primula could not imagine that the remote and distant stranger with whom she shared her home would have any interest in a ten-year-old peccadillo. If she spoke of it to him, he might see that as a bid for present attention, and Primula's pride rebelled from being thought a supplicant, even by him.

Fortunately she was a calm, level-headed person who could face facts unblinkingly. Primula dabbed at her eyes savagely with a lace handkerchief. Severn was a bad lot. He was heartless. He'd proved it.

Not only had he refused to take her part with Georgie yesterday, he had even encouraged him in his raking. She had waited up to see her husband home, hoping every minute he had changed his mind about the party. But it had been four o'clock when Severn had come in, and he had been well foxed. He had not changed from the proud wild boy she had known, and it was time to give up the stubborn hope that he would. It was time.

Therefore, she would think about Georgie. And about some method, not relying upon kindness, for getting Severn to Almack's, now that vouchers had been secured. She was no more trapped, she was possessed of no less love, than she had been before her marriage. It had been enough then. It would be enough now.

Primula took a deep steadying breath. If only Mama and Papa weren't in Scotland! She dared not confide her vexation to a letter, soothing as that would be, but she thought now that she might tell Papa the whole. The advice he would give her would be no different than that she would give herself: be strong. Survive. She had done it for ten years. She could do it now.

She thought longingly for a moment of posting up to join her parents at Lord Rannoch's. But no. Abandon the venue of her social triumph? Make a present to the gossips of the trouble in her marriage? No and no. The world would see a fond wife and an admirable husband—and the world would see Severn at her side at Almack's.

But first Georgie. She lifted the lid from the box that stood on the table and sighed her approval.

Madame Bouchard, the hatter, had delivered yet another of her stunning creations. It might distract Georgie into talk of the latest mode and cause him to make unwise promises. Reverently Primula lifted the creation from its deep nest of silver paper.

It was perilously high in the poke, and nested among the curling white ostrich plumes were some treasures from India—half a dozen peacock feathers, spangled blue and violet and green in the morning light. A daring conceit, but Lady Severn dared much. With one reverent finger she traced a band of the glistening straw braid that made up the hat.

So engrossed was Lady Severn in contemplating George Lambton's instantaneous surrender to the charms of her bonnet that she ignored the opening of the door.

"M'lady," the abigail began.

"I can see that she's here," came Severn's voice from the hall. "Now let me in."

Lord Severn did not look as though he had been out of bed for any length of time. His unpomaded hair was tousled in a fashion that owed less to art than to haste, his biscuit-colored trousers were sadly pulled, and his limp collar points were innocent of the addition of any cravat. Primula could see the light gleam in the soft hollow of his undefended throat, and his flaunting of the intimacy angered her. She took the time to set the bonnet on her head before turning.

"Well, my Lord Severn, you come in fine time this morning," she said. "Oh, don't hover, Claggett, you know that I am going out and I am sure that Lord Severn has other things to do."

The abigail curtseyed and left. As Primula heard the door click behind her, she realized with an undignified thrill that this was the first time since her marriage that she had been completely alone with Lord Severn.

"Well?" she said, more briskly than was perhaps flattering.

Lord Severn was equally blunt. "Why did you marry me?"

Because like a fool I loved you. And I thought you might love me. No. She would not make him a present of her heart twice. Primula forced a trill of laughter.

"La, sir, why does any woman marry? It is ungallant to ask us our reasons, Lord Severn—and at such an hour! But I am so glad you are here—I'm going out, and I meant to ask your advice about this bonnet before I did." Primula turned back to the mirror. She could see him in the glass as she made an elegant bow in blue-green silk ribbon beneath her chin.

"Do you think the ribbon tied so? No; certainly not; you are quite right. Nothing conventional will do. How about so?" She shifted the ribbon about to the other side and made the loops of the bow even more extreme.

"My lady wife . . ." She watched him watch her as she primped and preened. She almost regretted her hastiness in cutting him off. Why should he ask such a question? And what might she answer if he asked it again?

"Are these things really important to you?" he asked instead, indicating the bonnet.

They are all I have—and all I ever will have! "As important as breathing, my lord—in fact, far more! Why, one can study to give up breathing altogether for a minute or so, but fashion? Never! As well to give up Society, and that's nonsense. You can never rest a moment, in this gay mad social whirl of ours, or you lose your place entirely." She would rather be thought heartless than heartbroken, if those were the only choices offered to her.

"And what about *my* place in Society?"

She longed to cradle him in her arms—that, or slap him silly. It was grossly unfair of him to raise hopeful doubts in her now.

"That, my lord, is entirely up to you. If you mean to be a hermit, however, you must let me know—I shall have no trouble finding for myself a suitable *gallant* to do the pretty in public. It is quite fashionable, never fear."

"Oh, fashionable," said Severn dismissively. "But is it wise? My dear Lady Severn, I know that we are not perhaps on intimate terms, but—as I know my sisters have told you—I am well acquainted with reputation, and how to lose it. It is more fragile than you may think, and fashionable is often just a synonym for fast."

Primula's battered heart took refuge in fury. Here he came, demanding confidences from her and then lecturing her on her behavior—when he had not come close enough to her in a month of marriage to have formed any idea of it!

"What's never smirched is soonest laundered; *my* credit can stand a little eccentricity, even if yours cannot, Lord Severn. Or are you worried that my company is too fast for you?" She tossed her head as she turned her attention back to the mirror.

"I am wondering why a chit of a girl that I don't know from Mother Eve would stoop so low as to marry the Viscount Severn," he growled dangerously. His green eyes were snapping sparks; his fists were clenched as if he intended to beat the answer out of her.

Primula regarded him with wide brown eyes and studied ingenuousness. "For the consequence, of course, my lord. Is there any other reason anybody would wish to marry you?"

Her own words circled around in her head, mocking her—that, and the image of Severn's white-lipped fury when he stalked from the room. "Is there any other reason anybody would wish to marry you?" How *could* she have been so stupid?

Oblivious of the carriage's motion and her elaborate bonnet, she buried her face in her hands. How could she have made such a muddle of things, when all she meant was to live quietly with her husband and abjure all romantic nonsense? She would have been better employed offering him soft sweet answers to his questions; as soon as Lord Malhythe returned Severn would ask *him* the same question, after all, and Primula was willing to bet that the Earl would give him the truth.

Don't think about that now, she told herself desperately. She took a deep breath and forced her thoughts away from the painful and well-worn track. *While you keep your head, all about you are safe.* She dabbed at her eyes and inhaled stingingly from her bottle of salts, and as the carriage drew up before Colworth House she was able to face the servants with an air of composure.

Primula had been at Colworth House any number of times in the past year, attending the numerous parties that signalized her engagement. She knew perfectly well that to say it now looked neglected and abandoned was to engage in rankest air-dreaming. She strode up the steps and rang a brisk peal on the iron bell-pull.

The servant who opened the door was correct as always; his countenance as sphinxlike as if the Earl were still in residence.

"Is Mr. Lambton here?" she asked, handing in her card.

"I shall enquire, Lady Severn."

She awaited the footman's return in a parlor that had nothing at all of a Gothic air to it. It was, in fact, exceedingly normal—hardly the parlor of a man who would blackmail his son and chosen daughter-in-law into marrying. But what kind of man *would* do such a thing?

"Aunt Prim!"

Primula had never looked less auntlike. She was wearing an extravagant poke bonnet trimmed with plumes and peacock feathers, and a dashing pelisse made of several Kashmir shawls and trimmed with tigerskin.

"Oh, Georgie, for heaven's sake—you make me feel I should be at caps and crochets already," she said with a smile.

"Never," he said, recovering gallantly. "Has Saunders brought you everything you wish? I hope you will excuse me, but—"

"But you think I am here to read a scold over you, and you wish not to hear it, I know! But I shall have my say, and then you may go on your errand unscathed." Her smile made it impossible for a dutiful nephew to refuse; Georgie thought of his uncle with a startled moment's envy, and lowered himself gingerly to the seat beside her.

Primula was not quite certain what sort of depravity she expected to have left its mark on his features, but whatever she looked for wasn't there. She relaxed slightly.

"We will assume that I have asked you how you are finding London, and that you have asked me how your Mama is—though really, Georgie, she can hardly have gotten there yet, let alone written—and I have made certain that you have not forgotten about my party—which is Thursday week, remember—and you have told me that you are contemplating a toilette that will dazzle the *ton*—"

Here George Lambton smiled faintly.

"—and come directly to the point, which you are avoiding. Addie meant you to live under my roof while she was away, and I have yet to see you there." Primula stopped and looked at him steadfastly.

Georgie searched the walls of the room, but aid was not forthcoming, either from the ancient darkness of the paintings or the brittle vitreous glitter of the gimcracks in their glass cases. "No, Aunt Prim," he admitted.

Primula sighed. "It is not, Georgie, that I wish

to mew you up, or keep you from enjoying the liberties of a young man about town. . . ."

"It's just that you think I'll make a wretched muddle of it. Well, you're quite wrong there, my girl—er, Aunt Prim. I don't intend to sail in Dun Territory, or fall prey to Greeks and blacklegs, or—well, anything."

"It is my understanding that one never *expects* to get into trouble," said Primula rather tartly. "Georgie, do be sensible!"

"If by sensible you mean I should fall in with your wishes," said George Lambton perspicaciously, "I shan't. With Grandfather away in France, Uncle Severn is the head of the family, and if *he* sees nothing wrong with a man of nearly three-and-twenty residing in his own ancestral home for the Season, then there's nothing to gossip of in it, is there?"

Primula was caught between a strong desire to call her husband a niddering noddycock and a wish to throttle her nephew until he did what she wished. Since neither of these attractive courses was immediately possible, she simply smiled her brightest and most mendacious smile.

"Well! I see that nothing will persuade you—and so I must trust in your good sense. I hope this new separatism will not keep you from eating your dinner with us this Friday? I shall have to write something to your Mama, you know, and I do not wish to have to say that I haven't even seen you."

Georgie smiled with the relief of one who has been let off rather lighter than he suspects he deserves. "I shall certainly be there—and I promise, Aunt Prim, I shall do nothing disastrous without consulting you first."

And with that rather ambiguous promise, Primula had to be content.

Chapter 15

APRIL 18, 1817—EARLIER THAT MORNING

BOTH ASPASIA AND her housekeeper spent a restless night tending to the ills of their stray. Dr. Southland had come as summoned, but he could do little more for Miss Sarah Jane Emwilton than they could. He assured them that they could expect a sickly catarrh at the very least, and advised them in the most marrow-freezing terms to keep her wrapped up warm if they wished her to see the dawn.

So the two ladies plied their victim with hot bricks and hot plasters and heaped upon her every covering the house could afford, and in the end Dr. Southland was confounded. Miss Sarah Jane Emwilton dropped off into a rosy healthy sleep toward dawn, with no sign of the promised illness.

Aspasia watched the morning come over the row of discreet little houses facing one another across her cobbled close. Her elegant self was swathed in a dressing gown of sapphire velvet liberally ornamented with gold lace and bullion fringe. Her raven's-wing curls were covered with a mobcap of silk crepe trimmed in matching ribbands, and her blue eyes were troubled.

What was one to do with the little Emwilton girl?

Aspasia picked at a loose bit of lace at her wrist. She had been on her own since the age of fifteen, and she knew only one answer to that question. When a woman had been cast out by her family, and for that reason could not expect to marry (well or even otherwise), there were few alternatives.

She could go into service—but employers expected better character from their servants than they had themselves.

She could become a street vendor, selling violets or cress, and live in a squalor so unspeakable that death would be preferable.

Or she could go on the stage—but that was only a roundabout path to her only real choice: to find some man willing to take an interest in her, and in exchange agree to make a home for him without benefit of clergy.

It would not be hard. Sarah Jane Emwilton was not bad-looking. She had educated speech, and probably very pretty manners as well. Cocky Peg would almost certainly be grateful to make her acquaintance, and even, if she were lucky, introduce her to a pretty boy like George Lambton, who would make her descent beneath all respectability as painless as possible.

Aspasia sighed and refilled her glass. All that was left was to explain to the girl that, like Persephone, she had descended into the underworld—and unlike Persephone, she would never see the sun again.

Sarah Jane was certain it had all been a hideous dream. The turbot had been a little off at dinner, that was all. She was at Oakleys—didn't the linens tickle her nose with the scent of sun-bleaching and country washing? She was warm and safe and dry and wrapped in wool flannel. The other had simply not happened.

Then she opened her eyes on the opulent and unfamiliar room and reality jarred nastily into focus.

The room she saw was filled with delicate spindly French furniture picked out in enamels and gold. Past the foot of the bed she could see the ornate carving of a white alabaster fireplace inset with lapis plaques. The wall above it was graced with elaborate plasterwork of nymphs and cupids, and the mantelpiece itself was covered with a lady's elegant clutter—a lace shawl, a fan, a pair of gloves.

It was the most exquisite room Sarah Jane had ever seen. It was also most unmercifully intimidating, because she had no idea at all of how she had gotten here.

"Oh, good, you're awake—Cutty and I thought you might just sleep through until tomorrow. How do you feel?" The speaker was a vision in blue velvet, with a pink-and-white complexion that looked almost too vivid to be real. And, like the room, Sarah Jane could not remember ever having seen her before.

She tried to move and discovered that every muscle hurt.

"A good hot bath will fix that," said the dark-haired woman in answer to her wince. "The doctor will be so disappointed—he intended you for a bout of the influenza at the very least." The stranger sat down upon the bed. "My name is Aspasia—last night you told us yours was Sarah Jane Emwilton."

"Yes." Her throat seemed scraped raw, and the horror of the past two days rose up in her until she felt she'd choke on it. She sat up abruptly. "I—how did I come here, Lady Aspasia?"

Aspasia smiled a little bitterly. "Just 'Aspasia' will do, Miss Emwilton. As for how I found you, my carriage nearly ran over you on its way home from a party last night. How did you come to be in the road?"

"I . . . ," Sarah Jane began. To her consternation, tears filled her eyes and spilled over.

"Never mind," the woman called Aspasia said. "I daresay I can guess—and as for the whole, you can tell me after your bath."

A little more than an hour later Sarah Jane Emwilton was bathed, brushed, dressed—in a borrowed costume of rather dashing cut and hue—and ushered into the sitting room to breakfast with her mysterious patron.

She had belatedly discovered caution, and wondered if this might be some complex trap of Lord Drewmore's. But the maid who had accomplished her dressing seemed an army of rectitude in herself, and as no one appeared to pounce upon her, Sarah Jane allowed her suspicions to be laid completely to rest by the crisp clean linen and sparkling service of the breakfast parlor.

Her hostess was already at table when Sarah Jane came in, still in a state of what Sarah Jane's well-educated mind persisted in conceiving of as "voluptuous disarray." But the lady did look rather, well, gipsy-ish in her velvets and ribbons.

"Do sit down, Miss Emwilton, and have some breakfast. Then you may tell me as much as you care to, and we shall see what may be done."

Aspasia was not of the company that believed a faint stomach and light appetite won men's hearts. The breakfast set before Sarah Jane Emwilton was almost alarmingly hearty; nevertheless, two days' privation made certain that Sarah Jane did justice to it. And as the fried bread and the roast beef vanished, the tale of General Emwilton's death and Sarah Jane's search for employment appeared.

"—and of course Mrs. Courtenay was everything kind," Sarah Jane added, and faltered.

The name told Aspasia everything she needed to know. "But then Lord Drewmore took an interest in you," she finished.

Sarah Jane choked upon a last morsel of biscuit and went rather sickly pale.

"Don't look so startled," Aspasia said mockingly. "You're quite safe here—but as he's brought more girls to this way of life than any other, how shouldn't I know him? His sister-in-law is no angel either—she's the snare he uses to catch the pigeons he fancies." Aspasia's bitterness surprised even herself.

"But Mrs. Courtenay—What— What way of life?" Sarah Jane finally managed to stammer out.

"My dear Miss Emwilton, did you think I was a Quakeress come to preach you improving tracts? If so you must have an odd idea of the breed! No, your salvation was paid out of the wages of sin. You are among the muslin company, Miss Emwilton. And I am a whore."

She must tell Severn the truth of who she was. There was no help for it. He had asked why she had chosen to marry him; honor and decency demanded the honest truth. And if he laughed in her face—or made her the scandal of the *ton*—she could survive it. And if the news drove him straight back to his old rakehell habits, she would not take responsibility for them. Lord Malhythe had made this marriage, not Primula, and at five-and-thirty John Clerebold Acelet Rudwell, Lord Severn, had better be ready to take responsibility for his life.

It was a fine resolution. She wished Papa were here to lend her the courage to carry it out, but there was only Primula. Who would, in this as in all things, do her duty.

But not quite now.

The letters had been waiting for Primula when

she returned from Colworth House—yellow bills and vari-colored cards of invitation and one of stark and opulent cream much stained with the rigors of its journey. She had carried everything off to her primrose-yellow sitting room to read it—as if proof of her social success could be set against the failure of her marriage. Now Lady Severn turned to her mail.

Invitation, invitation, invitation—she set the best of those aside to consider later and discarded the impossible at once. The Viscountess Severn was far above Mrs. Hector Basingstoke's touch, and Primula Greetwell-as-was was too wise ever to attend one of Caroline, Countess of Coldmeece's soirees.

Bills—they could wait until the end of the quarter. She stuffed them into a pigeonhole of her golden marquetry desk without looking at them; she was quite rich enough that her tradesman's duns held no terrors. That left two letters. She recognized Lady Lockridge's illegible scrawl on the first and tore it open. Two books of vouchers fell out, each pasteboard ticket imprinted with the date of its Assembly.

She had her vouchers for Almack's—and precious little hope of inducing Severn to go there with her. By the time the Season was over its prize matrimonial catch would have made her a prize laughingstock—and partly through her own efforts!

Primula flung the vouchers down with a muffled ladylike oath. The remaining letter crackled unopened beneath her fist. Prepared to wish its sender at Jericho, Primula broke the wafer that sealed it.

The lines staggered back and forth across the page, and the penpoint, digging into the soft vellum, had sent sprays of ink across the paper. Primula read several paragraphs before she realized who the sender was, then started over from the beginning, peering frowningly at the crabbed script.

Adeline Lambton had arrived in Tilling, Primula read, to find her husband gravely ill. The terror Primula read in Addie's careful choice of words dismissed any suspicion of this being merely another case of the Lamb's vaunted-and-laughable hypochondria; the doctors Addie had summoned were gently preparing her for the worst.

Then Primula got to the last line, and crumpled the page in exasperation. *"I pray you,"* Mrs. Lambton wrote, *"do not distress Georgie with the news of his Papa's Grave Condition. He is a Sensitive Soul, and I cannot bear to—"* What Mrs. Lambton could not bear was indecipherable; a large blob of ink had smirched it, and failing time to recopy it, Mrs. Lambton had trusted to her friend's indulgence to read the letter as it was.

Primula sighed. So Georgie was not to know. Well, she could see the point of that; he would drive his mother half-mad hovering about his father's sickroom. But it was equally true that Addie was now in no case to bully Georgie into proper behavior.

Which meant Severn must. Which meant, Primula realized with a groan, that she herself could not make a clean breast of matters yet. Not while she could not trust Severn not to be petty and ruin Georgie for misdirected spite. Or perhaps she only wished any excuse to put off betraying herself.

Fortunately Primula did not have to decide where the burden of ignobility lay. When she tapped hesitantly on the doors to Severn's rooms they were opened by his peculiar manservant.

Loach regarded Lady Severn with a bright brown gaze.

"His Grace isn't here, seemingly," Loach said. Over his shoulder Primula could see a wide desk covered in paper: the disarray of a room in use.

Loach stepped back and held the door wide. "In

a rare taking was His Grace. First 'un wouldn't get up out of un's bed, and then needs must rush about like tiger with his tail caught. Worriting, is His Grace's state o' mind."

Primula followed this speech with extreme difficulty. She stepped into the room across the slippery surface of the tigerskin rug.

"Severn has gone out?" she hazarded. "Did he say when he would return?"

"Said I might meet 'un at devil—begging Your Grace's pardon—soon as ask after 'un. Worriting."

Primula collapsed onto a chair with a moan. "Worrying! I—" Barely in time she recollected herself. "Well. If he's out, he's out. I'll leave him a note—and please do tell him that I must see him just as soon as he returns."

She might just as easily have returned to her own study to pen the stiff and formal little message, but instead she crossed to Severn's desk to write it there. Since Loach was still present, Primula did *not* wail in despair and bury her face in her hands. With calm control she began searching Severn's desk for pen, paper, and inkwell.

She wanted to love her husband. She wanted her husband to love her. She wanted Severn to be someone worth loving, and feared that he wasn't, and thought that being so concerned about whether he was, in some sense, worthy of her made her a very unworthy person indeed. And she could not even hate the Earl of Malhythe for pitching her into this muddle because it was difficult to hate someone so completely incomprehensible.

"Is Your Grace after wanting help?" asked Loach.

"No, thank you, Mr. Loach. I shall contrive."

A drawer at last yielded the supplies she sought. She reached for a sheet of the thick fine paper embossed with Severn's crest and was distracted by the glitter of something farther back. She pulled the drawer all the way open.

It was a small chamois bag. The strings had come unknotted, and its contents spilled out; rough spheres of blue and green and red, the glowing round perfection of pearls.

Oblivious to Loach, Primula spilled the bag's contents onto the surface of the desk. Sun glinted off the starshine caught deep in one blood-red rocking surface; rough-cut diamonds starred the papers with their attendant prisms.

A fortune—shoved negligently into a desk and ignored by its owner. Primula glanced back at the drawer and saw that there were other bags there, each of which remained tightly tied.

"His Grace don't lack for money, Your Grace; don't fret 'ee on that head."

Aghast at her own curiosity, Primula scooped the plundered trove back into its bag and tied it tight. "That's as may be—but he most certainly will lack these if he leaves them lying about! They should be in a strongbox, at the least—and I daresay there may be more." At a loss for what to do, she dropped the bag back into the drawer and heard it chink as it landed.

"Aye, prodigal is His Grace, but look'ee, he says to me, there's no cause to be puffing off our blunt in hiring Runners and bank vaults. T'would be impertinent, says 'ee."

"I— But—" Primula took a deep breath. "Thank you for telling me, Mr. Loach, but I believe His Grace—I mean Lord Severn!—to be misguided. I shall speak to him about it." She dipped a quill into the inkwell and began to write.

The more she knew—or thought she knew—the more confused she became—until it was a wonder, Primula thought crossly, not only that anyone ever knew anything, but that anyone wanted to know anything.

A thousand years ago—so it seemed—Malhythe had sat in her parents' drawing room and told her that if Severn did not choose to please him by marrying the girl of his choice Severn would be left penniless. And this vow, Primula had thought until today, carried enough weight with Lord Severn that he had married exactly as his father chose.

Did Malhythe, she wondered, know how rich Severn was? Even to her inexpert scrutiny the gems in her husband's desk represented great wealth—far more than that of the Earldom of Malhythe, and certainly far more than the portion of it that comprised Severn's revenues.

Either Severn had bent to the Earl of Malhythe's will over an amount of money that he must consider trifling, or his acquiescence had been paid for in another coin entirely.

For the first time Primula wondered: What did *Severn* seek from his return to England?

"I can't do it! I *can't*!" Sarah Jane Emwilton wailed, flinging herself away from Aspasia's outstretched hand. She came to a stop at the sitting room window and stared blindly out over the rooftops of St. John's Wood.

"Miss Emwilton—Sarah Jane—I beg you; be reasonable."

"No!"

"Then tell me—what else can you do?"

The strained, tear-sodden face turned to her would have softened the hardest heart, but if sympathy were any cure for the evils of the world, there would be far fewer of them. "What else can you do?" Aspasia repeated.

In the last hour she had put Sarah Jane in possession of such particulars of her life as she felt it necessary for her to know and obtained enough of Sarah Jane's history to convince her that her case was, if not hopeless, then the next best thing.

No father, no brothers, no aunt or married sister who might take her up. Her mother living in furnished rooms—and looking to Sarah Jane for help with her support, as likely as not.

"Lord Drewmore will put the story about, if only for spite's sake—and he will not omit to name names. You must consider that your reputation will be—not such as to commend you to prospective employers."

"Save of one sort." Sarah Jane's voice was bitter.

"Save of one sort," Aspasia agreed.

Sarah Jane retreated from the window and stood facing Aspasia across the breakfast table, her hands fretting with the scrollwork of the back of her chair.

"I— You have been all that is kind, Aspasia. I am sorry that I cannot be more conciliating. But you must see that—" Her brave politeness dissolved; the corners of Sarah Jane's mouth crumpled and the tears came.

Aspasia rounded the table and folded her in a roses-and-chinchilla embrace. "Here, now, hush. Don't fret, Jenny; no one is asking you to hawk your virtue on the street. I'm sure your mother will never listen to gossip from Drewmore's direction, and she need never know the rest, if you're discreet. Mrs. Leacock—"

"If that is my only possible fate you should have left me in the road, Aspasia—it would have been kinder," Sarah Jane said with forlorn dignity.

Aspasia gazed into the miserable blue eyes and saw the determination there. With sinking heart she recognized that the life of the half-world was not for Sarah Jane; Miss Emwilton's was a heart that would break rather than bend.

"I . . . do not know what else can be done. Your

reputation hangs on Drewmore's word, and without it you can neither marry nor earn your bread in any respectable fashion. But I will do what I can," Aspasia promised reluctantly.

The radiant look of hope on Sarah Jane Emwilton's face would certainly have been more than enough payment if Aspasia had thought she had any chance of success whatever. With unwonted vehemence she rang for Mrs. Clutterbuck and told her to bring the carriage around, then went off to dress.

Mr. George Lambton, innocent of all the heartburnings and hand-wringings his conduct occasioned, sallied forth with the serenity of a young man in love.

His *amoreuse* had given him her direction the night before, and if he could not achieve an interview with her this morning, he could at least leave his tokens of an affection he hoped would ripen.

Of course she wasn't a respectable woman, but respectable women meant respectability, and that was something that Georgie did not feel at all ready to cope with. Someday his would be the sole responsibility for the happiness and future of one of the gently bred maidens of the *ton*, but at the moment such a course looked like a great deal of work for very little reward, and Georgie was in no hurry to undertake it. The society of the delightful lady he had met at Bad Barham's party last night, on the other hand, augered an ease and good fellowship that Georgie did not associate with women of his own class, and he intended to pursue it. She seemed very expensive—perhaps even famous—and though his gaming debts were heavy, his other expenses were slight, and he had no doubt of being able to go the distance. If she were indeed casting her net for a new protector, Mr. George Lambton was more than willing to oblige.

These glorious reflections occupied him quite pleasantly for the time the carriage took to traverse the stretch of road that lay between Piccadilly and St. John's Wood.

Aspasia had been very clear in her instructions to her housekeeper: no one was to be allowed into the house in her absence. If there were any hope of the miracle that would restore Sarah Jane Emwilton's reputation at all, it could not be accomplished once it was known that she had spent even five minutes beneath the roof of a notorious Cyprian. Thus, in her absence, Aspasia's door was closed to the friends and cicisbeos who normally gathered there.

It was, naturally, not closed to Dr. Emory Southland, coming to enquire after the health of his patient. And, equally naturally though unfortunately, it was not closed to the young gentleman caller that Dr. Southland met upon the steps and happily brought in with him.

Sarah Jane was just sealing up a carefully worded letter to her mother when Mrs. Clutterbuck opened the door to the salon.

"It's Doctor Southland to see you, Miss," the housekeeper said. Sarah Jane rose and turned to confront, not Dr. Southland, but a very Pink of the *Ton* in biscuit-colored superfine trousers, a dazzling waistcoat of peach silk, and pointed moroccan slippers he could certainly have not managed to walk half a mile in. Sarah Jane was attempting to believe that he was Dr. Southland when he turned to address a remark to a companion behind him. That companion was almost certainly a doctor, from the large leather bag he carried to his grey trousers and hammertail coat.

"Heavens, Cutty, is this my little patient, now? She looks quite recovered to me."

"And so she would be, but Miss Aspasia said she was to have complete quiet," said Mrs. Clutterbuck, with a meaningful glare at Mr. Lambton.

"Oh, nothing of the sort," said Dr. Southland obliviously. "Sound as a drum, I should say. Come over here, lovey, and let me earn my not inconsiderable fee. And then, I'm sure, you'll drink a glass of canary with us?"

Sarah Jane was almost certain he meant to be kind, but nothing in her brief existence had prepared her for the freedom of a life of ruin. To be addressed with such cozening familiarity, to be offered spirits, to be abandoned to the company of these strangers without even a shawl to cover the indelicate dress that her benefactress had loaned her— Sarah Jane backed up against the writing-desk, her mouth working soundlessly.

"Here, now—Mr. Lambton, brandy!" Dr. Southland rapped out to his new acquaintance. Georgie thrust his parcels into the hands of the astonished Mrs. Clutterbuck and flung himself out of the room.

Dr. Southland crossed to Sarah Jane. "Nerves sadly shattered, if I don't mistake." He uncorked a vial under her nose and she choked on pungent spirits of ammonia. Caught off balance, she allowed him to lead her to a chair. "Soo, lass, there's nowt to fear," he said, lapsing into the broad Yorkshire of his childhood.

Sarah Jane cast a look of agonized appeal at Aspasia's housekeeper, but while Mrs. Clutterbuck looked sympathetic in the extreme, she obviously did not think that Miss Emwilton was in the least need of rescue.

"Here we are!" said Georgie, plunging through the door with a looted decanter.

"I'll thank you for that, young sir!" said Cutty

briskly. "As I told you on the step, Miss Aspasia's from home, and—"

"But surely she'll be back in a moment or two?" Dr. Southland said pacifically. He poured a generous splash of brandy into a tumbler and put it to Sarah Jane's lips. "Drink up, now."

Miss Emwilton had little choice but to comply. A glow seemed to radiate from her stomach to the tips of her fingers and toes, and she looked at Dr. Southland in wonderment. He smiled reassuringly and pulled up a chair to sit beside her and take her pulse.

"Nothing at all wrong here," he said a moment later, patting her hand. Mrs. Clutterbuck appeared with a tray bearing a decanter and three glasses, and he stood and poured all three full.

"A toast, then, to your recovery, young lady," he said, handing glasses around. "And Cutty, you must tell your excellent mistress that I'm desolate to have missed her, but I just stopped for a look-in on my way to an accouchement, and I really must go." Dr. Southland poured himself a second glass, and drank that, and then picked up his bag and hurried off down the stairs.

"Hello," said Georgie to the flabbergasted Sarah Jane Emwilton.

"Shall we have him out, Miss?" said the formidable Mrs. Clutterbuck.

"Oh, I say! It hardly seems fair," protested Georgie, "when she said I might call upon her, to be denied the company of not one, but two goddesses," he finished plaintively.

"I don't believe we have been introduced," said Sarah Jane faintly.

"I am George Lambton, your devoted slave. And you . . . ?"

"I . . . ?" began Sarah Jane.

* * *

It was with heavy heart that Aspasia ascended her own doorstep.

Mrs. Leacock could offer no hope; if Sarah Jane Emwilton balked at joining the muslin company, one could hardly expect her to be happy as an actress, and those members of the canting lay who trafficked in the illusion of respectability while in search of lucre could discover among themselves no need for Sarah Jane's talents. The only good that came from that interview was the knowledge that Lord Drewmore had not yet made his latest scrape public.

But he would. And then Sarah Jane, disgraced, could return beneath her mother's roof—if that good lady did not cast her off to preserve her own reputation—or embrace in truth the life that Drewmore had chosen for her. She experimented with a cheerful smile for Sarah Jane's benefit as her housekeeper opened the door.

"I tried to stop him, Miss, but he said as he'd wait!" Mrs. Clutterbuck said.

"Who?"

"Mr. George Lambton—" the housekeeper began, before realizing that she was speaking to the empty air.

Aspasia heard conversation in her drawing room before she opened the door. Her feelings were only slightly mollified to see that by Sarah Jane's stricken face she was entirely sensible of the mess she was in.

"Why, Mr. Lambton!" Aspasia cried gaily. "How wonderful of you to come."

George Lambton turned away from his current partner with slight but unmistakable reluctance and Aspasia repressed the urge to laugh out loud. So Boy Lambton was smitten with young Sarah

Jane Emwilton, was he? Well, that would solve all their problems right there. . . .

If Sarah Jane would be willing to live beneath Mr. Lambton's protection.

Which she wouldn't.

Mr. Lambton rose and bowed over Aspasia's hand. "I have just been conversing with your delightful—"

"Sister," Aspasia supplied.

"To be sure. And perhaps you will be able to persuade her of the propriety of attending a little supper party I am giving on the twenty-fifth. Can I not tempt you both? The company shall be just as you like, and Lord Malhythe keeps a notable chef."

Aspasia was quite tempted—after all, it would be very quiet—until Mr. Lambton uttered the fateful name.

"Lord Malhythe! Never say he is giving this party!" Aspasia exclaimed.

"Well . . . no. But I've got Colworth House all to myself while he's away, and—"

Aspasia had not survived as long as she had in her present life without the ability to think furiously while uttering gracious inanities. A quarter of an hour later Mr. Lambton left, entirely in alt while having been promised nothing. Aspasia stood at the parlor door until she heard the downstairs door thud shut and the clatter of carriage wheels on the cobbles. Then she collapsed into a chair.

"Well, there's the cat among the pigeons and no mistake! And Malhythe's grandson, to boot. Damn!"

"Aspasia!" gasped Sarah Jane, more shocked by this rough language than by most of the morning's events.

Aspasia smiled at her. "Well, there's nothing to be done about it now, is there? I shall have to speak to Cutty; I told her she was not to admit anyone."

"He came in with Dr. Southland. The doctor says

I am quite recovered, though my nerves are sadly shattered," Sarah Jane offered hopefully.

"And so they should be, and I'm afraid I've brought no news that will help. He would be Lord Malhythe's grandson," Aspasia added despairingly.

"Do you not care for the family?" asked Sarah Jane doubtfully. "I must tell you, then, that my godmother's daughter recently married Lord Malhythe's son—I had hoped, perhaps, if you knew her direction. . . ."

"I couldn't set one foot over her doorstep," Aspasia said flatly.

"But *I* could! If Lord Drewmore hasn't—I know Primula will be able to help; if I can just *explain*—"

Aspasia bit her lip. She could not bear to crush Sarah Jane's stubborn hope, or remind her that now that George Lambton had seen her here, the possibility of redemption was even farther away than before.

"Let me write, first," temporized Aspasia. "Or better yet—you will write her and tell her you are stopping in town with friends. Then if she will agree to see you—"

"But why shouldn't she agree. . . . Oh, I see," Sarah Jane said flatly.

Aspasia went over to her and patted her hand. "It will be much better for her to refuse to see you than to be thrown into the street in broad daylight when you come to call."

"Primula's not like that! You'll see," said Sarah Jane stoutly. She held her chin very high as she sat down to the desk to write her letter.

Chapter 16

APRIL 18, 1817

SEVERN HAD FLUNG himself out of the house to make the round of his several clubs, as if to reassure himself that he still found London as dreadful as heretofore.

Primula had married him for his title. She'd said so. And it was appalling how much that hurt.

Once he had considered himself a marketable commodity, and laughed at the shifts hopeful mamas employed to secure him as he dangled himself before them on the marriage mart. It was not that he was—or had been—a desirable *parti* that galled him.

It was that Primula should have no other use for him than that.

Well, what did he want? wondered Severn sourly. Did he want her to love him for himself alone? She'd be a fool if she did.

And his lady wife was no fool. Severn chewed his lower lip mediatatively. A woman who retained her reputation in the face of all he had done to her was no fool. She need not have waited ten years to marry—nor need she have married him; there must have been others willing to stand the office.

So why *had* she married him?

Did he want to know?

With the ease of returning familiarity Severn made his way down St. James and then turned onto Piccadilly. The shop-window splendors of a post-Waterloo London failed to hold him; he was casting his mind about for a refuge that might suit him when he was hailed from the window of a carriage that bore the Rudwell crest.

"Ho! Lord Severn! May I take you up?" George Lambton asked.

Georgie was as self-pleased as any other young man; moments after Severn had seated himself beside him on the leather bench-seat of the Earl's town carriage, Mr. Lambton had put him in receipt of the news of his morning's visit, the raven-haired charmer who had so tantalized him, the hardly-less-delectible Fair Unknown who had such an intriguing air of reserve about her, and his hopes of both or either of them on a future occasion.

Severn, while wrestling with the novel impulse to keep someone out of trouble, was a model listener. His attention was only fully summoned when the carriage rocked to a stop in front of the Albany Hotel.

"Do come up if you like; I'll only be a moment, but he's said I might bring my friends if I choose," Georgie said.

Severn was curious about what god had superseded him in Mr. Lambton's private pantheon. With an ironic flourish, he followed his nephew up the Albany's narrow stairs.

Severn's first thought was that the rooms were blessedly warm; his second was that the ancient in the Bath chair at the room's center had eyes as yellow as the tiger's.

"Lord Warltawk, this is my uncle, Viscount Severn," said Georgie importantly. He disposed himself upon an ottoman with the ease of long familiarity.

"Ah, Malhythe's cub. At last. My dear Lord Severn, it gives me very great pleasure to meet you." Warltawk extended his hand.

Warltawk wore a great many rings, and his hand glittered like a dragon's scales. Lord Severn came forward, not certain whether the very old man expected him to shake the hand or kiss the rings. Then he took a closer look at the hand's glittering freight and froze.

There were not two rings like it in the world. Its stone was a long oval of tiger-yellow Chinese topaz. Its reverse had been carved with the five flying black swans of the Rudwell crest; their lacquerwork inlay made the birds appear to be caught in the stone, flying endlessly through a golden world. The setting was of the reddish Eastern gold set with the rarest of stones, the red-black oriental ruby. Severn had given the orders for its creation himself, and it had been one of the gifts he distributed to his family upon his return to England.

It was on Warltawk's hand now.

"Ah, sir, so you admire my ring. Delightful, is it not, to be the recipient of these little gestures of affection?"

Severn had given it to Georgie's mother.

"One must think so, sir," said Severn, bowing.

When Severn was young and wicked, Warltawk's fame had been the touchstone on which one proved one's own depravity. But Warltawk had been a god of the Elder Days, like Sixteen-String Jack or Francis Dashwood, whose like would not come again. Severn had been certain Warltawk was dead and buried long since—and from the look of the man now, he was at least half right.

Warltawk Kingbreaker. What was such a man

doing as Georgie's companion? It was obvious that George Lambton and the ancient Lord Warltawk were on the closest of terms. The perspiration rolled down Georgie's face and darkened the goldenrod hair in the oven-heat of the room, but he cheerfully prattled on, reminding Warltawk of past conversations they had had.

Severn would rather have conversed with a cobra.

It was not that fault could be found in anything Warltawk said . . . quite. It was more in his way of looking at things, until generosity became stupidity and cruelty became wit. The scorn he heaped upon the doings of Bad Jack Barham was such that anyone hearing it would long to outstrip Barham's depravities, and his method of dismissing the topic of the new-met Cyprians would induce anyone to bring him new and spicier *on-dits* from that quarter.

Severn said little, though he was conscious of Lord Warltawk's eyes constantly on him. At last the visit was over and he and Mr. Lambton rose to go.

"And what do you do upon the *ton*, Lord Severn?" Warltawk asked. "It seems we have heard very little of you since your return."

"If that is so, Lord Warltawk, it is because I have done very little. I prefer a quiet life."

The reptilian old man smiled. "As you did in your youth. It would be foolish to force your nature into paths it was not meant for. Blood will tell, Lord Severn, I assure you."

Severn bowed.

The curbside daylight was sweet and clean by comparison with the rooms above; Severn took a deep breath.

"You damned young puppy—how long have you been staking your mother's jewels at the tables?"

George Lambton's face bore the affronted shock of pure innocence, and his pleased smile vanished. "I'm afraid I haven't the slightest idea what you're talking about, Uncle," he said stiffly.

"You won't convince me Addie gave Lord Warltawk that ring—I had it made myself in China and gave it to her when I came back."

Georgie's brow cleared, though he still looked hurt. "Oh, I see. I'm sorry you saw it, then. Mama didn't fancy it above half—said it looked positively popish—so she gave it to me. Of course one couldn't wear it, precisely," George added, and seemed to feel that this disposed adequately of the matter of the ring.

"Yet Warltawk was wearing it," Severn said rather sharply. "How is it you come to know a man like that, Georgie—let alone game with him for such deep stakes?"

"I wish you'd get cards out of your head," Georgie said pettishly. "I'd never bet with him—he'd skin me sure as daylight, and then tell me how it was done. Warltawk knows all the sharps that catch the flats." A footman jumped down from his perch to hold the door of the carriage, and Georgie stepped up, his back stiff with insult. Severn followed after.

"So it was a gift, then?" Try as he might, Severn could not keep the nagging note of worry from his voice.

"You're as bad as Mama!" Georgie snapped. The carriage rocked as the door slammed to and the footman mounted the steps at the back. "I suppose a man mayn't give a friend of his a gift or two if he likes? I'm more than seven, you know, and my money's mine to dispose of."

Which was unfortunately true, Severn thought as the carriage wheeled off. The generous allowance that was George Lambton's through his mother's marriage-portion had become his absolutely upon his twenty-first birthday. He might now ruin himself in quarterly installments just as he pleased. And that included taking up such perverse and unsavory company as Christian, Baron Warltawk.

"Georgie—" Severn began again. The face Mr. George Lambton turned to him was stubborn in its youth, and bore a stamp of wildness that Severn recognized with kindred knowledge. Press Georgie on this matter now and he'd lose any authority he had with Georgie forever.

Had Malhythe ever thought such thoughts, looking at him?

"Certainly your money's yours to dispose of," Severn said easily. "And that young lovely you met this morning undoubtedly has a dozen or so ways to help. Perhaps I might join you on your next venture there—you said there are two of them, after all."

Georgie laughed, his mood lightening, and promised that Severn might accompany him on his next journey to St. John's Wood. The rest of the journey to Severn's own door was passed in idle gossip, and not once did Severn say anything even remotely uncomplimentary about Lord Warltawk.

Instead he resolved to write Adeline Lambton the moment he reached home, and then to use his little influence to ensure that Georgie went home when summoned. This was no time for Georgie's father to be sham-sick in bed—from all Severn knew, the company Georgie was keeping now was far more dangerous than that of the most rapacious lightskirt.

Chapter 17

APRIL 18, 1817

AFTER A NUMBER of tries, some covering several sheets of paper, extending long past the time the candles were lit and the curtains drawn against the dusk, Severn concluded that the writing of this letter was not in him.

He had beguiled native princes with ease, and cajoled his superiors in India with hardly a pause for reflection, but the simple explanation of why George Lambton must return home at once was beyond him.

Lord Warltawk was bad company—but would Addie believe it, when her rakehell brother said so? Any enumeration of Georgie's sins would be written off to a spiteful desire to make trouble, Severn had realized despairingly, and indeed it was just the sort of prank that his younger self had delighted to indulge in.

In fine, to convince Adeline of anything, he must first convince her that he was a changed individual, and he did not think he could. His wife, on the other hand. . . .

With sudden energy, Severn rang for Loach and demanded his evening dress. Primula, he belatedly remembered, had asked to see him—and so she would.

* * *

Primula met her husband outside her dressing-room door.

"Severn!" she said.

"You? Here?" he answered mockingly. "But it's my house, you know—or is it yours?—and I've a fancy to dine with my wife. That is, if you have nothing more important to command you?"

"No—nothing," she said, and Severn offered his arm.

She had told Badgley that she would be dining alone this evening, but Severn must have given orders otherwise, as covers were laid for two on the linen-swathed mahogany expanse of the dining table. Severn seated Primula at his right hand.

"Now, Lady Severn, we will converse as married people do," he said firmly, as the footman placed wide plates of clear turtle soup before them.

"Yes, my lord," Primula said demurely. The branches of lit candles gave off a heavy scent, and she concentrated on their steady flames as she waited for the servants to go.

"I should like to apologize for my conduct this morning," she said when they were alone. Severn's green eyes glinted in the candlelight and he inclined his head.

"The fault was mine," he said. "I . . . expected too much of you. One should use people according to their capacity."

"Should one?" Primula was nettled. "How pleasant to be omniscient and know exactly what everyone is good for before you meet them." She bit her lip and applied herself to her soup.

"In my experience, it is what they are bad for that one generally discovers, and that really doesn't take too long." He frowned. "Lady Severn, there is no need for us to be enemies."

Primula cast him a sidewise glance beneath her

lashes. "There is no reason—yet—for us to be friends, Lord Severn." And every reason to be enemies, once he knew who she was.

"I am corrected," Severn said gravely. The footman came to clear the soup away and produce the savory.

So matters went throughout the meal. Primula could never quite bring herself to apologize, and still less to break her promise to the Earl of Malhythe and tell Severn who she was and on what terms she had married him.

"But perhaps there is a matter that I can assist you with, Lady Severn," her husband announced as the footman withdrew for the last time, leaving behind the cut-crystal decanter gleaming on an expanse of snowy-white linen. "Your note did say that you wished to speak to me."

For a moment Primula hesitated. Then she summoned her resolve and pushed forward, no matter how unpleasant the task. "I do not expect you to share my feelings in this matter, my lord, but I will tell you plainly that Addie will not approve of the company Georgie is keeping. When she left she meant for him to live here, but you—"

"But my wicked self confounded all her plans. So Addie will not approve. By all means tell her so. Write and make everything clear to her, and have her summon home her erring skylark—you may make me the goat, if you like," Severn added lightly.

"If it would do the least good, I would," Primula retorted. "I meant to write to Adeline myself, but I had a letter from her this morning, and Lamb is seriously ill. She does not wish Georgie to know, for fear he will come home and make his Papa's condition worse. I can't possibly write and tell her what Georgie is doing! So it is plain, Lord Severn, that you must tell Georgie not to—"

"Not to what?" asked Severn. "Not to follow in his uncle's footsteps? And do you suppose he will pay any heed to that at all? You amaze me, my lady wife—I thought you were smarter than that."

"Oh, no," said Primula bitterly. "I'm not clever at all. I thought you wanted to come home to England to be one of us again—but all you want to do is pout and posture and pretend. You are *selfish*, Lord Severn, and I thought—"

"What did you think?" Severn demanded. Primula started to rise from the table, but his hand settled about her wrist with a merciless gentleness. "What did you think when my father came to you and offered you my name and person? Did you—"

"I thought he was a monster! I think you are a monster too!"

"And your husband, my blushing bride. Shall we ascend the marital stair together, Lady Severn, and see if like calls to like?" He got to his feet, his mouth pulled into harsh lines by the desperate need to resolve—somehow—his torment.

"How dare you?" Primula whispered, her dark eyes fixed upon his face. Slowly Severn let go of her wrist.

"You have not changed," she said, like a judge passing sentence. "You are no more than you ever were. Perhaps I am no better, but at least I am not in love with my own selfishness." Passion brought a crimson flush to Primula's cheeks, and tears of pure fury glittered in her dark eyes. Severn took a step toward her.

"*No!* I don't ever want to have anything to do with you again!" At a pace barely less than a run Primula made for the double doors of the dining room. She flung one open and rushed through it, and its lazy impact with the wall woke a soft ocean of rolling echoes.

Severn stood watching the doorway for a long

time, a familiar dull pain coiling about his heart. *"You have not changed,"* she'd said, and how could he if no one would believe it of him?

It was as impossible as the task of bringing Georgie to hand.

"But you will have to see me again, my lady wife. You wanted me to go to your opera-party, and so you shall have me—the leopard, in all his spots!"

Chapter 18

APRIL 22, 1817

FOR THE NEXT four days Lord and Lady Severn presented a facade of unruffled serenity to the outside world.

Lady Severn continued to pay her morning calls. Lord Severn continued to sleep until noon.

Lady Severn attended her *affaires*. Lord Severn attended his clubs.

Lady Severn occupied herself with her party: dinner at Kitmatgar House before the Opera, and a cold supper to be served in the theater itself. Lord Severn flung himself deeper into the pointless frivolity of a young man of means: park-sauntering, coffee houses, and late nights over cards. The calls he paid were of a sort unmentionable in polite circles, upon ladies who were anything but.

And through it all his mind turned upon two problems: his wife and his nephew.

Georgie was somewhat easier, and Severn had been trained to plan in an unscrupulous and unforgiving school. In the days that followed their first meeting he heard more of Lord Warltawk, and none of it nice. His circle was vast, and surprisingly young, and George Lambton fit into it like a lamb among wolves. So the lamb must be removed from the killing-ground, and since Severn had neither the authority nor the force to do so, something must be found to supplant Warltawk in Georgie's interests.

Unfortunately Severn could not imagine what it was. By the evening of Primula's fete, Severn had feelings of charity for the absent Earl of Malhythe that would quite have surprised the old devil.

She looked every inch the ice-matron, Primula thought, gazing critically into her mirror. She wore a dress of oyster-white satin with an overdress of blue net; a liberal selection of the Rudwell sapphires and diamonds ornamented her, from the glittering buckles on her slippers to the drops that flashed in her ears. Her evening shawl was the same blue net as her overdress, embroidered with enough silver and lace to seem more substantial than it was. Her fan and her gloves waited nearby for her to add them to her costume. She looked the consummate Viscountess.

And that would have to suffice, because now, truly, thoroughly, she knew it was all she would ever have. Severn might carry his paradoxes to the grave; she knew the one thing she needed to: he did not intend to make a marriage of their match. She was as alone as she had been before, and the responsibility for those entrusted to her care was hers alone.

And there was nothing she could think of to do about her nephew. In desperation she had even thought of writing to the Earl of Malhythe, but his man of business had taken great pleasure in informing her that Malhythe's whereabouts were not to be communicated to the likes of her; she might write if she liked, but all letters would be held at Colworth House against Lord Malhythe's return, which was to be at some indefinite future date.

She dared not write to invoke Georgie's other uncles, since that would almost certainly betray the secret that Addie had entrusted to her. And Severn had already failed her.

Severn! Try as she might, her thoughts always returned to him.

If only Sir Rowland and Lady Greetwell were not so very far away! She was certain that Papa could bring Georgie to heel, that Mama would have some blistering common sense to soothe her sore heart. They were safe, now, from anything the Polite World might do, now that Lord Severn had been forced to make the repairs to her reputation that honor demanded. They were safe.

They were also in Scotland with Laird Rannoch. And they might as well be on the moon for all the good they could do her from there.

She was absolutely alone. And for the first time in her life she had absolutely no idea of what to do.

There was a knock at the door. She waited, but no servant entered, and at last she went and opened it.

Lord Severn stood there, his hand raised to knock again. He was garbed most correctly, from his starched collar points to the gleaming black toes of his elegant slippers. He wore the blue coat and buff trousers of those who followed Brummell's style, but the opulence of his vest and the sheer price of his rings and fobs and seals made the asceticism of the Beau seem a rather shabby thing.

She had not seen him since their disastrous dinner together, and now, when he smiled his crooked, self-mocking smile, she wanted to fling herself into his arms.

"Lord Severn. I did not expect you," Primula said coolly.

"Ah, Lady Ice. You look ravishing—if one might be ravished by an iceberg—so I will overlook the fact that you swore last week that I must attend this event for my own soul's health and your position in Society. I promised to do so, and I rarely forget a promise. Shall we go down, my dear? Our guests are waiting."

One can do a great deal of thinking in four days. The last year of Sarah Jane Emwilton's life had been a gradual unfolding of the knowledge, through a series of worsening shocks, that the world was neither a kind nor a forgiving place. So it was without real hope that she had written her letter to Primula. She was certain of Primula's sympathy, but the simple facts were damning.

She had traveled unescorted, up to town. She had gone to an assignation with Lord Drewmore. She had spent a night on the streets. And she had spent the last four days beneath the roof of a notorious courtesan.

Intellectually she knew she had been dealt a death blow. She had no more place in Society, and her leprous touch could only infect all she held dear. She might even preserve her chastity, and earn her bread in grinding labor, but aspire to the company of decent people she might not.

One can learn a great deal in four days. She now had a far clearer idea of Aspasia's life than she had before. Aspasia's protector (whom she had refused to name) was away now, but soon he would be back and not even the most charitable Cyprian could continue to give her houseroom then.

And after that came the streets, or a rented room that would make the drabness of Mama's Bath apartment look palatial by comparison.

Her whole soul rebelled from that, as it had from every shift and accommodation forced by straitened circumstances in the months since Papa had died. And because she was both a pragmatist who saw things quite clearly and still young enough to believe in miracles, she went to her hostess and made her request.

"Aspasia, may I go with you tonight?" Aspasia looked up from her dressing table mirror and set down the swansdown puff with which she had been applying pearl powder to her neck and shoulders.

"You know that I am going to the theater, Miss Emwilton," Aspasia said carefully.

"Yes, I know. Papa took Mama and me to the theater once—before. I liked it very much. I should like to go again, if it isn't too much trouble. If you would loan me a dress."

Aspasia's mouth made a little *moue* of sympathy. "I'm afraid most of my evening gowns aren't very respectable," she said gently.

"That's all right," Sarah Jane said stubbornly.

On this late-April evening Lord Severn was everything a gracious host should be. He kept the idle table talk flowing, he saw to the comfort of Primula's carefully chosen guests, he provided anecdotes of his Indian adventures that were fabulous but not scandalous, and the gathering at Kitmatgar House that evening would be quite forgiven for forgetting his past entirely.

Primula was certain he was only doing it to spite her.

Her feelings for her husband had gone far past the point that they might be considered appropriate or polite. Her servants had been quite willing to tell her that the husband she saw not-at-all had been much in the company of his nephew—and undoubtedly encouraging him to new excesses of rakehellishness. And then, for him to come here, and preside over the head of her table like a pattern-card of virtue—

Primula felt an urgent desire to march to the

head of the table, put her two hands firmly about that exquisitely cravatted neck, and throttle Lord Severn.

The Drury Lane Theatre had been opened in 1663, burnt to the cellars for the third time in 1809, and in 1812 been rebuilt more glorious than before. While its last incarnation had seen Kemble and Mrs. Siddons, the present structure had seen Edmund Kean act Shylock, a performance about which talk was still flourishing. Drury Lane was now, beyond doubt, the most dazzling showcase for the arts to be found in modern London, and London itself was a city that, so the wits said, reinvented itself hourly.

It lacked a week and more of May, when all the World would come to town, but the theater was still well attended. The Severns' party had arrived fashionably late: the curtain had risen on the main program an hour before, and a rather well-fed Hamlet was struggling to make his singing heard over the audience—from the penny-a-place groundlings around the orchestra pit to the Fashionable Pure—and Impure—who subscribed to their elegant boxes by the season.

Aspasia's elegant footman held out the silver beaker and replenished his mistress's cup of punch. Beside her Sarah Jane Emwilton sat, upright in low-cut sea-green lace, holding her own untasted silver cup. Her cheeks were expertly rouged, jade drops dangled from her ears, and her expression was both determined and lost.

Better for her to be altogether ruined at once, Aspasia thought, trying to harden her heart to Sarah Jane's misery. The letter Sarah Jane had written to Lady Severn had gone unanswered; and though Lord Drewmore had been mysteriously silent, the die was cast. Sarah Jane's future lay in the demimonde now.

Idly Aspasia fanned herself with her broad ostrich-plume fan, then raised it to peer through the spyglass concealed at its center. In the boxes surrounding her own she could see the deadlights and will-o'-the-wisps of the London society, scattered among the more respectable luminaries. Birth was no bar at the theater; the only requirement was to have money, or know someone who did.

Drewmore wasn't here tonight, thank God. Aspasia had heard rumors that he'd fled to the country, or even the Continent, but hardly dared to trust such good fortune. Lightfoot Bobby she saw, in a borrowed box with his hymn-singing sister and trying to catch the eye of Bad Jack Barham, whose box was crammed with rowdies and dashers pelting the pit with orange peels in a spirit of historical recreation.

Among the Old Respectables, as she privately termed them, were Lady Hawkchurch, in half-mourning, and the young Lord Hawkchurch. Some of Aspasia's friends had wept for his elder brothers, gone to grass on French battlefields, and it was a sure bet that the formidable old battle-ax would never see a round half-dozen of her grandchildren.

And then there was the Severn party.

They had been there when Sarah Jane and Aspasia arrived, impossible to miss. Sarah Jane had hurriedly put up her fan, but George Lambton had seen them. Still, Mr. Lambton's manners were very good, and so he had looked stricken rather than pleased. For fear she would wave to him, Aspasia supposed, and flaunt the connection.

But while some might boast of tangling grandfather and grandson in the same net, Aspasia had no desire to even pretend to do so. Not while it seemed that the time she would have with Malhythe would be so mercilessly brief. When he returned and saw what Severn had become he would marry again. And she would leave him.

Well, and that was the way of the world, and there was not a single blessed thing that she could do about it. Aspasia forced a bright smile, conscious that she was as watched as she was watching. The things that she could do something about seemed rather few. She could not, for example, take away her young companion's shame and fear and cause her to enter into a liaison with George Lambton upon the instant.

Oh, but ah, if she could. . . .

Lord Severn had not drunk deep at dinner, but that he had drunk at all could be accounted a species of self-flagellation. The expression upon the face of his lovely wife had been impossible to mistake: Primula had finally decided what to think of him.

And the irony of it all was that at the moment she had come to despise him, Severn had finally decided he was not despicable.

It was true that the sins of his young manhood could still make him cringe with shame. It was equally true, however, that he was proud of much that he had done in India. Of his third life there was little yet to say; he had done little either for good or ill since he had returned to England—except, of course, to mire himself inexorably in the cunning trap his father had set for him, his marriage to this galling jade.

She looked as if she were made of snow—but that unfortunate simile made him think of how ardently he had desired snow when the baking winds of an Indian summer made her plains all but uninhabitable for the white men sent there to govern. He would lie upon his cot with the *punkah* fan sluggishly pushing the blood-hot air against his naked body and think of snow, cool and smooth, its rounded curves and shining white surface pressed against his body and molded to his seeking hands. . . .

Severn brought himself up short with a mental shake, still gazing at the wintercream slope of his wife's bare shoulders. He was willing even to credit the Earl of Malhythe with the sorcery that knew he would love his bartered bride as surely as she would hate him. And he knew the only cure for this fever was swift surgery. As soon as possible—tomorrow, no, tonight—he would tell her who he was, and let her hate him for something that was founded in truth.

The opera wandered to its second-act curtain, and the ballet came out before the screen. The house stirred, and many rose to their feet, preparing to mingle with their fellows.

At the Severn party, liveried footmen unpacked hampers of dainties. Lady Severn fluttered her fan in the midst of gallant gentlemen plying her with outrageous flattery. Even Sir Gerald Lockridge assayed a pleasantry, and his wife laughed in delight.

Primula laughed too; Sir Gerald, though an irreproachable husband, was usually inclined to the pedantic. Then she looked up, across the edge of their box, and her smile became rather hard.

"Sir Gerald, you'll spoil me, and then Lady Lockridge will be jealous!" she protested automatically.

"Jealousy," said Lady Lockridge, "is the green-eyed monster, Gerry says, and since my eyes are blue I couldn't possibly be jealous, now, could I?" she finished smugly. There was an appreciative round of male laughter, and she dimpled up at her husband. Primula excused herself and rose gracefully to her feet.

Yes, it was definitely Georgie letting himself into the box across the way and being greeted by its occupants. And it was impossible to mistake the quality of those occupants. Primula tried to look without looking, and fiddled with the carved fan looped upon her wrist.

"Are you quite all right?" her husband asked.

"I think we've lost Georgie," she answered, through gritted teeth. Severn looked, more openly than propriety allowed him too.

"Oh, it's a temporary dereliction. He'll be back for the third act, never fear."

"Is that all it means to you? Yes, of course it is—but I beg you, Lord Severn; he will listen to you."

"Not if I try to bring him up short over this." The harsh note in his voice made Primula look up at him. Severn smiled at her painfully.

"Have a little compassion, lady wife, on those whose only sin was being found out. And on Georgie—he's twenty-two, dear God, and you and Addie treat him like a boy of sixteen. There's no harm in a flutter among the demi-monde."

"I don't imagine you would think so!" snapped Primula, keeping her voice low with an effort. "And you will say the same to anything he does—'there's no harm in it'—until the day he is ruined. Severn—"

"I said before: as scandals go, it's both innocent and common. And I won't make myself look ridiculous wailing after him like a banshee nursemaid. It would hardly suit my reputation."

"Reputation!" Primula said bitterly. She watched as Georgie bowed over the blonde woman's hand. Her hand was all that Primula could see; she held a large painted fan up before her face.

"Oh, yes, reputation," Severn agreed softly. "Of all people on this earth, Lady Severn, you should know best how far one will go to save a reputation."

Primula drew breath to reply—damning confession and accusation all in one—and Lydia Mainwaring dropped neatly into the silence thus created.

"Lord Severn, you have been so quiet this evening, how are we to know what to think of you? Everyone was surprised enough to find you here—and Almack's will be even duller, don't you think, after the things you have done?" She gave every evidence of wishing to corner her prey at the front of the box; Primula snapped open her fan and moved back toward her.

"Almack's can hardly be duller than a six month's sea voyage," Severn said, following his wife.

"Then is the cat belled?" asked Mr. Rainford. "Is the legendary Lord Severn taking up the yoke of frivolity, now that the Patronesses have given the nod? I admit I will be sorry to lose your wife's company of a Wednesday evening. It is such charming company, after all."

Severn regarded his guests with a bland, noncommittal expression. His gaze roved among them until it fell upon the face of his wife.

"The vouchers arrived. I didn't tell you," Primula said, as if every word had been extracted by torture.

"But you told all our friends. How respectable," said Severn.

It was only the sort of thing that everyone else did, George Lambton told himself firmly as he made his way to Aspasia's opera box. And though he would return directly to his Aunt Prim's party, and though she would most virtuously pretend not to see him, Georgie was kind and well mannered enough that he would not have gone at all save for the pretty blonde seated beside Aspasia. He had been trying for the past week to see her again without success. Tonight, if he did nothing else, he would learn her name.

The door he scratched at was opened by a liveried footman, and as he entered, Aspasia turned and smiled upon him.

"Why Mr. Lambton, we were hoping you would come to us. Jenny and I—but you have met my sister, Jenny Fair—remarked you when we entered, with your so-respectable friends!" Her eyes laughed and her mouth turned upward in a teasing, carmined smile, but he had eyes only for the girl who sat beside her.

"Jenny Fair," said Georgie. "May I sit down?"

Sarah Jane turned her head away, and set her jaw so her mouth did not tremble.

"Please do, Mr. Lambton," Aspasia's voice was mercilessly kind.

Georgie accepted a silver cup of punch and drained it, and by that time Sarah Jane had nerved herself to look at him.

"How do you find the opera, Mr. Lambton?" she asked in a low voice.

He smiled. "Afraid I haven't much use for those cat-squallings. Came to oblige a lady—well, my aunt, actually, but she's still a lady—Lady Severn, in fact." With an inclination of his head he indicated the box that held the party of which he spoke, and the cup she held slipped through Sarah Jane's nerveless fingers. Aspasia caught it, but not before it had emptied itself on Sarah Jane's skirt.

"Why is it, Mr. Lambton, that your mere presence causes us to pour libations to you?" Aspasia interrupted teasingly. "It is a great gift, to be sure, if hard on our poor servants. Of course your aunt is Lady Severn, and her husband is your uncle, Lord Severn. Lord Severn's father, if I do not mistake, is the Earl of Malhythe, while *his* father—"

"I'm deuced sorry, Miss Jenny," Georgie burst

out. "She's right, you know: happens all the time. When I first met her, in fact."

"And I am well aware that you still owe me the compensation of a game of whist, Mr. Lambton," Aspasia answered.

He extracted a silk pocket-square and laid it gently over the wet spot on Sarah Jane's dress. The cup, refilled, appeared at her hand, and under Aspasia's bullying gaze she gulped it, shuddering only a little.

"Do you play, Miss Jenny?"

"Only a little; Mama said it was fast, but Papa—" Sarah Jane stopped in appalled silence.

"Then Mr. Lambton can teach you, if he will stoop so far," Aspasia said ruthlessly. "Will you, Mr. Lambton?"

"I would be delighted." Georgie rose to his feet and bowed, first over one hand then the other. "May I call upon you soon?"

"Yes," said Sarah Jane miserably. "Make it soon."

The theater evening proceeded to its expected close; the pleasure-party members departed to their various residences, and Lady Severn's party was pronounced a great success.

Lord and Lady Severn and Mr. George Lambton shared a carriage in demure silence. After stopping at Colworth House so that Mr. Lambton could alight, it proceeded to the Severns' most fashionable and new-built residence.

Their servants stood awaiting them in the dark hallway, blinking sleepily. Each as self-absorbed as if alone, Lord and Lady Severn disposed of their outer garments to their waiting minions. Then they ascended the staircase to the first floor—Primula to her solitary bedroom, Severn to his.

An hour later, washed and suitably gowned and

nestled among her bedclothes, Primula sat upright against a bulwark of pillows and tried to concentrate upon the book of sermons she had brought to put her to sleep. The single candle at her bedside stretched the shadows into fantastic shapes. When it fluttered in the draft the shadows leaped and jerked, but Primula didn't mind them. The only emotion she was conscious of was a flat despair, a weariness that even outweighed fury.

Severn had proved that he was not what she had set her heart on all those years ago—and if he was not it, then it did not exist anywhere.

The candle flame flattened in a sudden new draft, and as Primula grabbed for it to shield it she saw the door to her bedroom slide quietly open.

"What are you doing here?" Primula said to her husband.

"Surely a man may enter his wife's bedroom." Severn closed the door behind him. A green silk dressing gown was flung over his evening dress, and in the dim light his cat's eyes were black.

Primula pulled the bedcovers up to her neck. "I don't want you here," she said flatly.

Severn sighed and leaned back against the wall. So far from her candle's light, his face was a featureless white blur in shadow.

"Then why did you marry me," he said, "if you didn't want me here?"

"Because Lord Malhythe asked me to." To tell the truth at last, however unwillingly, made her giddy.

"Oh, yes. I know that. That's common gossip," Severn said patiently. "And why did you say yes?"

Primula's mouth twisted with remembered bitterness. "Is not a title and an establishment, and a sweet compliant husband, reason enough? Go to bed, Severn, you've been drinking, and you know it doesn't suit you."

"Yes I have and no it doesn't and no, it's not enough. Not for you. Tell me the truth, or I'll—"

"You'll what?" Primula demanded, flinging back the bedcovers and reaching for a robe.

"I'll—Dear God, Primula, must we be enemies?" He took a few quick steps forward and fell, unsteadily, into a chair.

"No. Not enemies." She picked up the candle and walked toward him. The circle of light crept up his body until it illuminated all of him, and she stood over him like a torch-wielding goddess come to pass sentence. "But if I told you the truth—*if* I told you—you wouldn't like it."

Severn looked up into the candle's bright flame and laughed. His skin was sheened with fever. "Wouldn't like it? Why, what sweet compliant husband would object to knowing that he'd married slightly *shopworn* goods? Not that I can object—unless there were others between John Cunningham and myself."

The candle danced wildly and fell. Severn caught it and cursed at the spill of hot beeswax across his hand. Primula pressed her fists to her bosom in a gesture unconsciously theatrical, her heart hammering as she fought the sudden rush of faintness.

"You knew. From the very first, you *knew*." And all the heartburning hours she had spent wondering whether to keep the Earl's secret were wasted, because Severn already knew.

"And wondered, my sweet compliant *amiable* wife. What sort of woman would happily trip down the aisle with her seducer?"

The ugliness in his voice revived her as no cordial could. Primula threw back her head and glared at him.

"In case you have the slightest interest in the details, my lord Severn, I had no choice." She hesitated—back to the bed, or ring the bell that would summon all the servants to witness this new scandal?

" 'I had no choice.' Very pretty. You should go on the stage. Which is where, be it known, I expected to find you." Severn, too, swayed to his feet, but Primula's thoughts were no longer on retreat.

"After my disgrace? *My* disgrace? Why not yours? All I did was trust and love you—you set out cold-bloodedly to make my life a lie and ruin me."

"Apparently I didn't succeed."

"Are you sorry?"

He hesitated as if actually considering the matter, and Primula's hands clenched into fists.

"I . . . No. I'm not sorry. I'm glad. But I don't understand. I—"

"You pretended to marry me, took me to Guildford for two weeks, and then threw me out of your carriage on my parents' doorstep."

"I'm sorry," Severn said.

The simple inadequacy of it made tears prickle behind her eyes, and Primula raised her hand as if to ward off the pain. Carefully Severn set the candle on a near-by table; the light gilded his jaw and cast his eyes into shadow. Then he spoke again.

"No, I'm *not* sorry. If I hadn't done . . . what I did, I would never have married you *this* time." With new assurance he closed the distance between them and gripped her shoulders lightly.

"What I did to you ten years ago is unforgivable. But I want you to forgive it. Because I want you for my wife. John Cunningham lied, but I'm telling the truth. I love you, Primula."

"If you are lying—" Primula began. The tears rose up in her throat and choked her.

"Not to you. Never again. Come to me, my love. Oh, Prim, I have waited so long to come home."

And then she did cry—as though her heart were breaking, when in fact it was healing itself with

Severn at its center, just as he had been since Primula was sixteen years old.

Eventually her tears dried, and she sighed and looked up into her husband's face.

"You *knew*," Primula repeated numbly.

Severn smiled; a wry, foolish, hopeful grin. "I got to England three weeks before the wedding; Father locked me up in an inn ten miles out of town until my wedding day. I couldn't think why the date he'd chose was so plaguey familiar—until I heard your name. And then I was sure that . . . I don't know, any more." He buried his face in her hair. Primula stiffened, but did not protest. "How did— What did—Your father never knew, I'll swear to that," he added.

"I never told them," Primula said in a voice slightly hoarse from crying. "Mama cried so! I wished I could die and not have to hear her weep. I think they must have guessed what had happened, but if I wouldn't say, they could only accept that or throw me out.

"But Lord Malhythe knew. I don't know how. He came to me last year and said he would make what had happened public knowledge if I didn't agree to marry you. I had no choice."

"The devil!" Severn's arms tightened with his fury until Primula squirmed in protest. "But surely, my heart's life, ten years later no one would care . . . ?"

"Oh, Severn, do I look as if I am made of wood? I didn't care for myself—but I'd never kept quiet for myself. What do you suppose would have happened if I went to Papa and said: I have been disgraced by Viscount Severn? He would have challenged you to a duel, wouldn't he, or your father if you were gone?"

"Yes," Severn said slowly, thinking about it.

"Any man would. And I was in a coach bound for Dover before the day was out."

"And do you think Lord Malhythe would have refused to meet him—or have deloped if he did? Lord Malhythe is a very fine shot, you know, and Papa would have been dead—because of me.

"And Mama would have stood by me, of course—but who would stand by Mama, once the news of her daughter's disgrace was presented to the *ton*? Certainly no one would bring their daughters beneath the same roof as I, and Mama could not call upon people who would not call upon her in return. So Papa would have been dead, and Mama deserted by all of her friends—or enough of them to hurt, anyway—all because I could not keep silent. And one year, or ten years, or a hundred years later it would still be true.

"The only thing I could do was what I did."

Severn buried his face in her hair again—after a moment Primula realized he was weeping. "Ah, dear God, and I thought you were heartless," she heard him say.

It was most pleasant to sit so upon her husband's knee, with the clean smell of his linen in her nostrils and his arms hard and warm around her. And though nothing was settled—not his character, not her duplicity—she was obscurely comforted, as if a long season of pain had come to an end. He loved her and he knew the truth. The rest they could face together.

"I'm not a very successful rake, am I?" Severn spoke at last. "God, I shouldn't drink. Got no head for it anymore; you lose that in India, if you live. All it ever does is make me sick and bring on a bout of fever. But I had to talk to you, and I couldn't manage it sober. I couldn't stand it; that—if—"

Primula took him by the shoulders and shook him gently.

"Oh, Severn! Come to bed, my love."

* * *

"I will not be sold!" Sarah Jane Emwilton stormed up and down the dimly lit parlor.

"Sold is better than given away. Or stolen," Aspasia said with maddening calmness. "You have no other choice, Jenny. I'm sorry."

"Don't call me that! That's not my name!"

"Jane, Jenny, Jennykins . . . Do you want to give him your full name and direction and make your mother a scandal? Do you think I was christened Aspasia? Georgie seems kind enough; I might almost trust him to keep a secret; tell him the truth entire if you want to break your heart! What can he do, even if he wanted to do all he could? Lady Severn will not answer your letter—you saw her there tonight, and the accident that sent you to the Theater with me instead of her cannot be reversed."

"I can't . . ." Sarah Jane said.

"Then you'll die." Sarah Jane stared up at her; Aspasia's eyes were dark in the candlelight. "You'll die," she repeatedly flatly. "Jenny, sometimes they can be kind . . ."

"Please!" Sarah Jane pressed her hands over her mouth as if to cram the words back. She sobbed and ran from the room.

Chapter 19

APRIL 23, 1817, AND ONWARD

THE LATE APRIL weather was horrible, but neither the Viscount nor Viscountess Severn cared. For at last they were able to do what they should have done from the very beginning—talk.

"But why?" Severn demanded for the thousandth baffled time.

Thick rain hammered against the windows and slid gluily down the panes. The cold silver of daylight mingled with the hot gold of the candles, and the breakfast remains, on the tray pushed to the foot of the bed, bore mute witness to how long this question had been asked.

"Oh, Severn, *I* don't know! Papa asked the same thing, you know, and all I could tell him was what Lord Malhythe had said—that he wished to make you sorry."

"And you weren't to tell me that you knew . . . who I had been."

Primula sighed and rubbed her cheek against his woolen-clad shoulders. Loach had entered their bedchamber with the sun, and that strange old man's indignation at Severn's naked and unprotected state was almost funny. Nothing would do but that "His Grace" must rise at once and be properly dressed for bed—the dire threats of what would obtain if he did not were as colorful as they were incomprehensible to Severn's giggling wife.

"Not until a year had passed. He promised . . . that no harm would come to me because of you—oh, he talked a great deal of nonsense about settlements and incomes, but he never told me anything more than that."

"Except that if you would not agree to the marriage, he would make your life a hell on earth," Severn said broodingly. "How fortunate for him that he is not in London at this present."

"I suppose so," Primula said, more interested in studying her husband's face by daylight. The brass-bronze hair was almost its normal color now, no longer faded by alien suns but heavily streaked with grey. The lines of torment about the generous, mobile mouth had softened.

"But you know, Severn, as soon as I married you he had no more power over me. Once we were wed, no one would care very much if we had . . . anticipated the wedding."

"By ten years or so. I dare swear you'd have found the entrée to Almack's a deuced sight harder to come by, though."

"Yes, but do pay attention, Severn. Lord Malhythe had discovered the name of the woman his son had ruined—that's me, you know. He went to her and proposed that his son would marry her, sight unseen, and not (in fact) knowing who she was. All Lord Malhythe required of her was her silence; she must on no account tell the wicked Lord Severn that she knew him for her seducer. What does he gain? The marriage is made in any event, and unless he wants a great scandal and has the means to arrange an Act of Parliament, there can be no divorce. So what does he gain?"

"I don't know." Severn's voice was languid, his attention obviously elsewhere. He extended an exploratory finger and began to smooth Primula's brown curls around it. "I don't care." He planted a kiss upon her neck just below her ear. "And I'll think about it later, dearest wife."

"Oh yes, my lord rake—but, mind, I still expect you to come to Almack's with me—after all we have been to one another!"

But the questions so easily put aside would not go away entirely, and later Primula wondered: Did Lord Malhythe have yet another plan to destroy their happiness now that they had at last found it?

George Lambton availed himself of Aspasia's invitation before too many days had passed. Though he would be loath to admit it, unlimited freedom was already proving to be a bore—since unlimited freedom seemed to most of his friends to mean unlimited license. Once his curiosity had been satisfied as to what sort of party the likes of Bad Jack Barham gave, there seemed to be no reason ever to attend another.

So while Georgie shared with all the young men of his age and class a taste for showy horseflesh, deep play, and the niceties of fashion, his bloodstock was sound, his gaming rewarded skill before luck, and his tailor's bills had so far been settled with reasonable promptitude. And his parties, when the time came to host some, would be more fun and less notorious than the ones Lightfoot Bobby Gressingham was always saying were all the crack.

But for such parties a hostess was essential—a frivolous, scandalous charmer who would dazzle his guests and nonetheless shoulder the real work of arranging things. Georgie, like all the Rudwell line, liked his comforts.

He was received in the parlor of the little house in St. John's Wood with all the panoply of a favored guest. Malmsey and sugared almonds were set out for him, and blonde Jenny played a popular air upon the pianoforte while brunette Aspasia sang a naughty little ditty that would much have shocked the tune's composer.

"But heavens!— Look at the time!" Aspasia said unconvincingly when she had finished. "I know you will excuse me, Mr. Lambton, as I will leave Jenny to entertain you, but there is an errand I simply *must* run. You will be here when I get back, won't you, sir?"

"I—of course," Georgie said, rising to his feet. Aspasia blew him a kiss and exited the room with a practiced flirt of her black curls.

There was a silence, during which Sarah Jane stared straight ahead at the music spread out before her and the ticking of the ornamental porcelain clock on the mantelpiece was the loudest sound in the room.

"She means you to take me into keeping, you know," Sarah Jane said at last, "but it won't work, Mr. Lambton. I know it is my only hope—and I have tried very hard to be ruined—but it won't work. So you may as well save your breath."

Georgie, made uncomfortable by this plain speaking, sat down abruptly in his chair only to rise again and stride about the room with his hands in his pockets. Eventually he came to an abrupt stop in front of Sarah Jane.

"Are you saying you *ain't* ruined?" he demanded inelegantly.

Her shoulders slumped. "Oh, no. I am ruined, I think. I—tell me, Mr. Lambton, can you keep a secret? Aspasia thinks you can."

Put off-stride by this novel change of subject, Georgie stared at her for a moment. "Keep a secret? What about?"

"About me. It is only fair to tell you; you have

been very kind. But you must promise me never to tell it to another living soul."

"Well, I—"

"Swear it!" Sarah Jane commanded.

"Very well, Miss Jenny. Whatever you tell me here will remain our secret, I swear it." He sat down beside her on the piano bench.

Sarah Jane smiled bitterly. "My name is not Jenny. It is Sarah Jane Emwilton. My father was General Horatio Emwilton—and I have some claim of a connection with your family, I believe."

Sarah Jane told her story briefly: her months as a governess, the supposed summons to town from her employer, Lord Drewmore's proposition and its aftermath.

"Aspasia tells me there is no hope of mending my reputation—too many people know, you see," Sarah Jane finished.

Georgie had gone white, then red, several times during the course of her narrative. Now, flushing hotly, he rose to his feet. "If my silence can—can serve you in any way, Miss Emwilton, rest assured that—that I will do everything—or not do anything, I mean—"

"Oh, dear Mr. Lambton, it is not you! But Mrs. Courtenay must have come home by now and found I have run off, and Lord Drewmore is bound to put the tale about. Even if I just went home to Mama, gossip would certainly follow! We should be thrown out of our lodgings."

"But you have done nothing," Georgie protested.

Tears glittered in Sarah Jane's eyes. "Oh, Mr. Lambton—to hear you say that means more to me than I can say. But now I have the reputation for doing things, and . . ." She closed her eyes tightly and covered her face with her hands.

Awkwardly Georgie pressed his handkerchief into her hands.

"That devil Drewmore! I'll call him out!" he promised.

"You can't!" said Sarah Jane, stifling her tears. "And it would do no good, even if you were to kill him. I've thought and thought and thought. I'm quite ruined, and even if there were any help for it I have no one to help me. I even wrote to—a friend—and she wouldn't answer my letter!"

"Then she is no one worthy of your friendship," said Georgie firmly. "It all sounds deuced smokey, but there's always a way out, even when you've got your back to a wall—m'uncle always says, anyway, and I suspect he's right. I know someone who may be able to help. Miss Emwilton, may I ask you to place yourself utterly in my hands?"

"It is what Aspasia intended," Sarah Jane reminded him with a shaky attempt at mirth. But Georgie was able to extract the promise that he wanted. Sarah Jane would do nothing, rash or otherwise—until he had set the matter (naming no names) before a friend of his who was both wise and well-connected. Without waiting for Aspasia to return he took his leave, and bowed chastely over Sarah Jane Emwilton's hand as he did so.

Chapter 20

APRIL 1817

"WELL, YOUNG LAMBTON, what brings you to call upon me with such promptitude? Surely my company cannot compete with all the wonders of London." The aged yellow eyes watched him closely as Georgie doffed his hat and bowed.

"You do yourself too little honor, Lord Warltawk," Georgie said with prompt politeness.

"I merely recognize that all men have limitations—most of all in their capacity for boredom. Myself among them, I might add. I have never enjoyed being bored."

"I hope, then, that I will not bore you, sir. There is a matter upon which I would appreciate the favor of some advice, and I can think of no one who could better advise me."

"So you feel yourself obligated to aid this nameless young jade?" Warltawk said when Georgie had finished. For the last quarter-hour he had sat, silent and motionless as an Egyptian mummy, while Georgie had related the tale of Sarah Jane's predicament, leaving out only the names of the principal actors in the farce. As he retold the story, Georgie found himself struck as he had not been before by the unfairness of it—Sarah Jane had done nothing but her best to be kind, and was rewarded for it by a fate worse than death—not swift execution, but slow starvation.

"Yes, Lord Warltawk. I . . . gave her my word that I would do all that I could to help her."

Lord Warltawk smiled—a death's-head stretching of pale parchment skin. "Well, Mr. Lambton, if the situation is as you described it, and your word has been pledged, there is one thing you may do for your fair *incognita.* A drastic measure, I will grant you, but it will in one stroke end her troubles and redeem your honor, if you are brave enough to take it."

"Anything, sir!" Georgie said rashly.

"Warltawk leaned forward. "Marry the girl."

George Lambton recoiled as if a snake had suddenly been thrown at him, and Warltawk laughed mockingly.

Georgie flushed hotly. "Marry the girl, you said, sir?" He spoke with determined resoluteness.

"But of course that's hardly possible, is it? Your dear mother would never approve—"

"Sarah Jane's family is as good as any!" Georgie protested.

"And better than some, surely, who embark upon a career such as hers *after* they are married," Warltawk purred. "But pray do not rip up at me, my dear Lambton. I put no obstacle in the way of the execution of your plans. In fact, I would offer you every assistance . . . if you were actually serious."

"I *am* serious, my lord!"

"About marrying a young woman . . . under a cloud, shall we say? Without the knowledge or consent of your family?"

"I need none," Georgie declared stoutly. "And if you think that marrying her will serve—"

"My dear young man, I think that marrying the

chit will serve admirably," Warltawk said with a note of stifled laughter in his voice.

"Then I shall do it."

"I applaud your instincts." A faint flush had appeared upon Warltawk's ancient yellowed cheeks, and his tiger's eyes glowed bright with eagerness. "It is true, then, that even in these debased days breeding will out. Rest assured, my dear Lambton, that I stand ready to aid you by every means at my disposal. I shall arrange for a coach and horses at once, and you may elope to Gretna in perfect safety."

"Gretna," said Georgie, trying to sound pleased. It was true that once over the Border, and in the realm of Scots law, merely announcing their intent to wed would make Sarah Jane Emwilton and himself as truly married as if they had plighted their troth in St. George's Hanover Square in front of their assembled families, but it would also add one more soupçon of scandal to a situation that could bear none.

"Have you an alternative? Oh, it may be that I can provide a Special License, but would it be wise to remain here in town with your new bride?"

The matter having thus been presented to him, George Lambton could not see any way in which the situation would be improved by presenting his new bride to Lord and Lady Severn—and his mother.

"It would not be," Lord Warltawk concluded. "Take her away, spend a month or so beyond the petty-minded reach of English law, and when you return at the height of the Season, who is to say that your honorable bride has ever set foot in London before?"

Georgie sighed with relief at another obstacle surmounted, but he was badly confused. He was quite certain that his uncle, his mother, and even his grandfather would—while believing every word of his story—come up with a different answer than marriage. Georgie was not stupid, merely inexperienced; he did not think that Lord Warltawk was as convinced of Sarah Jane's innocence as he was. Yet Warltawk was counseling that Georgie marry a woman that Warltawk must believe profoundly unsuitable.

He would not think of it now. There was no better answer. He had sworn he would help her, and she would be safe the moment the ring was on her finger. Any past scandal could be hushed up, or lived down, or at worst, they could retire from town and live quietly on Georgie's generous income.

"Well? Or is this more trouble than you are prepared to undertake?"

He did not want to do it. But this marriage was, at worst, an inconvenience to him. It was Sarah Jane Emwilton's only hope of a life that did not end in the gutters of the London streets—for an act she had not committed, and a crime she had been no party to.

"No, sir. It is not. Please let me know how long you will need to make your arrangements, Lord Warltawk, and pray accept my deepest gratitude for all the trouble you are going to on my behalf."

Chapter 21

APRIL 1817

PRIMULA CONFESSED HER bet with Mrs. Mainwaring, having learned a healthy distaste of secrets, and endured a scalding lecture from her husband on the folly of even such mild scandal.

"All it does, my girl, is blunt your sense of what *is* scandalous, bores you, disgusts your friends, and leads you to— Well, never mind what it leads you to, but I'll tell you this: Do you think I began my career by debauching virgins such as yourself? I began with milder pastimes, and never saw anything wrong with each increase!"

"I—" Primula began.

"And don't tell me your character will stand it—because in the first place, *mine* won't, and in the second, eventually you'll fall into something *yours* won't."

Primula nodded meekly. "Then you'll speak to Georgie, Severn, about his behavior?" she asked, dimpling.

Severn laughed, and kissed her, and, even more delightfully, promised to.

"But I can't just forbid it—nobody's forbidden him anything in far too long except Addie, who forbids far too much. I'd rather make him stop than make him mind—" Severn frowned off into space.

"You might—" Primula blushed. "You might buy the woman off, Severn."

"Woman? What woman? I wish to God it were as simple as a woman," Severn said bitterly, and would not confide in her further.

But he had chosen to win her bet for her, and so the very last Wednesday in April found Lord and Lady Severn—and the ghost of old scandal—dancing meek attendance upon the *ton* at Almack's.

It was not a new experience for Primula, who had spent every Wednesday of the previous Season reveling in the often-mocked delights of Seventh Heaven. She herself had found the dancing enjoyable, the conversation pleasant, and the sense of social superiority intoxicating (which she knew betokened a grievous want of moral fibre, but which she was helpless to resist).

It might even be imagined, by the credulous, that Lord Severn had been here before. But if he had been, it was many years and many sins ago, and in a persona altogether different.

"Why Lydia, dear—you must not be so formal! Why, here is Severn—*so* anxious to see you again, you know!—and surely you will not deny him the pleasure of making up a figure with you?" Primula thought Lydia might pay her on the spot, so great was her consternation.

"Of course not," said Mrs. Mainwaring with a defiant toss of her head and a glance at her escort. He bowed, and Severn bowed also.

But others were not so forbearing. By the end of the evening Primula had quite managed to forget that she had ever wished her husband to take his place beside her in Society.

It had been ten years, but she was finding, as Severn had found before her, that society did not forget. It went so far, in fact, as to refuse to believe that ten years had passed, and thought of Severn as the same callow rakeshame that his father had banished.

But he was not. Primula believed that with all her heart and was furious that no one else seemed to see it.

Even her friends treated him with a certain distance. Oh, they were willing enough to acknowledge him—Mr. Rainford and the Lockridges had attended her theater party, after all—but their acknowledgment was tempered with a wariness that set Primula's teeth on edge.

"Give them time," Severn said, handing her a glass of punch as they stood by the refreshment table.

"They are—" began Primula, fuming.

"—the same people you have commended to me these past two months. It is like hunting tiger; if you are quiet and patient for long enough, eventually the beast pounces and devours the sacrificial goat. I shall cease to interest King Mob soon."

"Severn!" Primula said, protesting even as she laughed.

"Oh, yes," Severn assured her. "I shall become very dull and respectable. I should have realized it was more fun than being wicked—why else do so many people embrace it, after all? And I do have a wife who forgives me all my numerous shortcomings."

"People are looking," Primula observed, plying her fan.

"And so they should; it's a rare enough sight; an uxorious husband and an intelligent wife. O jewel among women—"

"Severn, people *are* looking."

"Then take me home where they won't be able to stare at me—providing you are finished trooping the matrimonial colors, that is."

"In a while, my lord," Primula said. "I would not

wish our friends to think you are not enjoying yourself."

The while stretched to another hour, then two, and it was quite late—or very early—when Lord and Lady Severn reached their own doorstep. On balance Primula was satisfied with the way things had gone; by the end of the Season Severn should be solidly reestablished, and those who shunned him now would clamor for his presence at their parties.

But Primula's satisfaction did not long survive her arrival in her dressing-room.

She pulled off her gloves and flung them down upon her dressing-table. One of them caught upon a folded billet of rose-colored parchment sticking up out of the litter of boxes and bottles; retrieving the glove, Primula pulled the letter free.

Occasionally she opened her mail while dressing; this letter must have slipped from among its fellows and been wedged between the mirror and her pounce-box, undiscovered until now.

A strong scent of violet and musk emanated from the missive, and Primula could not imagine who could be writing to her who used such perfume. Still in her ballgown, she sank slowly to the padded stool before her dressing-table mirror and broke open the seal on the letter.

She read it all the way through to the end in disbelief, then read it again more slowly. Sarah Jane Emwilton, her mother's goddaughter, had been ruined by Lord Drewmore and had taken refuge beneath the roof of a courtesan.

Primula covered her mouth with her hand, torn between mad laughter and tears. Why hadn't Lady Emwilton written to Mama before things had reached such a pass? Sarah Jane, a governess? There was absolutely no need—why, Sarah Jane could have come to live with *her*—

Primula pulled herself up short, curtailing the desperate lunge into might-have-been. She looked at the date again. Almost a week ago! She must answer it at once, before Sarah Jane thought she meant to cut her; she must write to Mama—

And tell her what? Slow tears of weariness and exasperation—and sympathy—trickled down Primula's cheeks. She had saved her own reputation through sheer luck, loving parents, and the fact that she had absolutely no need to earn her bread. Sarah Jane was in a far worse state.

What could she do? And, worse, if trying to save Sarah Jane meant ruining Severn, which would she choose?

Chapter 22

MAY 1, 1817

ON A DAY traditionally associated with license and riot—the First of May—Mr. George Lambton pulled up in a very smart rented coach-and-six in front of the little house in St. John's Wood. The coach was sturdy and the horses stout, as befit an equipage intended to carry its occupants all the way to the Border.

In his pocket reposed a Special License, along with the address of a parson who had the living in the village of Little Fakenham, a few hours to the north. His heart was full of doubts, though none of them pertained to the course of action he had chosen.

He knew that Lord Warltawk's fortune was long expended—in fact, Georgie had been the agent of a few small loans to his lordship, as well as making his mentor a modest gift or two; he was as well placed as any man in London to say how his lordship's finances stood.

And they did not run to the expense—thirty guineas—of a Special License, or the cost of the handsome coach, well provisioned, which Warltawk had insisted on bearing.

Georgie frowned. He wished he could discuss this with Severn, but that would require disclosing the whole of his plan—of which Severn might very well disapprove.

Mama would certainly disapprove—and well she might, he supposed. If he had not been distantly connected to Miss Emwilton, he would certainly have thought twice before making such a sweeping promise of aid.

But he *had* promised, and Georgie had been raised as an Englishman, in a tradition of service and sacrifice that had been old when Conqueror William had beached his boats. He had promised to help Miss Emwilton, and this was the only way he could.

But it was not a way that would meet with universal approval, and Georgie badly wanted to know why Warltawk wished him to do it so much.

But that could wait. At the moment, Georgie felt a pressing need to marry.

Sarah Jane Emwilton had lived in a state of nervous hope since she had met with Georgie. She had not confided the details of that meeting to Aspasia, but her high spirits communicated themselves to her hostess, and Aspasia was so merry that Sarah Jane felt quite guilty. Aspasia had even insisted on searching her wardrobe for dresses that could be made over to suit her, swearing that these were merely a paltry prelude to those that Sarah Jane might one day call her own.

Sarah Jane, hoping for quite a different resolution to her troubles, could not bear to disillusion her hostess—or perhaps herself. Wise in the ways of the demi-monde, Aspasia might simply tell her that she had no right to hope—and that Sarah Jane could not bear.

And so it was that, decked in borrowed finery, Sarah Jane was sitting and sewing in Aspasia's parlor when Mr. George Lambton came to call.

Mrs. Clutterbuck quickly ushered him into her presence. Georgie's blond handsomeness was perfected by a coat of russet superfine, a waistcoat of dull gold embroidered satin, and neat biscuit-colored pantaloons finished off by gleaming slippers of Turkish leather. In one hand he held his curly fur-felt beaver, gloves of Cork tan, and a slender malacca cane with a cloudy amber head. In all his neatness and fashionable understatement, he was like an emissary from the sunlit world of cool reason and common sense, and Sarah Jane, unreasonably, could have wept to behold him.

"Good morning, Miss Emwilton," he began, as calmly as if she were any well-bred hostess in her own parlor.

"Good morning, Mr. Lambton," Sarah Jane returned gravely. "Would you care for a glass of wine? Our hostess can offer a tolerably fine *oporto*, I understand."

Mr. Lambton set his paraphernalia on a low table and seated himself upon the chair at Sarah Jane's right. He indicated he was not averse to the refreshment offered, and Sarah Jane, accordingly, sent the housekeeper off in search of it. Once she had left, Georgie leaned forward confidingly.

"Miss Emwilton, I have spoken to the acquaintance I mentioned to you, and set forth—without names—the full particulars of your plight. He advanced to me a solution which I believe to be a just, true, and only reasonable resolution, and accordingly I have come to tender it to you."

"A solution?" Sarah Jane penetrated to the heart of this polysyllabic rodomontade with the incisiveness of the desperate. "There is something you can do to help me, Mr. Lambton?"

Georgie opened his mouth to reply, and closed it again as Mrs. Clutterbuck entered with her tray.

"Now here you are, young gentleman, and as nice

a glass of port as you'll get anywhere," she said encouragingly. She poured out a glass, hovered for a moment, and then bustled off, with a conspiratorial glance at Sarah Jane.

"Er, yes," said Georgie, as flustered by Mrs. Clutterbuck's conspiratory mien as Sarah Jane had been. "If you will marry me, Miss Emwilton, I daresay your problem will be solved."

There was a long pause.

"Marry you?" Sarah Jane stood and flung the dress she was altering to the floor. "How dare—" But he dared because she was in the situation that she was, and there was nothing she could do if he chose to mock her. Sarah Jane sat down again.

"I have a Special License," Georgie said apologetically. He produced it and offered it to her. Sarah Jane looked at the stiff cream vellum with its dangling episcopal seal and felt the blood thunder in her ears. Georgie quickly offered her his untasted glass of port.

"It was all I could think of," he went on. "I know it is perhaps not quite what you could like, but Lord Warltawk said it would serve, and I know I can bring Mama around—she and Aunt Prim are special friends, you know, and you are a connection of hers. If you will say yes, we can marry this afternoon in Little Fakenham—and then perhaps we could visit Aunt Catherine. She is Lady Rannoch, you know, so we would be in Scotland, and she is generally glad to see me. We could write Mama from there—and your mother, too—and then. . . . Well, no one need know any more than that I took you away from Oakleys and that we have been married for ever so long."

Sarah Jane had never heard of Lord Warltawk, his scandalous past or his notorious present, nor had she any reason to suspect that his interests in George Lambton might be less than benign. She only saw the hesitant stubbornness with which Mr. Lambton proffered this mad and foolish plan, and it won her heart forever.

"Your proposal does me very great honor, Mr. Lambton," she said slowly. There was a pause while they looked at each other, and then Sarah Jane forced herself to go on. "I hope you have considered that it may not work—that instead of redeeming me, it may ruin you?"

"Well, then," said Georgie stoutly, "I shall be ruined. Papa don't go about much, and I should like to see anybody say a word against Mama! No; you'll see—it will work out very well. And I dare to say—we might make one another comfortable, Miss Emwilton."

"Sarah Jane," whispered Sarah Jane. "If I am to marry you, George, you must call me Sarah Jane."

Aspasia returned home from a morning of shopping and calls among her friends to the news, conveyed by Mrs. Clutterbuck, that George Lambton had called, and—following an interview between him and Sarah Jane that Mrs. Clutterbuck had not been privileged to hear—Sarah Jane had asked her assistance, packed several bandboxes with the new wardrobe of Aspasia's furnishing, and departed with Mr. Lambton in a coach and six.

"Oh, Cutty, how wonderful! I admit I shall miss her company, but Georgie will be very good to her, don't you think? Where is he taking her, did they say?"

"No, lamb. It was all talk of the horses left standing—I made so bold as to give Miss Jenny a half-dozen of your good lace kerchiefs, and to make certain she had a bit of money about her."

"Cutty, you are a treasure! For all that poets and mooncalves say that love alone is enough, I have never known a good set of clean sheets and a hot water bottle to hinder matters—never mind the ability to tip a coachman." But despite her expressed delight, in her heart Aspasia was not so sanguine. There were many pitfalls to the Cyprian's life, and Sarah Jane had not been willing to listen to advice on avoiding them.

Her heart was further troubled by the billet she saw propped meaningfully upon her mantelpiece, and her composure was shattered entirely when she read it.

"Dear Aspasia, By the time you read this I shall be Mrs. George Lambton. . . ."

Oh, Colley, thought Aspasia in despairing entreaty. When the Earl of Malhythe came home to discover that his grandson had eloped with a member-of-the-muslin-company-by-courtesy who had been living beneath her roof—!

She scanned the rest of the note quickly. They were marrying by Special License in a town called Little Fakenham, and proceeding to Scotland. Little Fakenham was four hours from here at least, and in a heavy traveling coach might be farther.

"Cutty!" Aspasia cried, vigorously pulling at the bellrope. The housekeeper was at her side instantly.

"They've eloped, the damn fools! When did they leave? Order my phaeton—and pack me a case, I'm going after them!"

Primula had agonized all the next day over what she must do. She wrote and destroyed a dozen notes before settling desperately upon a few brief lines that baldly stated that she had received Sarah Jane's letter and would write again soon. She fared better in writing to her mother—the letter to Lady Greetwell was discreet to the point of incomprehensibility when it discussed Sarah Jane Emwilton's mysterious problem, but at least she managed to make it clear that here was a matter that her mama must solve at once.

As a woman who had well-learned her lesson in the folly of keeping secrets, Primula knew that the next step she must take was to put the matter before her husband, but that she dreaded to do. Not because he would be angry—she did not fear him—but because it would make him unhappy. Primula very much feared that Sarah Jane's was a problem with no solution, and she did not wish to see Severn break his heart on it for her sake.

But then it was May Day, and she had made up her mind to tell him today—by writing it down and slipping the letter under his door, if necessary—when Badgley announced a caller.

The woman he ushered into her presence was heavily veiled, and if not for the fact that the tulle was a whimsical shade of mauve, would have presented an appearance of deep mourning. Badgley followed her in, radiating disapproval.

"Miss Wakefield to see you, my lady," he said stiffly.

The veiled figure advanced into the room. "Send your servant away," she said, gesturing with a gloved hand. "What I have to say is for your ears alone, Lady Severn."

"Pray be seated, Miss Wakefield," she said, nodding to Badgley to dismiss him. "I fancy I know why you are here." The day she had dreaded had come: one of Severn's youthful follies—one of Severn's *other* youthful follies—had come to present herself.

"Well," said Aspasia, throwing back her veil. "*That* should give them a great deal to talk of in the servants' hall! Now. I am most pleased to make your acquaintance, Lady Severn. I am Aspasia, the mistress of your father-in-law, the Earl of Malhythe. I have come to tell you that your nephew,

George Lambton, has eloped with a protégée of mine—"

"Sarah Jane Emwilton," said Primula, white to the lips.

"So you *did* get her letter! She wondered why you did not write. That was a cunning note you finally sent; it came yesterday; a masterpiece of tact. I'm sorry I had to burn it, but it would not have done Jenny any good. This marriage would do her a great deal, but it will do Georgie none, and as I have a fondness for the family I have come to you. They have a Special License and are bound for Little Fakenham. If you have a fast coach we may be able to stop them."

Primula rose to her feet and took a deep breath. "Yes. We must go at once." It felt as if someone else planned the words, but she felt her lips move. Georgie and Sarah Jane! Two innocents, but a scandal volatile as phlogiston. "But it will take an hour to get the coach put to—did you leave a hack standing, Miss Wakefield?"

"No. I came in my phaeton, Lady Severn."

"Then it will have to do." Primula rang for Badgley. The promptitude with which he answered suggested that he had been loitering just outside the door.

"Badgley, is Lord Severn at home?"

Aspasia, reveiled, made a minatory gesture that Primula ignored.

"No, my lady." Badgley looked sidewise at the veiled woman, a plain hint that he could easily handle any evictions that needed to be made. "His lordship did not say when he would be back, neither."

"Oh." For a moment Primula felt betrayed. How could she leave these matters to Severn's handling if he was not here? Then her natural air of command asserted itself. "Send Claggett to me—I shall be going out. And bring me pen and paper—at once."

"But you cannot be serious!" protested Aspasia when the servant had gone. "To drive to Little Fakenham in an open chaise—you would be exposed to every gawker and park-saunterer between here and there—and worse if my phaeton should overturn! Think of your reputation, Lady Severn!"

Primula laughed. "You are a fine one to worry about reputation, Miss Wakefield! We shall both be veiled, and it *is* an emergency. It is just as well you asked for me, all things considered," Primula added, "but I do wish Severn were here."

"Severn would not have done me the least good," Aspasia said tartly, "for to be frank, I cannot see he would be the slightest use in *stopping* a scandal."

"Then you do not know Severn!" Primula flashed—and then, reluctantly: "Do you?"

Aspasia threw back her head and laughed. "Rest yourself on that head, my lady Viscountess—I have met your husband once, in very public circumstances, and have no desire to pursue the acquaintance. His father is the better man," she added consideringly, and Primula blushed.

Half an hour later the ladies were spanking down New Oxford Road—past Tyburn, past St. John's Wood—in Aspasia's leaf-sprung yellow-wheeled double-bodied phaeton. A pair of well-bred greys carried it forward at a steady twelve miles an hour, and at a little over twice the speed of the conveyance they were pursuing, they enjoyed the confident hope that they could overtake the young people before they succeeded in tying a knot that only Parliament could break.

Despite her misgivings about the propriety of the

vehicle, Aspasia was an excellent whipster, and even Primula, safe in the passenger's seat with Claggett sharing the jumpseat with the luggage, had to admire her driving as she threaded the equipage around the obstacles of Outer London without slackening speed. Enough young bucks addressed whistles and cat-calls to the supposed spectacle of two of the Fashionable Impure out for a morning's airing to make Primula almost wish she had waited for her carriage, but to do so would have insured Georgie's marriage. Oh, if only she had gotten Sarah Jane's letter earlier—if only Georgie had not conceived this mad plan—if only it were not perfectly calculated to flick Severn on the raw.

Once the city and nearby towns were behind them Aspasia sent the thong of her tasseled whip sailing out over the ears of the horses, and the phaeton picked up speed.

An uneasy truce had formed between the two ladies. Primula did not feel that someone such as Aspasia had any right to form a judgment of Severn's character, while a small guilty voice inside her insisted that Aspasia was among those best qualified to do so. And she had rescued Sarah Jane when Sarah Jane's need had been dire, and succored her as best she could.

"For my part, Lady Severn, I never thought I would meet you—oh, not to speak to, though I fancy I saw you at the theater last week—and since I have, my curiosity is intense. What on earth did Malhythe offer you to marry Severn? I tell you frankly *I* would not have done it, not for respectability and ten thousand pounds besides!" Aspasia spoke without turning her eyes from the road.

"He proposed the match, Miss Wakefield, and my parents thought it suitable."

"Oh, don't rip up at me," begged Aspasia, taking

the horses neatly around a lumbering bullock-cart and steadfastly ignoring its driver. "I am good-hearted, in my fashion, and even humble. I do not presume to be able to winkle Georgie out of parson's mousetrap; that requires a lady of quality. Malhythe told me when he sent for Severn that he knew the match was agreeable to *him*—but his reputation seems to have survived his absence without losing one iota of color, and surely your parents knew it."

"Lord Malhythe spoke to you of Severn's marriage?" Primula asked, sidestepping the rest.

"He did. He told me—as I am sure is no secret—that if Severn continued to behave as he did before, he—Lord Malhythe—would remarry and leave the estate elsewhere."

"If he thought that would influence Severn, he is mistaken. My husband is a very rich man."

"And my lover is a very powerful one. And I imagine that no one of the four of us wishes to see George Lambton make this mistake. I will grant you that Jenny is as pure and innocent as any *ton*-ish virgin—and it makes no difference. In reputation, Lady Severn, appearance is all."

Aspasia seemed to know the countryside well; she turned off down a lane at the outskirts of Little Fakenham and headed the phaeton toward the spire of a large country church. The horses were beginning to flag, and she slowed them to a trot, but if they were not here before Georgie's coach they were only an instant or so behind.

In fact the coach, coming from a direction that suggested it had recently been lost, was just now pulling up before the building that must be the vicarage.

"There they are!" cried Primula, rising to her feet and pointing. The carriage jolted, and she sat down again abruptly.

From this far coign of vantage Primula saw the coach door open. She saw the flash of an enameled crest upon its black lacquer door. She saw a distant russet figure lean out and remove its hat to reveal a bright flag of blond hair.

She saw the figure retreat hastily into the coach, and the coach begin to move.

"Georgie!" said Primula, though he could not possibly hear her. Aspasia said nothing, but plied her whip to good effect, coaxing her tired team to a faster pace. The phaeton jolted alarmingly as it hit the rough stones of the paving.

The coach horses found their stride, and Primula could hear the clatter of their hooves blend into a solid powerful thunder as the phaeton closed the distance between the two vehicles.

The oddly assorted company swept through Little Fakenham and around the curving tree-lined sweep of country lane that led back to the Great North Road. The coach rocked violently, but flung about as its inhabitants must be, they fared far better than the occupants of the phaeton.

Grit worked its way between Primula's teeth, and flung clods stung her face even through the heavy veil she wore. Claggett wailed her discontent, having been thrown to the floor atop the bandboxes at the first instant, and the phaeton seemed to bounce, more than roll, in pursuit of its object.

Aspasia's greys were the best that money could buy, but they were far from fresh. They advanced to within a finger's-breadth of the coach's near wheel and hung there grimly, but the coach showed no sign of stopping, and in the end something had to give.

It was the rear-left wheel of the phaeton. The axle sheared through and dropped the rear end of the vehicle with a bone-settling jar. The horses, terrified, set themselves to bolt, and Aspasia only just managed to pull them up to a trembling stand before the phaeton parted ways with the axle tree forever.

"Well," Aspasia said rallyingly, "I told you it was too light for the roads. I suppose we must wish them very happy, for we certainly aren't going to catch them now."

John Rudwell, Viscount Severn, arrived home in the flower of his maturity at four o'clock of the afternoon of May first, 1817, secure in the knowledge that all problems have solutions. They took time to find, and longer to apply, but for the first time in many years he had no doubt of their existence.

He had spent his morning trying to find Georgie, having conceived a simple plan to detach his young nephew from Warltawk's unwholesome influence. He would take Georgie with him to Paris in search of Lord Malhythe. Severn found he needed to speak to his father, and Warltawk could hardly work mischief on Georgie with the width of the Channel between them.

It was true that Mr. Lambton had not been at home to try this conclusion upon, but that hardly was a flaw of the plan. Severn left a message for him and went away to an idle afternoon at his clubs, testing the waters of respectability. The *ton* was suspicious, and overnice in its requirements, but he felt certain of mastering it in the end. Primula—his helpmeet—would help him, and whatever labyrinthine vengeance Lord Malhythe had intended would vanish like morning mist in the sunlight of reason.

This was his opinion when he entered his home.

He felt the electric impulse of trouble the moment he crossed his threshold. Servants who might reasonably have been somewhere else were loitering about the hall, obviously waiting for his return.

Badgley, ferociously correct, hovered importantly near a heavy silver salver.

"Lady Severn left you a message, my lord. She said you was to have it as soon as you came in. And there is another message, my lord."

Severn scooped both of the folded cards off the tray. One was Primula's, the other sealed with a device he did not recognize. He swept the populous hall with a glance.

"Thank you, Badgley," murmured his lordship sweetly. He bolted up the steps to his study, leaving several disappointed servants behind.

"Rare doings today, Your Grace." Loach rose to his feet from his seat by Severn's grate. If the servant found things difficult—or even different—here in England, Severn was not privileged to possess the information. He flung himself into a chair and Loach began to make up the fire.

"Well, something seems to have stirred up the servants—not that anyone'll tell me about it, of course." Idly Severn broke the seal on Primula's letter.

"Heh! And what would such an 'un say to Your Grace, what with women all over flummery like heathens coming for to see Her Grace, and Her Grace dashing off with them with no more kit nor a bandbox?"

"Women?" said Severn, removing his attention with difficulty from the letter. "An Indian woman came to see Prim?"

"Are Your Grace sickening for the fever, and it not even come on for summer yet? Her were all over veils, her was, like a dead sperrut, and didn't Her Grace see her all alone? Aye—and make off with her too, her did."

Severn stared at the note. Primula had gone away with a veiled woman. The note in his hand said that he must not expect her back for a day or so. He tapped it against the heel of his other hand.

"Did she say where she were—*was*—going, Loach?" Perhaps the other letter held the explanation to the first.

"Her didn't talk to likes o' me—nor anyone. Fetch paper, her says. Fetch box—and Jeems to walk two grey horses up nor down square whole half-an-hour, nearly, and yon gowkie painted all over roses!"

The decoration of the conveyance seemed to annoy Loach as much as all the rest, and Severn could not think of anyone he knew that had a chaise painted with roses and drawn by a pair of greys. He broke the seal on the other letter.

"My dear Lord Severn," he read in an ornate and unfamiliar antique script, *"please do me the honor of calling upon me at your earliest convenience, in regard to a matter that you will find of interest."*

The signature was Warltawk's.

Severn swore half-heartedly and allowed himself to believe for a moment that Warltawk had somehow kidnapped Primula. But the notion was ridiculous, and besides, Prim had more sense than actually to go.

Which was more than he had.

"Be a good fellow, Loach, and lay out my evening-dress. Knee-breeches, and the emeralds. And call up the coach. I am going to pay an evening call upon ancient history."

"And Her Grace?" said Loach, turning a worried monkey face to his master. "Will 'un be bringing Her Grace home?"

"I don't know," said Severn.

Though the phaeton was in pieces, its occupants had not taken much harm. But by the time a passerby had been hailed and pressed into service, a coach had come from the Arm and Hammer in Little Fakenham to take them back there, and the horses been looked over by the blacksmith and pronounced sound, it was too late to do anything at all except engage lodgings for the night.

Aspasia dealt with matters with a cool mendacity that impressed Primula. A story of a race, a bet, a cousin following with a coach and luggage, were quickly unveiled for the landlord, and the quality of the horses and the sovereigns presented for his inspection enabled them to secure the coffee room to their private use, and the promise of a bedchamber well-lit and aired.

"Which will undoubtedly contain fleas, at the very least," sighed Aspasia, sinking down upon the bench beneath the window. "Oh, well, at least we will be able to go back to town in more comfort than we left it."

"Back?" said Primula, stretching out her hands to the coal-fire in the grate. "But we must go on—and catch them."

"And what then? They may be married even now—and they are certainly more than two hours ahead of us."

"And they may not be married—or their coach may have thrown a wheel, just as ours did—or—I don't know—but I *do* know that I will not have Sarah Jane thinking that she is alone, and with no one to turn to, just as—" Primula stopped, and Aspasia regarded her with wide blue eyes that saw too much.

"No," said Lord Malhythe's Cyprian. "We won't let her be left alone, Lady Severn. Now I will ring for the maid, and we will bespeak a hearty dinner, and see if in all this dismal little town there is a coach that may be hired. And tomorrow, as you say, we shall see if we may find them."

* * *

It took Sarah Jane Emwilton the better part of an hour to persuade Georgie to turn the coach about, but when he did, the phaeton that had accosted them in the Little Fakenham churchyard was nowhere to be seen.

"P'raps they have gone back to town," said Georgie.

"Perhaps they are waiting for us in Little Fakenham. Oh, Georgie, Primula wanted to stop you—she wouldn't have come for any other reason! But how did she know?"

"Devil if I know," Georgie lied cheerfully. He had his scandalized suspicions as to the identity of the other occupant of the phantom phaeton, and no intention of sharing them with his affianced bride.

"Well, we can't go on. Oh, Georgie, I know I agreed, and I know you will think me intolerably sheep-hearted, but I simply cannot ask you to do something that—that so many people will mislike!" Sarah Jane wrung her hands, crumpling one of Aspasia's best lace handkerchiefs to an unrecognizable mess.

"Now see here, Sarah Jane—of course they won't like it. But they'll get used to it—and they can't do that until we do it." He gave instructions to the driver to turn the coach again, and after much backing and jouncing they once again headed north. "There must be dozens of village churches about," he said cheerfully. "I daresay we'll find something that will do somewhere along the way."

Chapter 23

MAY 1, 1817

THE LAMPS WERE being lit as Lord Severn arrived at Warltawk's rooms. He did not doubt that Warltawk would receive him. There was an air of feline cruelty about this affair that Severn thought he had left behind him in the East; Warltawk would not wait to give him his news.

Nor did he. Severn was barely seated when Lord Warltawk, irreproachably dressed but jeweled in the fashion of an earlier day, broached the subject of the call.

"Ten years ago, Lord Severn, you seduced and debauched a young virgin of good family. Today your nephew has rung a small change upon your escapade—he has eloped with, and intends to marry, a young prostitute who has made her debut beneath the roof of your father's mistress."

Severn sat very still, his cat's eyes glinting green in the candlelight. At last he said: "And have you a reason for confiding this intelligence to me, sir?"

Warltawk laughed, an almost soundless rasping. "You are cool, sir! Blood will tell—I told your father so, on the occasion of your birth. He may prink and patch at the sacred Rudwell consequence all he likes, but this atop the other will put an end to any pretense of respectability he may foster."

"If it is known." Severn regarded his adversary as steadily as if over the barrel of a dueling pistol.

"You anticipate me, my lord. Some wine?"

The wine was brought and poured. Severn used the pause to try to imagine what Warltawk's motive was for telling him was. He could think of no reason, not even blackmail.

"The reason I have chosen to disclose this to you," Warltawk resumed when his servant had retired, "is that the girl's state is not a matter of common knowledge. Malhythe's doxy knows, and our dear Mr. Lambton, but the only other person—besides yourself, my dear Lord Severn—is the man who ruined her. It should gall any scion of the Rudwell line to take Lord Drewmore's leavings, but it seems that it has not. And Lord Drewmore, sir, maintains his silence at my behest."

So it was blackmail, then. "And you have called me here to tell me precisely what, Lord Warltawk?"

The old monster's eyes glowed appreciatively. "That Lord Drewmore's silence depends on my goodwill, my arrogant young hotspur."

Lord Severn rose to his feet. "I apologize for contradicting one so much my elder, Lord Warltawk, but Lord Drewmore's life depends on his silence. If he should choose to circulate such a vicious and unfounded rumor about any member of my family, I shall certainly shoot him. You may depend upon that, sir, and so must he."

In a lesser man, the silence that followed would have bespoken incredulity. Warltawk searched Severn's face for any sign of bluff or hesitation, and found none.

"You will find I am a dangerous man to cross, Lord Severn," he said at last.

Severn bowed. "I imagine that you are, my lord.

But I have crossed dangerous men in my time, sir. Good evening."

Was it true? The streetlights, as the coach passed, flung bars of yellow light through the venetian blinds of its windows. Light, then shadow, in an uncanny counterpoint to Severn's thoughts.

Why tell such a story if it were *not* true?

What did Warltawk hope to gain from masterminding the affair?

And where was Primula?

Unbidden, the image rose up in Severn's mind—Georgie, at Covent Garden, bowing over the hand of an expensive barque of frailty named Aspasia. Was Aspasia his father's mistress? Did she drive a rose-painted chaise, and had she come armed with knowledge of the elopement to Primula?

It made a horrible, surreal kind of sense. And whatever truth and lies might be mingled in Warltawk's farrago of nastiness, Severn must assume that Georgie was heading for the border with his shopworn prize, and catch him if he could.

Chapter 24

MAY 2, 1817

THE SERVANTS AT the Arm and Hammer roused Lady Severn and her companion long before dawn. They washed and dressed by chill candlelight and made a scant breakfast as the greys were being put to the rented carriage.

"I suppose there is no way to persuade you to turn back, Lady Severn?" Aspasia asked as she sipped her coffee.

Primula worried her lower lip between her teeth. "He must be going to the Rannochs'," she said, as if she had not heard. "Even if he has used his Special License, which we do not know he has, he will want to go away from town for a while—and if he does *not* use it, he must cross the border into Scotland. And once there, he is sure to go to his aunt—Mama is there, so even if he does not, it is plainly the first place I must go." She glanced quickly at Aspasia. "I am sorry to trouble you, Miss—"

"I beg you will call me Aspasia," she interrupted quickly. "It is my professional name, in its fashion. I hope you may be right; that they have lost their wits and are simply bolting for Gretna. Everything will be much simpler if they are."

"Let us hope for it then, Miss—Aspasia. Perhaps we shall have great good luck indeed, and their carriage will have lost a wheel as well. With luck, we might meet them before we have traveled half a league."

Severn borrowed and provisioned a heavy-sprung racing curricle; its iron-shod wheels and tempered steel fittings ensured he would come to no grief on the road. Next he wrote letters: to Primula, to Georgie at Colworth House (in the event that all of this was merely a Banbury tale), and one to Lord Drewmore. This last letter was charmingly frank, and advised his lordship to seek a long repairing lease upon the Continent in preference to indulging in idle gossip.

Severn then occupied the rest of the night in preparing a long letter to his father, which he hoped Malhythe would have no occasion ever to see.

Dawn was breaking over the housetops as Severn and Loach entered the curricle, and the first steeples were just catching dawn fire as Severn turned the team's heads northward and set himself to catch something that might not even be there at all.

They searched all that day. It would have been bad enough if there were simply no word, but the coachman and postilions Aspasia had hired inquired at every change of horses, and what they heard was worse than nothing.

"Landlord says there was just such a coach and gennumun as you say, Miss. Traveling with his sister, and the baggage coach lost." The coachman spat upon the ground to indicate what he thought of such sisters and missing baggage.

"Thank you. Please give him this," Aspasia placed a silver coin in the driver's hand, "and this for yourself. When did they leave?" It was already nearly noon, and the inside of the coach was stiflingly close. They had been traveling since dawn, and both ladies felt faint with hunger and the constant jostling.

"He said the horses were put to nine o'clock of the church steeple."

"Oh, I can't go another inch!" wailed Primula, but even as Aspasia suggested they stop, she shook her head. They were only three hours behind—surely they would overtake them soon.

But George Lambton and Sarah Jane Emwilton were not on the road ahead, and when the landlord at the next inn they pulled into had not seen them, Aspasia bullied Primula into stopping there, telling her that if she would not think of her own comfort she should look to her servants'.

"For they have been hired with the carriage, you know, and are just as likely to turn about and leave us if they do not like the conditions under which they are worked. Let us stop and eat, Lady Severn, and if we do not hear further of them ahead, we will turn back."

"If they are not ahead of us, they must be behind us, you mean. You are right, I suppose, Aspasia—but it is so very hard to stop when they might be just over the hill!"

Aspasia nodded and pushed open the door of the coach. Uncertainty nagged at her as well, but at the moment it was as much folly to go on as it was to stop.

An hour later they set off again. And despite every exertion of horse and man, they had nothing more of the fleeing pair than news of their passage when darkness forced them to stop once more.

Lord Severn had two advantages over both of the parties he pursued. For the first, this was not the first time he had hunted prey that did not wish to be found. For the second, he knew that this was what he was doing, and came prepared for it.

As a result, by nine o'clock in the morning he had reached the Arm and Hammer, heard the story of the disintegration of the phaeton, and understood that Primula and Aspasia had spent the night here and hired a coach in the morning. The Arm and Hammer's postilion, who had ridden Aspasia's greys back from the first change, confirmed that the ladies were heading north.

"They was looking for someone, capting—if I had a yellow-boy for every inn-yard we stopped at I could buy this here establishment." The postilion was a red-headed lad with freckles, and looked willing to spin this fine gentleman as elaborate a story as imagination could fuel, if only he were asked.

Severn tipped him instead—if not a sovereign, a shilling—and wheeled out of the inn-yard. The first change he would have to make of his team was still some hours distant; with the others a day ahead he was not troubling himself with the hope of arriving before they did anything.

He stopped for lunch and a change of cattle at the inn where Georgie had spent the night, and over several glasses of heavy-wet with the landlord obtained the full particulars about Mr. George Lambton and his "sister"—as well as of the veiled ladies in the hired coach who pursued them.

"Right Quality, they was, me lord, especially that black-headed one, saving your lordship's grace. Plain to see they was close as sisters—in fact, I reckon they was sisters, and that young scamp was making off with a third of them."

"I imagine you're right," Severn said and treated mine host to another.

From Loach Severn learned—once they were safely on the road once more—that Georgie and his "sister" had taken separate rooms, and, further, one of the hostelry's maidservants had been engaged not only to spend the night in "Miss Lambton's" room, but to accompany her on the following day.

Keeping his horses' ears centered between the ditches occupied only a portion of Severn's mind, unfortunately. The greater part was left free to mull over what he had learned.

And even if he refused to consider the riddle of his wife traveling in the company of a notorious Paphian, his nephew provided more than enough food for thought.

Warltawk had said the girl was a whore. And Severn had believed him, as there seemed little point for Warltawk to go to all this trouble else. But inn servants have sharp eyes, and sharper noses for scandal—and not only did they agree that Georgie's companion was a lady of Quality, her actions bore them out.

Why?

Only let him catch them, Severn demanded of an uncaring Providence, and he would ask them.

Primula realized by the evening of the second day that she and Aspasia had no real hope of catching up to Georgie and Sarah Jane. But by then they were two days out of London, with two days more between her and return. She could not remember the contents of her hastily scribbled note to Lord Severn; she wondered what she had said.

"Ha'penny for your thoughts?" her companion said. They had not been lucky enough to bespeak a private parlor this evening, so they had retreated to make an awkward meal in their room. But life in the demi-monde seemed to prepare one for coping with hardship of this sort; Aspasia did not look in the least rumpled.

"Oh, Aspasia, I've been such a fool!" Primula said. She only wished she felt as tidy as Aspasia looked. "Whatever they were going to do they've undoubtedly done by now—and here I am, in the middle of nowhere—"

"And what will you say to Severn when he, reasonably or no, demands to know where you've been? My dear, tell him the truth. It's not such a bad truth, when all's said and done, and he can't turn you off, you know."

"The truth!" Primula said as scornfully as if she had been a liar all her life. "You don't understand: running off—in an open chaise—with—well, *you*. It just isn't respectable!"

Aspasia laughed, so openly that Primula was forced to join in. "No, Lady Severn. You are quite right. It isn't respectable. And does that matter so much to your Lord Severn—and do you care?" she added shrewdly.

"Yes, I care. And yes, it does matter to Severn. Maybe it wouldn't, if—if he hadn't been so wild as a boy. But nobody will believe that he has changed!"

"And so he must be more respectable than the best of them to be thought as respectable as the least of them." Aspasia smiled. "So. Will you turn back tomorrow? I am afraid you're right—Georgie has had time and enough to work whatever mischief his heart is set on."

"But he will still need good advice," Primula said, contradicting herself once more. "And the damage to my marriage is done now, however bad it is. We must go on."

Chapter 25

MAY 4, 1817

THE EARL OF Malhythe, his business in France concluded, returned to his native land. His secretary, whose business it was to keep him informed in all things, had written him of the Greetwells' visit to his daughter, of his grandson's protracted and solitary stay in London, and of his only son's ventures into Society.

Accordingly, his homebound ship landed at Newcastle instead of Dover, and he made his leisurely way north and west to the home of the Laird of Rannoch, metaphorically nestled on the shores of Solway Firth.

A servant had been sent on ahead of him, and thus the occupants of Lymond House showed no surprise when, on a bright morning in early May, Lord Malhythe's carriage drew up to the front portico and his lordship descended.

His second daughter, Catherine, greeted him warily as he advanced into her drawing room. All the Rudwell girls went somewhat in awe of their draconian papa, and for Malhythe to appear so unexpectedly, in the wake of her brother Severn's inexplicable wedding just this spring, made Catherine decidedly uneasy.

"Hello, Papa, I trust you had a pleasant journey," she said, rising on tiptoe to salute his cheek.

"It was tolerable. I trust that Sir Rowland and Lady Greetwell are enjoying their stay with you?"

"Why . . . yes, Papa," said Catherine. "Sir Rowland has been out nearly every day—he is out now—and says that his book on Scottish wildflowers is nearly complete. Your rooms are ready for you," she offered tentatively.

"And so I will retire to them. Please convey my respects to Sir Rowland when he returns, Catherine, and ask him if I may have a moment of his time. I fancy I have a topic that will interest him."

Chapter 26

MAY 4, 1817

LORD SEVERN HAD begun to feel that the chase was an end in itself when he pulled into yet another inn-yard a few miles south of the Scots border. He had been on the road four days and was heartily sick of everything connected with it. The knowledge that travels had been harder and often made for less reason in India did nothing at all to console him for the privations of the current journey.

When he reached the end of at least part of his quest, he barely realized it. He had to look twice before he realized that the slender figure alighting from the mud-spattered coach was his wife.

With an equally mud-spattered oath he tossed the reins to Loach and flung himself from his curricle.

"Primula!"

Primula had gone from despairing of catching the eloping couple to real worry about their safety. Since yesterday not one of the inns she and Aspasia had stopped at had been willing to admit of seeing Sarah Jane and Georgie, and the border was now only a few miles away. Her mind was on anything but her own problems when she heard a familiar voice call her name.

"Primula!"

And there was Severn, windblown and mud-spattered, springing from a much-tried racing curricle and searching her face with worried eyes.

"Severn!" She ran forward and flung herself into his arms—and felt giddy with relief when his arms closed around her as if they would never open. "Did you—did you get my note?"

"Yes, and a prettier piece of nonsense was never committed to paper. But never mind that now. Where's Georgie—have you found him?"

"No." Primula did not stop to question how Severn could be so *au courant* with her troubles. "We always seem to be just a little behind—and today we have had no word of him at all. I can only imagine what Sarah Jane must feel—she is my mother's goddaughter, and she used to stay with us when her Papa, General Emwilton, was following the drum. Georgie is *eloping* with Sarah Jane Emwilton," she added helpfully, after a glance at Severn's face.

"Georgie is eloping with your mother's goddaughter?" Severn said blankly.

"Yes, of course he is! You see, there's been a little trouble, and—"

"They're here!" Aspasia, seeing Primula sidetracked, had proceeded upon the matter at hand. Now, armed with desperate news, she ventured to interrupt Lord Severn and his lady.

"Here?" Primula broke away from Severn and turned to Aspasia.

Aspasia gestured toward the road. "They stopped here to change horses—the ostler is certain it's George Lambton, and Jenny was with him. They left about half an hour ago—if we hurry we can catch them this time!"

"Oh, we must!"

Aspasia headed for the coach and Primula turned to follow. Severn caught her arm. "Ride with me, sweetheart. If I don't get a full explanation of what the devil is going on this instant, my brain is going to crack in pieces!"

Lady Rannoch was oppressed, all morning and afternoon, by the sense of Great Events about to break over her head. She soothed her nerves as best she might by agitating her cook's—no subtlety was to be spared to make this evening's dinner a masterpiece—and hovering over her children, until Baby Margie suffered a nerve-storm in anticipation of another trip somewhere.

As for her father the Earl, he had retired to his rooms and had not been seen again—sleeping the sleep of the innocent, his vexed daughter had no doubt.

She could not imagine what business her father might have with the agreeable Sir Rowland, unless it might be about the mysterious marriage Sir Rowland's daughter had made with Lord Malhythe's son. Lady Rannoch had met Primula, and liked her, and had never managed to persuade the secret of her betrothal out of her. That there was a secret her ladyship was certain.

She even debated the wisdom of sending a footman out to the hills to find Sir Rowland among his botanical specimens and warn him of the interview in the offing, but in the end she delayed too long. Sir Rowland Greetwell ambled through the front door of Lymond House just as the sun was beginning to set. His servant followed behind, carrying his specimen case and easels. As Sir Rowland entered the front hall, Lord Malhythe descended the stairs.

"Come in, Sir Rowland. I have come to tell you a story."

In a fashion made breathless and staccato by the whipping of the wind and the pounding of the horse's hooves, Primula related Sarah Jane's story to Severn as best she knew it, ignoring Loach just as Severn did. Behind the curricle ran Aspasia's coach, its leaders a scant two lengths behind Severn's wheels.

Severn listened quietly to Primula's explanation, and nothing on the subject of her own flight of fancy was said.

"—and I didn't know what else to do but follow them, and then when I knew it was too late to catch them it was too late to turn back—and I'm afraid it will be a very great scandal when everyone finds out they are married, Severn."

"Cheer up, darling, if there are any two people in England who know how to outface a scandal it is us. My lord the Earl of Malhythe will certainly contribute his mite—Father can hardly object to the girl's family, after all, seeing as it is yours—and if the children will only keep their heads I'm sure we can contrive something."

"But Lord Drewmore—" Primula began.

"Drewmore will not talk," said Severn. His voice carried such an air of finality, even over the thunder of the coachwheels, that Primula did not enquire further.

The road was thin of traffic here, and they were only a few miles from the border. The landscape rose and fell in slow swells like a frozen sea, and every swale might conceal George Lambton's coach. Finally, far ahead, they saw the smear of dust that must be it.

"Hold hard, darling," Severn told her, "here we go." He leaned forward and flicked the whip over the horse's backs. Instantly their stride lengthened. Their necks stretched and ears flattened, and Primula was pressed back in her seat by a rush of speed that was literally breathtaking.

"We shall look pretty fools if it isn't him, but I

somehow suspect it is!" Severn shouted over the pounding of the hooves.

The coach drew nearer. Primula had heard it described so many times in the past week that she recognized it instantly. It was as mud-spattered and sorely tried as the other two vehicles in this mad chase, and it showed no sign of stopping.

"We'll have to force them off!" Severn said, coaxing yet another burst of speed from his horses. A wide white grin split his tanned features, and Primula wondered that she had ever thought him thoroughly domestic.

Inch by inch, the curricle edged around the coach. Primula, windwhipped, could see a faint white blur of faces at the dust-frosted window. Then they were past, and pulling away, until the coach was one length—then two—then more—behind.

And Severn slewed the curricle across the road.

"Out you get, darling," he said. He lifted Primula from the curricle and then jumped to the ground. "In case they don't stop," he added, giving her an encouraging shove toward the roadside.

Then the coach was there, and for all the driver's whip-cracking and swearing, Severn held the heads of his team, and there was nothing for the coach to do but stop.

The coachman snarled inarticulately and reached for the cudgel he carried beneath the box. He straightened with it in his hand and prepared to descend, when the sound of a cocking pistol stopped him.

"It's only that I abhor violence," said Severn apologetically from over the barrel. "Do stay where you are, my good man—it's your passengers I want to talk to."

As if on cue the coach door opened, and George Lambton jumped to the ground. That young man, who had had the advantage of being able to pack for his journey and proceed in a traveling coach, looked very little the worse for wear, but an astute observer could mark the new lines of wariness and concern about his eyes and mouth.

"Hello, Uncle Severn," he said.

"Georgie!" Primula flung herself forward and threw her arms about him. "Oh, Georgie, we were so worried—we followed you all the way here!" She pushed him back to look at him. "And where is Sarah Jane?"

"Here." Sarah Jane Emwilton teetered in the doorway of the coach. The sapphire-blue wool dress she wore had a modest lace fichu made up high around the neck, but there was little she could do to disguise the dashing color that turned her blue eyes bluer, or make the fast and fashionable cut of it any less so. "It is all right, Primula. I have not married him."

"Oh, Sarah Jane," said Primula, "of course you haven't!"

Georgie lifted her down from the coach and she fled to Primula's arms to weep. Georgie looked at Severn in bewilderment.

"Though you might as well make up your mind to it; you've been over the Border these last two miles," Severn said.

From her vantage point on the low hill Aspasia saw the two young couples unite. She saw the amber flash that was George Lambton flinging his hat into the air, and saw him turn to the blue-gowned woman at his side and kiss her.

She saw the rake with the tarnished hair and (apparently) burnished conscience embrace Sarah Jane as well, and then his nephew. All seemed to be ending well, just as it did in Shakespeare. She turned to Primula's maid.

"Well, Claggett, I don't think we'll be traveling together any longer. But I would like to offer my appreciation for your services this past week." She reached into her purse and held out a gold sovereign to the maid.

Claggett drew herself up and reached for Primula's bandbox. "If you'll excuse me, Miss," she said stiffly, and reached for the doorhandle.

Aspasia watched her trudge up the road. After a while she dropped the coin back into her purse, where it chinked as it landed on its fellows.

So much for the universal opinion that no servant ever refused vails. She would write a letter to the *Morning Post* about it. Aspasia sat quietly for a moment, and then tapped on the sliding panel between her and her coachman.

"Turn about, driver, and let us see if we can make the Bull and Bear by evening!"

The carriage backed and filled as it turned, and Aspasia settled back against the cushions. It would be a dreary trip back to town, but perhaps Colley would be there at the end of it. She need have no fear of losing him, now. Severn was a good boy.

The clatter of the wheels settled to a steady rumble as the horses picked up speed.

Chapter 27

JOURNEYS END IN LOVERS' MEETINGS
MAY 5, 1817

LORD MALHYTHE WAS closeted with Sir Rowland well into the evening, but what was said on that occasion no one afterward ever knew.

It was enough, thought Lady Rannoch, that her father and her new sister-in-law's father should emerge, suitably dressed, and take their places at the dinner table. Lord Malhythe's complexion was as sallow as ever, and Sir Rowland's conversation was as droll. Catherine was moved to hope that the matter that had brought her father so far out of his way could be passed over thus, and leave not a social ripple in its wake.

She continued in her hopes while the gentlemen lingered over their wine—until, in fact, the carriage drew up at her door.

"Who can that be at this hour?" Lady Rannoch said to Lady Greetwell.

Lady Greetwell looked up from her letter-case and frowned inquiringly. In that morning's post a very disturbing letter had come from her daughter Primula, and she was debating whether its contents should be shared with Sir Rowland, and might even necessitate cutting their visit short to return to London.

"I'd better go see," Lady Rannoch decided, rising

to her feet. She was halfway to the double doors of the salon when they opened, and her butler entered, bearing cards on a tray.

"The Viscount and Viscountess Severn, Mr. George Lambton, and Miss Sarah Jane Emwilton to see you, my lady."

"Johnnie?" said Lady Rannoch in disbelief. "Send him in—send them all in—and go tell Angus at once!"

The battered travelers were shown in—and Lady Rannoch, who had not seen Primula since her wedding-day, thought that she looked even more radiant now.

"Johnnie, what are you doing here?" Lady Rannoch asked dangerously.

"Not what you expect, sister dear. In fact, not what you'll believe."

"And you, Georgie—why are you here when your Papa is so ill?" Lady Rannoch had a kind heart, but even her partisans called her sieve-witted.

"Papa? Ill?" said Georgie in horror. "*Truly* ill?"

"Gravely so, but recovering," said the Earl of Malhythe, entering the room with Lord Rannoch and Sir Rowland. "And he will be delighted to see you—as will I, once you have refreshed yourself."

Catherine cast a beseeching glance upon her husband, but the Laird of Rannoch was as bewildered as she.

"If you will come with me, Prim—and Miss Emwilton?" Lady Rannoch attempted to shoo the ladies from the room, but Primula stood fast by her husband's side.

"I must speak with you, sir." Severn faced his father unblinkingly.

"And I, it seems, with you." Malhythe waved an expressive hand. "But not in all your dirt, or before you have eaten. And then perhaps you will be so good as to explain to all of us how you come to be traveling in such great haste with Lady Greetwell's goddaughter, your nephew, and your wife."

Severn ran his hand through his dust-dulled hair. "I can answer that in one word, my lord—but it can wait." He turned away, and Lady Rannoch and the Rannoch butler each took charge of their portion of the party.

"It seems we are in for a wait," the Earl of Malhythe observed placidly. "Do either of you gentlemen care for a hand of piquet?"

It was more than an hour later when the party reassembled in the drawing room. Sarah Jane and Primula were still damp from their baths, and Sarah Jane's eyes were red with weeping.

Despite inclinations to the contrary, the spell of Malhythe's personality held firm. In the fashion of an earlier day he had caused to be placed a half-circle of delicate gilt chairs facing the fireplace, and it was there he took his stand, an elegant figure in snowy linen and deep rose broadcloth, when the others reentered.

Severn made a wry face at the tableau, and seated himself aggressively at its center. Primula sat at his right, with Lady Greetwell beside her, and Sir Rowland beside her. Georgie sat at Severn's left with Sarah Jane beside him, and the Rannochs filled up the two empty chairs at the end.

"As good as a play," murmured the irrepressible Laird of Rannoch to his wife. He settled back and prepared to be entertained.

Severn looked at his father, the expression on his face unpleasantly close to a sneer. "Well, sir? We are waiting."

"I have explained to your father, Lady Severn,

the circumstances of your betrothal and marriage," Malhythe said, ignoring his son. "You may now consider yourself released from any vows of silence you may have been sworn to."

Primula glanced at her father, who smiled at her encouragingly. Head high, she faced the Earl of Malhythe.

"I have long considered myself released from such vows. I have kept no secrets from my husband."

Malhythe seemed unperturbed. "And do you wish to go on living as man and wife with Lord Severn now?"

"What is the meaning of this farce?" Severn interrupted roughly.

"It is the last act, my lord, so pray be silent. Lady Severn?"

"Yes," whispered Primula.

Lady Greetwell looked on in bewilderment. "Later, Jenny," said her husband.

"Then I am satisfied, and I will meddle no further in your lives. Severn may rest assured that he will succeed me not only in my title, but in Rudbek Manor and the considerable all that pertains thereto."

"For which I should undoubtedly be grateful—save for the fact that I don't need your charity!" Severn was on his feet and had taken a dangerous half-step toward Lord Malhythe. "I came back from India a rich man—should Rudbek go on the block tomorrow I can buy it—and Colworth House as well!"

"I am delighted to hear that that is the case. Can you tell me then, if money is no object, precisely why you acceded to all my admittedly peculiar conditions for your return?"

"Because you asked me to!" roared Severn.

There was a pause. Malhythe raised one elegant eyebrow.

"I see. May we now turn to the matter of my grandson and Miss Emwilton?"

"You owe me an explanation, sir! You owe Primula—my *wife*!—an explanation, an apology, and—"

"Severn, don't," begged Primula, pulling at his sleeve. When that had no effect, she stood and put her hand on his arm.

"I owe you, sir, nothing beyond what I have given you. Your wife had her explanation long since," Malhythe answered.

"It wasn't much of one, Lord Malhythe," Primula said. Her voice was quiet, but clear. "You said you wanted Severn to suffer by marrying me. But you never told me why."

"I see," said Lord Malhythe. "You are correct, Lady Severn. My explanation was incomplete. If you will allow me to discover what brings Mr. Lambton here before I tender a fuller one, I believe his answers may have some bearing upon your question."

Primula inclined her head. She found her knees suddenly shaky and leaned upon Severn. Slowly the two of them sat down.

"I accept the relationship that stands between Miss Emwilton and my daughter-in-law, your aunt. May I now know the reason she was traveling to Scotland with your party at this most unseasonable time of year?" Malhythe asked his grandson.

No one could accuse George Lambton of cowardice. Faced with his formidable grandfather he did not stammer or hedge. "Miss Emwilton and I were eloping to Gretna, sir. Aunt Prim and Uncle Severn were not with us—until today, that is. They were trying to stop us."

There was a pause, in which Severn took the opportunity to marvel at the sweeping tact that omitted Aspasia entirely from the events.

"I see. And why were you eloping to Gretna Green with General Sir Horatio Emwilton's daughter? I beg you, young Lambton, spare me the obvious answer."

"I thought, sir, that once we were married Mama—and you, sir—might say what you liked, but you couldn't stop us. I had a Special License—but I thought Uncle Severn was right behind us, so we didn't dare stop and use it. Sarah Jane had her maid with her—from the very first!—and I'd meant to come here anyway, so that Aunt Kate could write to Mama."

"Thank you, I don't think," murmured Lady Rannoch.

"It was necessary that I marry Miss Emwilton, Grandfather. I promised."

"A gentleman's promise must always be kept. I see."

"*What* do you see?" demanded Severn. "Do you see that Lord Warltawk—a crony of yours, sir, so I collect!—plotted to place Miss Emwilton in an intolerable situation, and then, thinking it would be his ruin, forced Georgie—"

Malhythe raised a hand. "Before you go on, Severn, I beg you will allow me to correct a misapprehension—and, as it happens, provide your lady wife with the balance of her explanation."

Old habit held; Severn fell silent, and though Malhythe said nothing for at least a minute, there was no sound in the room. For a moment he looked almost indecisive, then he drew a deep breath and spoke.

"Lord Warltawk is not my crony, though my association with him has been longer than you know. He is my father."

Severn stared.

"But—" Georgie protested, then fell silent, blushing. Malhythe smiled slightly, two spots of color flaming high in his sallow cheeks—the only evidence of any emotion.

"Christian Warltawk was a notorious rake. He enjoyed proving he was above the law. He was born in 1719; before he was banished to France in 'sixty-nine he enjoyed an immoderate success in this one of his two chosen avocations. The other, it will come as no surprise to you, was treason, but let that pass; it hardly matters now. What does matter is that your grandmother, Severn, was one of his conquests. On the day you were born, Severn, Warltawk sent me compelling proof of my paternity—I was his son, and not, as I had always been led to believe, my mother's husband's. Had he not been in France the truth might have come out sooner; we share a common look.

"So far as I know he managed to sire no other living children. I and my descendants are thus his only family, in some sense; he has always interested himself in us."

"He said that blood would tell," Severn said, from a throat suddenly dry. "When he told me that Georgie had eloped, he said that blood would tell." Severn shut his mouth tight on the rest of what Warltawk had said, though surely nearly everyone in the room knew it.

"I think he hoped it would," Malhythe said to his son. "There is a streak of viciousness in all our line that comes from him, and it wants very little to bring it out. If I had known a moment sooner of my paternity the line would have died with me. He timed his revelation very well, but Warltawk has always been dangerously clever. I have seen him in myself every moment since, and have dedicated my life to seeing that blood, if not the line, stopped forever."

"He is my grandfather," said Severn reluctantly. "And I—"

"That heritage was strong in you, as it was in me. I refused to see it for too long—the girls, after all, had been reared strictly and showed no sign of it. When I realized what you had become I could not afford to be gentle in breaking you of Warltawk's tastes. The stakes were too high.

"There is your explanation, Lady Severn. You were my son's acid test, and he has passed it. Are you satisfied?"

"Yes," said Primula, and Severn said, almost inaudibly, "Thank you, Father."

"Well," said Lord Rannoch briskly, rising to his feet, "genealogy's a fascinating subject—though a bit dicey, finding out who your ancestors were—*hem!*—but that's still a little distance from settling these two young people."

"I shall write to Sarah at once," said Lady Greetwell firmly. "She shall make her home with us, Rowland, and on that head I will hear no discussion. As for Sarah Jane, I imagine that among ourselves we can account for her time in a manner that will raise no eyebrows?"

"Of course, my dear," said Sir Rowland.

"As you say, Lady Greetwell," said Lord Rannoch. "And afterward?"

"We wish to marry," said Georgie firmly, taking Sarah Jane by the arm and drawing her toward his grandfather.

"You have my blessing, grandson. No doubt Adeline will manage to cope somehow. Perhaps Lady Severn will give a ball to introduce you into society."

"Yes, sir," said Georgie doubtfully. Severn caught his eye and winked.

"Declare yourself married and you are so, young Georgie," the Laird of Rannoch said. "This is Scotland, you know, and we are all your witnesses." He rotated slowly, his gaze taking in the whole room, and all its assembled and dumbstruck inhabitants.

Georgie looked at Sarah Jane. "Then—will you marry me, Sarah Jane? I want you for my wife."

There was a ripple of interest from the room, and Sarah Jane blushed a nearly inarticulate scarlet.

"Oh, yes! Yes I will!"

Champagne had been poured, and the evening degenerated, anticlimactically, into a family party. Primula had told the truth to her mother at last, but in the face of her daughter's present happiness Lady Greetwell found it difficult to be as outraged with her son-in-law as conscience demanded.

Severn gazed across the room at his father, demoted almost instantly from capricious ogre to mortal man by the revelation of his paternity. Malhythe was speaking with Sir Rowland, as unconcernedly as if Primula's ruination did not lie between them.

"What will happen to Lord Warltawk?" Primula came up behind Severn and slipped her arm through his. Severn looked down at her and smiled.

"When he hears how matters have fallen out, the shock will probably kill him. Let him be. He is an old man. And his power is broken."

Epilogue

AUGUST 1817

THE HOT SUMMER sun spilled in through the high narrow windows of the bedroom of the little house in St. John's Wood. Despite the hour, the room was inhabited. Despite propriety, the room's inhabitant was sprawled, in a state of high deshabille, across her bedsheets of Chinese silk and Mechlin lace, playing Patience with a hand-painted deck.

"Married—eloped—dueled. Married—eloped—ruined." Aspasia said as she placed the cards on the counterpane one by one. "It certainly has been an interesting Season, to be sure," she said to herself.

The matters she had stirred into motion—or tried to stop—had all reached their preordained conclusions. Drewmore and his wild lot were off to the Continent—where Aspasia herself might go, when things were dull and cold here. The halfhearted Cyprian Jenny Fair was gone; Sarah Jane Emwilton was most legally and respectably married to the Earl of Malhythe's grandson, and the pair had spent a happy Season beneath Lady Severn's roof. It was rumored, one heard, that Lady Severn meant to present her husband with a pledge of her affection in the Spring.

"Married—married—*not* married." And she, Aspasia, was just as she had always been. She stretched luxuriantly, making the most of the sunlight. Redemption, she faintly suspected, would be too boring—and the only thing she really wanted was hers already.

There was a tap at the door.

"Lord Malhythe to see you, Miss," Cutty said, swinging the door open wide.

Aspasia sat up swiftly, drawing her pegnoir into some semblance of order. The cards she had laid out spilled every which way, starring the carpet with a court of hearts and diamonds.

"Colley? Come in, my love, I am here."

A Message from Rosemary Edghill

I am always eager to add to my knowledge of the Regency period. If you found any errors of fact in this book, please let me know. Send a description of my errors (including page number and book title, please!) and a citation of your source to:

Rosemary Elizabeth Edghill
P.O. Box 364
Lagrangeville, New York 12540-0364

All letters enclosing an SASE will receive a reply.

—Rosemary Edghill